I0554526

SIGN YOUR
LIFE AWAY

*From the Case Files and Personal
Journals of Cheyenne Bruce,
Private Investigator, Book Two*

Lella Rae

MasterPieces Unlimited

*To my children and their spouses: Michael,
Carol (Luke), Samuel, Alex, and Claire (Diane).
I love you more than you could ever know.*

PROLOGUE

February, 1972

I was in my car when the news came over the radio that Royal Blue was dead. Shocked, the world stopped moving for a while. The traffic slowed, then lined the shoulder as if the drivers and passengers were waiting for a prolonged funeral procession to pass. It had been the middle of winter. A fine rain had misted the windshields and polished the pavement. Time had hung suspended while we absorbed the terrible facts, listened in open-mouthed wonder at the rumors and arranged our private grief.

I had sat with my hands gripping the wheel, looking at the buildings of Seattle's skyline dismally rising like empty boxes through the watery air. The city had seemed suddenly, subtly altered, though I knew the change was only in my perspective. A blue convertible, its rag top glistening with wet, full of sobbing teen-aged girls, had sped by with the radio blaring. It had swerved sharply to avoid a slowing bus, skidded a little, then continued its frantic race with mortality.

Royal Blue, dead! It hadn't seemed possible. I had owned none of his records or tapes—my tastes ran to Neil Diamond, The Beatles, Simon and Garfunkel. Royal Blue's music was more popular with the younger crowd but I had recognized his genius. His were the records that stayed at the top of the charts week after week and then were studied and analyzed long after that.

After the news bulletin, the radio station had played one of his quieter, more lyrical ballads and I had let his voice fill my head. His words took on a new, more profound meaning for me. Had he known, when he had written that song, that he would take his own life? I wondered.

Once or twice in a lifetime there arises a star the brilliance of Royal Blue. His style and good looks had shot him to the top where he had stayed for more than a decade. Everyone knew of his humble beginnings, his devotion to his family and now we listened, in stunned silence, to the news of his death. We had all heard the dirty whisperings of drugs and liquor and too much pressure on a man too sensitive to endure, but they no longer mattered.

Whatever the truth, he was dead. Gradually other stars would appear and glow while still others would wink out. But none would match Royal Blue's radiance. The world would become used to his loss, but like the ripples on a pond, his essence would never really die. The surface of the music world would never again settle into stillness.

I drove on that day, little knowing that with the passing of years my life would become entangled with the lives of those Royal Blue had loved. Though I didn't yet know the players, they were waiting in my future to affect me to the end of my life. Although the case was finished long ago, I dream about it still. In my sleep I'm standing on the edge of hell with a madman.

ONE

Saturday, December 31, 1983

The end of 1983 had come as a welcome relief to me. I was looking forward to a new year, a new home and a new office. Only six weeks before, I had been, literally, facing homelessness. The last case I had handled could have had a tragic ending, but my wounds had healed and my life finally seemed to be on the upswing. I had wrapped up a missing person case that had haunted me for five and a half years. I had solved three murders, and I was all set to move into a beautiful new home and office due to my former client's generosity. You might say I was flying high.

My name is Cheyenne Bruce and I was a private investigator then. I was also psychic. I still am. The psychic part came in very handy as a private investigator, though I mostly didn't mention it to clients because then they would have wanted to know their futures and it never worked that way. Once upon a time, I had rented a dingy room in the basement of the Pike Place Market and exploited the public's belief in the occult. I'm not proud of that aspect of my past. I have run into outright fear from people when they find out what I can do. I get feelings from people. Some would call them vibes, some foreshadowing, though that implies that I can predict the future and I can't. What I can do is know if someone is experiencing guilt, bitterness, joy, desperation, hatred, love or any other emotion. And I can tell whether or not they are lying or about to lie. Whatever you call it, I get information about what people are feeling by touching them. Once in a while, a house or building will give me vibes too. At least, I will hear the echoes of the people who had once lived or worked there. I have learned over the years to filter out most of it. Otherwise, the noise, the chatter, the emotions would drive me insane.

It was true, my life had most definitely improved. For one thing, Christmas was over. I hadn't handled Christmas well since my mother died. For another, one of my favorite people was helping me pack to move into my new place.

Easy Radford – Ezekial Zachary Radford on his driver's license – was the Chaplain of the Seattle Police Department. According to that same driver's license, he was 35, which made him three years younger than I was. He had dark brown hair, almost black really, denim blue eyes that were quite alluring and was about five inches taller than my five foot six. Something the driver's license did not say is that

Easy was not always all that easy. In fact, he could be a little stodgy and, though I would never have told him outright, he was a bit of a sexist too.

Sexist or not, I was glad to have Easy's help. We had packed most of my belongings into cardboard cartons and I would be taking it all to my new residence in a rental truck the next day. Included in the load would be a huge cage carrying Mr. M, an Amazon Blue parrot my former landlady had foisted onto me just before she and her husband had moved to Spain. I hadn't wanted the bird but my new landlady, who was my former client, an actress named Magda St. Martin, loved him and was thrilled. *I* was thrilled to know that he would be living in her house and not mine.

"Tomorrow, I should be through with work by afternoon," Easy said after we had taped up the last box. He collapsed onto the sofa and reached for his water. "I'll help you get it all into the house then."

"By afternoon, I plan to have it all in, unpacked and put away," I told him. "I'm meeting with the Grayells tomorrow afternoon."

"You can't handle all of this by yourself," he said.

I didn't respond but gave him the *you're-treading-on-thin-ice* look. "Oh, I forgot," he said. "You don't have to take any of the furniture. Sweet deal, Magda throwing in furnishings too."

"Nice save," I said, but he didn't get it.

"She said Rolf had not kept up the interior," I told him. "I didn't see it after he left, but she said that since she was getting the apartment ready for the Grayells, she might as well get the cottage refurbished too." Rolf had been Magda's gardener. He had lived in the Caretaker's Cottage on the St. Martin estate. When he had left, Magda had offered it to me.

Easy's pager sounded then, as it so often did. He called in and then had to dash away. I was glad we were mostly finished. Sometimes, his pages came at the most inconvenient times, but once in a while, he got paged exactly when I needed him to be out of my hair.

I stacked the boxes by the door. The rental truck was sitting in the driveway. I could get everything into it myself and drive over to the new place in West Seattle the next morning. Then I could unload, also by myself, unpack, meet with the Grayells to show them their apartment in the big house...

I was still going over my mental checklist when the phone rang. It was Magda.

"How is it being back?" I asked her after we had gotten the greetings out of the way. She had returned to Los Angeles to work on a "project", as she called it. She had once been a well-known screen star until a plane crash had killed her third husband and almost burned her to death. She had recovered, though not without scars that were much more than skin deep. I had to admire her courage. We had become close after the case I had closed for her just six weeks earlier.

"Wonderful," she said. She sounded like it. She had suffered much in the past five or six years. I was pleased that she was finally getting to do what she wanted to do. "I'm directing a film, if you can believe that."

"Of course, I can believe it," I told her. "Where you're concerned, I can believe anything."

"How is the move going? Have you been over to the cottage yet?"

"Magda, it's absolutely beautiful." I meant it. "I don't think I can ever repay you."

"You repaid me already, Cheyenne, dear," she said. "Don't ever think you didn't. Is that lovely bird going to be there when I get home?"

"He'll be there," I said. "You should think twice about him, though. You *do* know he screams twice a day, right?"

"So you said." She laughed. "I'm sure it isn't as bad as that."

"Oh, yes," I said. "It is as bad as that. He's been here, at my apartment, for two days now. The vet says it's his way of calling for his mate, or letting her know it's time to come home or some damned thing. He screams. He literally screams. Twice. Every day. Loud."

She brushed my words off with another laugh.

"He'll be in the music room. He won't bother anyone." I wasn't so sure.

"Mrs. Grayell will have to deal with him," I said. "I warned her about him but she didn't seem perturbed at all."

"Did you do your background thing...your checkup...Did you check them out?" she asked. The Grayells were the new housekeeper and gardener couple Magda had hired after her former secretary/ housekeeper had had to leave. That was a whole different story. Magda had been without a caretaker for the big house for two weeks after she had hired someone who, it turned out, had a police record. When she had belatedly asked me to do a background check on him, I had found not only an arrest record but a warrant as well.

"I did. They're both squeaky clean. Neither one has ever been in the slightest bit of trouble. In fact, they look like they were born for their roles of Housekeeper and Gardener. I think she irons his jeans."

She laughed.

"I did the background checks on them both last week," I continued, "and I got glowing reports from their friends, references and their former employers."

"Did you get any, um...*feeling* from them?" she asked.

"I did." I knew exactly what she meant. She acted reluctant to mention my psychic abilities to me. For some reason, she thought it made me uncomfortable. It didn't. It was simply a part of me that I accepted. "I got good, healthy, honest feeling from both of them," I told her. It was true, but I was confident of them not so much because of what I had felt, but that neither one of them had ever been arrested. "Tomorrow, I'll show them the apartment, give them a tour of the house, and the keys and introduce them to Mr. M."

"Excellent," she said and broke off to speak to someone.

"Why are you working today?" I asked her when she returned.

"During the week we got behind in the shooting schedule. I forgot how much work this is!"

"I can tell that you love it," I said.

"I do! Oh! I have to go. They're calling me. But first, I wanted to tell you that I referred a client to you. She should be contacting you soon. I think it will be interesting. Oops. Must go. I'll call you tomorrow and tell you all about it." She disconnected before I had a chance to get any more information.

❉ ❉ ❉

E asy and I had arranged to spend New Year's Eve together at his place. I would have preferred mine, but all of my belongings were sitting in boxes in my living room. I wasn't looking forward to driving the dreaded truck, which I disliked more and more, to the University District where he lived. That meant extra mileage which equaled extra expense. *Oh well*, I thought. *What the hell? I may have a new client. I can afford it.*

When I got to Easy's, he was playing something truly awful on his turntable. It sounded like several hundred cats rhythmically screaming in unison. Sometimes I was amazed at what he called music. He claimed to be a music lover. I supposed owning thousands of records, and listening to all of them in turn, qualified him…

His apartment smelled like lasagna and garlic bread and I was suddenly starving. Easy ducked into his music room and switched out the album for something softer and a bit quieter. He had rented himself a two bedroom apartment for the specific purpose of lining one room with shelves of albums.

Music was only one of the things he collected. He also had covered his living room wall with scores of hats. Most of them unusual, some rare, he owned several dozen. He claimed he used the hats to cover the holes in his living room walls. I said he collected them because of the holes in his psychology theories. I once had read about a nurse in California who collected bedpans and lined her office wall with them. Given the choice, I would take hats.

We had a wonderful dinner. Easy knew Italian food was one of my favorites. He was a much better cook than I was, although I claimed that anyone could be a good cook if they didn't mind using lots of fat. I tried to avoid it if I could. Sometimes, though, like that night, it wasn't worth the effort and the food was delicious. I didn't allow myself more than a taste of the excellent wine, though, as I would be driving home.

"Are you staying until midnight?" Easy asked after we both had yawned.

"Do you honestly think we could stay awake?" I asked him. We were sitting on his sofa watching the new year begin in one time zone after another on the muted television. It was warm and comfortable with Easy's arm around me. I leaned into him and felt his love for me. Usually, that made my defenses slam into place, but that night his affection felt more comfortable and less urgent than it had in the past. I wondered if his feelings for me were changing. If they were, I had to admit, it would make me a little sad.

Easy got up and changed the record that had just finished for one of Frank Zappa's. Not exactly romantic, but, surprisingly, I liked him. His work was quirky and he was wonderfully and imaginatively talented. My kind of a guy.

Easy and I tended to avoid romantic music anyway. We were drawn to each other and were the best of friends. Easy would have preferred marriage and a big family while I tended to shy away from anything permanent. That night, though, we seemed to be in sync and I liked it. It was comfortable and I wondered why we couldn't be together like that all the time.

"I know I can't stay awake," he said.

"Let's call it a night," I told him. "You going to give me a 'welcome, 1984' kiss?"

"Gladly," he whispered and made good.

After a few minutes, I caught my breath. "I have to be up early tomorrow. Got a busy day." I guessed his feelings for me hadn't changed after all.

A few minutes later, I had headed out into the cold December night and the truck and I made our way back to my last night in the old Mercer Island apartment. The traffic wasn't bad. The partiers were still at it and not on the road yet. I was looking forward to a hot cup of tea and the start of a new year, little knowing that my life was about to change forever.

TWO

Sunday January 1, 1984

Halfway up Admiral Way, I ground the gears for what seemed the hundredth time. It was my second day of driving the truck and I was still not used to it. I almost stalled out at the top of the hill then rattled to a stop in front of my new home. On the front seat beside me, Mr. M squawked in alarm.

"What's the matter?" I asked him. "We're here now."

He muttered something unintelligible and I went around to the passenger side to take his cage into the house. He had spent his last night with me. I would hand him over to the Grayells when they moved into their apartment in the big house that afternoon.

Mr. M was no dainty chick. He was a fully grown Blue-fronted Amazon. His cage, complete with the branch he used for furniture, was almost too much for me to handle. Nevertheless, I wrestled it out of the truck and struggled up the walk. On the porch, I almost collided with a woman who had apparently been waiting for me.

"Oh!" I said, startled. "I'm sorry. I didn't see you there. Would you mind holding this for a moment while I find the right key?" I didn't wait for her to answer but pushed the cage at her and she raised her arms instinctively.

"*Konnichi-wa!*" Mr. M said, looking straight at her with one red-black eye.

"*Konnichi-wa,*" she answered in surprise, then looked a bit sheepish for having responded to a parrot.

After I had gotten the door open, I lifted the cage from her arms and put it on the floor in the foyer. "Come on in," I said. "Sorry about that. What can I do for you?"

She was young. She looked no older than eighteen and she was beautiful. Possibly the most perfect human being I had ever seen. Her face was oval, her features fragile and she had enormous, soft eyes the color of bittersweet chocolate. Her hair was that dark brown that was on the very edge of black; thick and healthy, cut simply, shining and as clean as fresh lemon juice.

"Are you Cheyenne Bruce?" she asked. Her voice was polished and I mentally added a year or two to her age. I nodded and she looked uncertain and eighteen again. And familiar. "You're a private detective?" I nodded again. Next, she was going to say that Cheyenne was an unusual name for a woman. She surprised me.

"I understand that you're a psychic too, and specialize in missing persons." She had a low voice that was startling in one so young, yet it seemed to belong with her and gave her an air of sensuality. She seemed entirely unconscious of the impression she made.

"I am," I said.

She gave the leaded glass window a glance, then took in the gleaming hardwood floors, the sofa and the shining mahogany side table. "This is an unusual place to have a private detective's office," she said.

"Well, this is it." It probably did seem a strange place for an office, this house sitting on the grounds of a mansion in West Seattle and tucked into a neighborhood of ordinary enough looking homes. Most people probably thought a private eye's office should be hiding in a seedier part of town.

"Come in and we can talk," I told her. I picked up Mr. M's cage again and carried it into the former sun room that was to be my office.

I put the cage on the floor and opened the drapes on the double glass doors. Winter light poured into the office of The Sign of the Cross, my agency.

I had to lift a box from the desk to the floor and move a couple of chairs around so there would somewhere for us to sit. She made no move to help me but stood by the doors looking out. I transferred another box closer toward the wall and looked her over.

Her suit was obviously expensive. My guess would be silk and I bet her underwear was too. The pink jacket, as pale as the inside of a conch, was cut in that simple design that only wealthy people wear for every day. If she owned a pair of cut-off jeans, which I doubted, they would have been the designer variety that sold for a hundred dollars or more a shot. She was slender and shorter than I, probably not over five feet two or three. Her carriage was regal though. There had been no bending over hot sinks full of dishes in her childhood. She fidgeted with her purse, probably for a cigarette, then changed her mind. The more I looked, the more I realized she was older than my first estimate.

"I hope you don't mind my coming on a Sunday," she said. She turned to me and examined me much as I had been eyeing her. "Magda St. Martin gave me your name, and I wanted to come as soon as I could. I'm Aïda Blue." She watched me for a couple of seconds.

I held my hand out to her. She took it without hesitation and I immediately placed a mental mark to the good by her name. Back then, some people weren't used to shaking hands with women. I thought they would be in the future, but, at that time, it could quickly turn awkward. "Have you heard of me?" she asked.

I nodded. "Of course. Everyone has. Your father was Royal Blue, the singer. I doubt there is anyone in the United States or in the whole world for that matter, who has not heard of you and your father both. I didn't realize that you were an adult." Of course, I should have realized it. Her father had died when she was nine or ten and it had been at least that many years since then.

She smiled. "I just had my twenty-first birthday last month. That's the reason I'm here."

I must have looked puzzled because she laughed. It was a wonderful sound, full of music. She made me feel tall and gawky, not to mention dusty.

"I'm sorry," she said. "I'm here to hire you. Now that I'm twenty-one, I've received some of my inheritance and I can afford to do it."

"What did you want me to do, Miss Blue?" It felt awkward calling her that, but something, possibly that indestructible poise, kept me from the familiarity of calling her Aïda until I had permission. She was, after all, something of a celebrity. I had seen her father's pictures, and later, her mother's and her childhood photos in *People Magazine* often.

"I want you to find someone for me." She wandered over to the cage and murmured a few words to Mr. M.

"That's what I'm here for," I said. "If you could hold on a minute, I'll try to find some forms for you to fill out. If I agree to accept your case, I will want you to sign a contract as well."

"Of course."

I moved a box out from the front of the file cabinet and shuffled around in one of the drawers.

"*Ikaga desu-ka*," she asked the bird softly.

I was astonished when he said, "*Genki desu.*" His Japanese was always lost on me.

Would you like a drink or something?" I asked belatedly. I rarely drank hard alcohol myself but I kept several bottles of it and various mixers around to serve my clients. I was pretty sure I had put some bottled water and soda into the refrigerator as well.

"Some water would be lovely," she said.

I brought two bottles from the kitchen then got her to sit down and gave her the forms to complete. "If you don't mind, I'm going to dash out to the truck for a load or two," I told her and took a quick sip of my water. She nodded without looking up.

I made several trips and nearly filled the office with boxes.

As I brought in the last one, she had her head bent over one of the forms and was busily writing. Mr. M seemed to be keeping his eye on her.

I had gotten an honest, positive feeling from her.

My mother had taught me to filter out most if not all of the feelings I got from people, but clients were a different story. I needed to know this woman so that I could successfully do whatever job she was hiring me for. My mother had told me, too, that if I didn't learn to ignore that which didn't involve me, then I would be inundated with the minutiae of other people's lives. I could almost hear her voice, I had heard the words so many times. *"Besides,"* she had said, *"you would never be surprised and sometimes it's pleasant to be surprised."* I had always thought she was wrong about that, though.

"I'm sorry I had to leave you like that," I said, and sat behind my cluttered desk with a sigh. "I have to finish this today so I can take the truck back in the morning."

"No problem," she said without glancing up at me.

I watched her shell-pink nails move over the paper. She held the pen like a child does, with her thumb wrapped around her index finger.

Mr. M muttered and was still.

I stood and leaned over to look at the papers she was filling out. The fragile scent of *Muguet* lingered around her. I had given her a standard missing person's request, background questionnaire and a genealogical survey several pages long. I needed to hear more about her case, though, before asking her to sign a contract. Normally, I would have asked questions prior to having her complete paperwork, but I had been bent on getting the boxes out of the truck.

"Just who is it you want me to find, Miss Blue?" I asked, doubt suddenly creeping over me like a quick summer fog.

She looked up at last and opened her huge brown eyes wide. "I want you to find my father."

THREE

Sunday, January 1, 1984

My belongings lay around us like dead soldiers on a battlefield.

Aïda sat across from me and stared intently into my face while I digested what she had said.

"Miss Blue," I said finally. She put her hand up to stop me. Her palm looked white and soft.

"I know what you're going to say. I've heard it already. I don't believe my father is dead." She gazed into my face as if daring me to contradict her. I didn't.

"Maybe you can tell me what makes you think that he's still alive."

She bent her head and fidgeted with her fingers in her lap, but said nothing.

"I'm sure you've heard all the rumors," I said. "Seen the photographs. Heard people talk about how he's been spotted in a Seven Eleven store in Muldraugh,

Kentucky, or in a video arcade in Farley, Iowa. Do you believe those rumors?"

She shook her head and stared at her hands like a schoolgirl waiting for me to finish a lecture on tardiness. The last of the morning light shone on the fine planes and curves of her face. She stood up in a smooth, graceful motion. "In my car, I have something that I think will help to convince you. It did me." She turned and went through the glass doors, leaving my office like a breath of perfume. When she was gone, the clutter around me looked even shabbier. My wonderful office, that had seemed a diamond earlier that morning, had suddenly turned to nothing but glass.

Mr. M watched me, cocking his head to one side and then the other. "What are you looking at?" I asked him. He ruffled his feathers but said nothing.

When Aïda returned, she was carrying a painting and a small bag. She propped the painting on the chair where she had been sitting and came around to my side of the desk to view it with me.

It was a nude. The woman was seated on a covered stool with her back to the viewer, her face turned so that one could partially see it. Around her neck, hung a pendant, but not in the conventional way. The *lavaliere*, an exquisite blue butterfly with silver filigree wings, hung at her back on a long chain, nearly to her waist. Her skin looked vibrant and full of life. I could almost see the faint flutter of her heart and felt that if I touched the canvas, it would be warm. The initials, the artists signature in the corner, were unreadable. They could have been Ns or Ws or Hs. My eyes, though were drawn again and again to the face and the graceful lines of the back. The woman looked very much like Aïda.

"I don't recognize the artist," I said. "He or she is extremely talented, though."

"He," she said somewhat curtly. "The artist is my father."

I nodded. "He was very good. I wasn't aware that he had been a painter."

"I don't think you understand," she said. "He painted this recently."

"Miss Blue, even if your father did paint this, it proves nothing. It's undated. He could have done it at any time. Perhaps when you were a child."

It was then that she pulled another painting, a much smaller one, from the bag she carried. It was a child of five or six, sitting in the same pose as the figure in the larger painting, though minus the butterfly.

"My father painted this portrait of me when I was five," she said.

She unbuttoned the top button of her blouse, reached in and pulled out a silver chain. Dangling from it was the silver butterfly pendant. "Do you see this?" she asked. Something seemed to have caught in her throat and turned her voice huskier. "My grandmother gave this to me just after my mother died. He couldn't have painted this before that time." She made a gesture at the larger painting. "He died when I was ten. This," she touched the gentle curves of the painted figure's breast just visible beyond the sweet sweep of her arm. "This is obviously a woman."

"But, honey, your father could have painted them both at the same time knowing what a beautiful woman you would turn out to be. Perhaps this is a portrait of your mother. She did look very much like you. Her pictures have been published too. I'm sorry, but this doesn't prove anything." I put my hand on her shoulder. I felt a bit of desperation there and some frustration as well.

"Look how he signed this, though," she said, pointing to the signature in the lower right corner of the small painting. It said "Blue" with a large capital B and much smaller, stylized "l-u-e". "Then, look at this." She gestured toward the Ws or Hs in the corner of the larger one. "If he had painted them at the same time, why wouldn't he have signed them the same? And what about the pendant?" she asked. She looked straight into my eyes.

I shrugged. "I don't know about the signatures, but the pendant could be something he had seen before. Was it *his* mother who gave it to you?"

She nodded. I thought I saw tears glistening in her

eyes, and I put my hand out to her again.

She stepped away from my hand and wandered to the window. Not harshly, but impatiently, as if I simply wasn't grasping the obvious. "You're psychic, aren't you?"

I didn't say anything.

"Magda told me you were," she said. Her mouth moved into a *moue* that was very close to becoming a pout.

"Magda may think I can do more than I can," I told her. It was not a lie.

"Nevertheless, I want you to locate my father."

"I do have psychic ability, honey, but I'm not a medium," I said and felt cruel for doing so, but she needed someone to help her face reality.

"I'm not looking for a medium. I'm certain this is my father's work. Recent work."

"Where did you get it?"

"I bought it at a...an antique store in San Francisco. More of a thrift store, really. I asked the woman where she had gotten it, but she gave me a rambling story about a mysterious stranger. I didn't believe her for a second. She said it might have been stolen. I think she told me that to add a little romance and intrigue to it." She didn't look intrigued, she looked miserable. "I want you to go to San Francisco and find out what you can from her."

"I can do that by phone," I told her, but she began shaking her head.

"I want you to go there and anywhere else you need to go to find him," she said.

"Do you think he's in San Francisco?"

"I don't know. But if you call the woman who sold me this painting, you won't be able to tell if she's lying or not, will you? Magda said you could do that by touching." Her brown eyes stared at mine.

She had me there.

"I don't know how the painting ended up in her shop," she said. "Maybe he *does* live there. Maybe he sold it to her. I don't know. But, I'm sure he isn't dead. I never *felt* that he was. Do you know what I mean?"

Unfortunately, I *did* know what she meant. "Honey, after my mother died, it didn't seem real to me either. And I was thirty years old. You were only nine or ten when your father died. Think about that."

She sighed. "I have," she said. "I've thought and thought about it. I've had eleven years to think. At first, I tried to tell myself the same thing. Everyone in the country—in the world—watched his funeral. I was there. I saw him. I touched him, and yet... It seems ridiculous, I know. Please Miss Bruce, I have the money. I have so much money I don't know what to do with it all. I want you to find my father."

I said nothing for a moment, thinking about what she had said. I wanted to help her but I wasn't at all sure that I could.

"I have another case to finish up, but it should be completed by tomorrow night. My fee is $35 an hour plus expenses. I'll need a retainer of $500. I'll also need you to complete these forms and sign a contract. Lastly, I'd like it if you would call me Cheyenne."

She smiled. Her teeth were perfect and white, small and even. "Only if you stop calling me 'Honey' and call me Aïda."

* * *

I was stacking books when the phone rang. It was Magda.

"Magda!" I said, glad for a break from unpacking. I always forgot from one time to the next, how much I hated moving. "I talked to Aïda Blue this morning."

"That's why I called, Cheyenne. You mean she's up there already? I just spoke to her about you yesterday. I was calling to tell you about the case, but I guess, by now, you know."

"Thank you for referring her," I said. "Unfortunately, I don't think there's much I can do for her. You don't seriously think her father is still alive, do you?"

Magda laughed. I was glad to hear it. "The important thing is that *she* believes he is. She and I were talking yesterday morning and she mentioned she'd like to find a good private eye in the Seattle area. Naturally, I thought of you."

"Why did she want to find someone specifically in Seattle?"

"Her father was born there, I believe. He used to have family in Seattle. Anyway, his attorney is in the area and his manager has settled there as well. I think Aïda has some idea that the business manager may have embezzled some of her father's money."

"Embezzled? She didn't say anything about that."

"She's a pretty mixed-up kid from what I saw, Cheyenne. Go easy on her."

"Oh, I will. I think it's a lost cause, though. I think she's suffering from some kind of delayed denial process. I guess that if she wants to spend some of her money to satisfy herself that her daddy is really dead, it's up to her. It's cheaper than several years' worth of analysis, anyway."

"Apparently, she's had that, too. She and I had quite a talk. I sent her to you because I know that you specialize in lost causes."

I laughed. I had just finished Magda's case, a lost cause if I had ever seen one. I almost hadn't solved it. For a while, I had thought I wouldn't live through it. "Come on, Magda, I said. "I'm the best detective you know."

"True!" she said, then switched gears. "You all moved in?"

"I have everything out of the old and into the new, if that's what you mean. I wouldn't have to do another thing if I didn't mind living out of packing boxes."

"What about that gorgeous bird? Did he survive the trauma?"

"So far."

"Did you get that handsome fella of yours to come help you move?" she asked, and I could hear laughter in her voice again.

Magda was convinced that I would be blissfully happy if I were married. I supposed that was a normal conviction for an actress who had had four husbands and wouldn't be averse to a fifth. I changed the subject and we chatted a few more minutes about more comfortable topics.

"I have to go, Magda," I told her, giving my watch a glance. "The Grayells will be here any minute."

"Good," she said. "I probably will be home in a week or two. I'll let you know."

When the call had ended, I turned and surveyed my new home and thought about how comfortable it would be once I had everything in its proper place. I had a big bedroom, a living room and a study, something I had always wanted, plus the sunroom which would be my office. There was a good-sized kitchen and the bathroom was even roomy. It had one of those old claw foot bathtubs which I loved.

My office had its own entrance; a lovely pair of French glass doors that gave it more than a touch of class. When the sun shone in the mornings, which it would do more often once the winter dreariness ended, it would brighten up even the most desperate character looking for a private eye.

Every time I stopped to take a look around at my new office, I had to reflect on how my life had changed. Just a month before, I had been living in a tiny basement apartment and was looking at having to move with no prospects in sight. The fee I had been paid to help Magda had been earmarked to make the last payment on my mother's hospital bills and I had known there would be nothing left. Magda had stepped in and offered me the cottage when it had become available and I had gratefully accepted.

At one o'clock, I hefted Mr. M's cage and locked up. I walked across the lawn to the front door of the big house just as the Grayells drove up.

It took me about an hour to give the couple a thorough tour of the house and describe their duties. Mrs. Grayell, who insisted I call her Georgina, kept referring to their new apartment as "the servants' quarters", but I knew Magda would see the Grayells as much more than merely servants. She had come to dearly love her previous housekeeper/

secretary.

Georgina seemed pleased that the new digs were located on the second floor of the big house rather than the third, and just as delighted with her new home and new job. Her husband, Daniel, was equally happy with the yard and the garage. I was well satisfied with the both of them and I knew Magda would be as well. We chatted easily about the neighborhood, the history of the house and their duties. I introduced them to Mr. M, then turned him and the keys over to them and left to go back to my own chores.

❋ ❋ ❋

I carried a huge stack of maps over to the corner where I was going to have my bookshelf when I got around to putting it together. I remembered, then, that Easy had planned to stop by that afternoon to help.

I caught him at his office and told him that I had a couple of errands I had to take care of before I would be available.

"I probably won't be able to make it until later anyway," he told me. "There's been a homicide on Capitol Hill. Maybe later this evening?"

"We could share a pizza," I said, knowing the reaction I would get.

"A pizza!? Who is this? The Cheyenne Bruce I know eats leaves, roots and twigs. I've never seen her touch anything as revoltingly fat laden as a pizza."

"Get off it, Easy" I said, laughing.

"I was going to offer to come over and help this evening," he said. I could hear the smile in his voice. "But, now, I'm a little afraid to. An alien may have taken over your mind."

"I should be home about sixish. Be here? I'll order some pizza. You bring the beer."

"Beer! Oh, my God!" I heard him say just before I disconnected.

After I hung up, I went into my new bathroom to shower. I'd have to find the proper box to dig out some clean clothes.

FOUR

Sunday, January 1, 1984

My first stop was K-Mart. They had exactly what I wanted. I bought thirty-seven cheap glass bud vases and tucked the receipt into my pocket. Someone else would be paying for them, not me.

On impulse, I stopped at Avenue Art Glass on the way home.

Ab Eberstein was the proprietor of the local stained glass shop. He actually lived in the apartment upstairs from the shop so he was in the store most days. Holidays, he said, meant nothing to him.

He gave me a hug when I came in. I had gotten to know Ab when I had worked on Magda's case. And, I could say I owed my life to him, though it probably wouldn't have come to that. He had been instrumental in getting the ambulance on its way when I had suffered a serious wound.

While visiting his store during the investigation, I had been so impressed with the art of making stained glass that Ab had encouraged me to take a class. Easy had given me a certificate for classes at Ab's shop when I had complained about being unable to afford them. It had been a perfect gift. I sincerely wished that I could have used it.

"I just can't quite afford the tools and the supplies yet," I explained to Ab. "I don't want to return the gift certificate, though. Could you hold it for me for a while until I feel that I can afford to go ahead with the class?"

He looked at me and chewed on his lower lip for such a long time, I was afraid he was going to turn me down.

Instead, he made me a counter offer. "Tell you what," he said. "You work here as an apprentice and I'll let you use all the supplies you need and you can use the shop tools."

"Ab, I would love that," I said. "But you know I have my own business. I wouldn't be able to spend enough time here to make it worth your while." My heart sank a little. It sounded like a dream to me. Being surrounded by those fascinating sheets of colored glass and learning how to create gloriously lovely pieces out of them was more than I could wish for.

"Not a problem, babe," he said. I had learned that he called most women "babe" and most men "buddy". I think it was so he didn't have to remember anyone's name. "You come in when you can, I'll teach you what I know. You can sweep up, watch the shop when I'm not here, act as cashier when we're busy. Whatever is needed and whenever you can."

We shook hands on the deal. I was thrilled. He told me he had entered an art contest and would be heading to a four-day art show in the summer. I only hoped I felt confident enough by then to run the shop for him while he was away. I silently vowed to spend every spare minute there I could.

By the time I left Ab and sped up the hill to home, it was quarter to six and Easy was waiting in his car. He opened the door when he saw me and climbed out. Striding toward me, tall and lean in the dark winter evening, his Native blood showed. His eyes flickered as if he had fire within him but kept the lid on so tightly that it could only gleam out of his eyes. He smiled as he came nearer.

❊ ❊ ❊

"I honestly think she's wasting her money," I told him. "She told me that she has started a foundation to bring music programs to underprivileged and ill children. It would be so much more useful if she spent her money there instead of having me look for her father who has been dead for over a decade."

Easy and I were finishing the last crusts of a Domino's pizza. Easy gathered the small pile of pepperoni slices I had picked off the pizza and pushed them into his mouth. We sat on the floor in front of my fireplace and leaned our backs against the sofa with our legs stretched out in front of us. I had lit the fire to burn some of the trash and kept it going to ward off the evening chill. I took a long pull of beer and let it slide down my throat. For a moment I watched the fire and let it hypnotize me.

"She can spend her money any way she wants, I guess," Easy said. "She has enough. She can do whatever she can think of. But, good for her for using some of it to benefit someone else."

He leaned back against the sofa and patted his stomach. He made groaning noises as if fat were overtaking him, but he looked as trim as ever. In fact, he was looking better by the minute. The light glinted off his blue eyes. One of his eyes is glass because of a childhood accident, and I saw the pupil of the real one dilate. When he saw me watching, he winked.

"She wants me to spend as much as I have to," I said. "She's insisting I go to San Francisco and look up that dealer who sold her the painting. I told her I'd make reservations and she said, 'fine.' Just like that. Didn't ask me how long I was going to be there, didn't ask me if I was planning to stay at the

St Francis. She didn't care." I belched softly. I loved pizza. At least I did right then.

"Are you going?" He suddenly looked doubtful.

"I guess so. I haven't made the plane reservations yet. I told Aïda that I could call her –the woman who sold Aïda the painting that is. But she pointed out to me that I wouldn't be able to use my psychic ability on her if I didn't meet her face to face. It really would be better to talk to her in person. Anyway, the client insisted, so yes, I'm going."

"I don't think it's necessary for you to go," he said. Lines appeared on his forehead.

"It may not be," I said, shrugging. "I don't particularly want to." What I wanted to do was get started working at the glass shop. I had considered mentioning my new apprenticeship to Easy but I thought he might be offended that I hadn't come to him for financial help.

"It seems like a waste of time to me," Easy said.

"I know. This whole thing is pretty silly. You and I and everyone else in the world knows that Royal Blue is dead. Everyone except a handful of crazies who think Elvis is alive, too and that the moon landing was faked."

"Have you tried your voodoo on it?"

I hate it when people call psychic ability 'voodoo' or 'witchcraft' or anything other than what it is. My agency's name, "The Sign of the Cross" and its logo were born when I made the mistake of telling a police officer about my ability to detect lying just by touching someone. He had made a cross with his fingers as though to ward off vampires. He thought it was hilarious. I didn't.

"No, I haven't tried *voodoo* yet. But, when I do, watch out for a big pain in your butt because it'll be me sticking a pin in it," I said, kidding, but not.

He grinned. "Sorry," he said. "What do you know so far?"

"Oh, hell, nothing. Everything. Doesn't everybody know practically everything there is to know about the man? She filled out standard forms and answered all the questions I threw at her, but she didn't tell me a thing I hadn't already heard."

"I think I read somewhere that he was pretty demanding and fired a maid in the middle of the night because she left a spoon by the edge of the sink." Easy picked up a stray piece of mushroom and looked at it before putting it into his mouth. "They say he had to have his house in perfect order. He was said to be vain and have a pretty good temper too."

"Jeez, you know more about him than I do. Why don't you take over for me? *You* go to San Francisco and find out where that painting came from. Probably somebody just painted a picture in art school. Except it's far too good to have been done by an amateur. It could have been copied from a photo, though. Just because someone painted a portrait that happens to look like Aïda, doesn't mean her father is the one who did it."

"Can you get an expert to look at it and tell you if it was done by the same artist who did his other works?"

"Aïda said she had taken it to someone along with a smaller piece that she'd had since she was a child. She showed it to me. It's essentially the same painting only of Aïda when she was five. The findings were inconclusive. They told her it could be the same artist or it could be someone imitating him. There *were* a few variations, I guess. The styles were slightly different, but that could be accounted for by the number of years between the two paintings and the growth of the artist. Aïda thinks that proves her father *did* paint it. Anyhow, it puts us right back where we were. The only thing I can do is go down to San Fran and talk to the antiques dealer myself. I took a picture of the painting so I can show it to her if I have to."

I snuck a look at Easy to see if he was going to try to talk me out of going. He had his eyes shut. His hands rested behind his head. I was very tempted to lean over to his ear and whisper "Let's go to bed," but I knew him. I knew how he felt about sex before marriage and he knew how I felt about marriage so I kept my mouth shut. I knew that I could probably coax him into my bed but I didn't want to have to deal with the crushing guilt he would feel afterward. Easy was raised by strict parents who ground guilt into his very center. Plus, he was raised Catholic and they are experts on guilt.

I stood up and went to the phone table. I riffled through my phone book and picked up the receiver. Finally, he opened his eyes when I made a reservation on United Airlines for the coming Tuesday. In one more quick call, I had a hotel room reserved too.

When I hung up, Easy was still looking at me. "Drive me to the airport?" I asked. He nodded and yawned.

I moved to the fireplace and put another log on the glowing coals. A lick of flame reached for the wood and played with it. When I turned around, Easy was still looking at me.

I don't know, maybe it was the fire or the comfortable feeling of being tired and well fed. Or maybe it was the beer. Maybe it was the realization that moving into a new place always awakened in me, that I was alone in the world. I should have been used to it. I *was* used to it but it was decidedly pleasant to be sharing the evening with Easy.

He stood up and yawned again. "I should let you get to bed. You must be exhausted."

"Actually, I have to do one thing before I can sleep," I said.

He frowned. "What do you have to do?"

"Just a bit of voodoo. Don't worry, it doesn't

involve going out."

He continued to watch me. I could tell he had something on his mind.

"You know, we still haven't had that talk," he said after a moment.

"Let's not have it now, Easy." I started to pick up the empty pizza box and the bottles that littered the coffee table.

"That's what you always say." He took the bottles out of my hands and put them back on the table.

"I'm not having a 'talk' now," I said. "I'm tired and I still have some work I have to do."

"I worry about you," he said. He put his arms around me and I had to resist the urge to move away from them.

"Remember, it was only a couple of weeks ago that you almost got yourself killed. I wish you were in a safer line of work."

"I didn't almost get myself killed," I said. "Not even close. Easy, please. We've been through this before. I'm...I'm tired of it." I was fully conscious of the fact that Easy loved me. Hell, I loved him too, but that didn't mean I wanted to get married. I had been there before and didn't want to go through it again.

"At some point—," he began, but I cut him off. I was getting a strong feeling from him that he was thinking about proposing and it terrified me.

"You wouldn't be happy married to me," I said.

He looked so startled I would have laughed if it had been any kind of laughing matter at all. But I could tell from the look on his face that I had been right. He *had* been thinking about it. "And I wouldn't be happy either," I added.

"You don't know that," he said.

"Yes, I do. You wouldn't be happy saddled with an agnostic for life. I think you know it, too. Yes, I know, at some point we're going to have to have a talk. Okay, we'll talk. Just not tonight."

The delight had gone out of the evening and I was tired and cold. He didn't look happy either, and that made me unhappy too.

After Easy had gone, I settled into a recliner in my living room. I closed my eyes and let my mind wander randomly, picturing Royal Blue as I had seen him on album covers, in movies and magazines. A bit of feeling flashed into my head and then out. I tried to relax, tried too hard and felt myself tighten up. My irritation with Easy was getting in the way, but I was determined not to let it intrude.

Frankly, I was more than a little frightened and it had nothing to do with my job or any physical danger. I had to admit to myself that I was scared of marriage. The first guy I'd been in love with was dead. The second, had left me without a word and I had never heard from him again. I didn't dwell on him so much. Oh sure, sometimes, in the very depth of night, I thought about Cam and wondered where he was. But I had never, ever stopped thinking about David.

"Come on," I said aloud in the silent house. "Let's get serious here." I relaxed again with a few deep breaths and found myself watching a series of photograph-like images flip through my mind at frantic speed. They were like unconnected movie stills, and they sped by so quickly I couldn't capture any of them, only a sense of dark blue eyes staring at me in reproach.

It wasn't what I would call productive. Suddenly, I was hit by a sharp pang that had once been exhaustingly familiar. I missed my mother. She would have known how to interpret what I had seen. I could describe only a sense of it, though it made no sense at all.

I must have dozed. When I awoke, the house was cold and quiet. I could hear the whispers of others who had lived there. I eased my sore muscles out of the chair and ran a hot, hot bath. Then, it was all I could do to drag myself out of the soothing water and climb into bed.

FIVE

Monday, January 2, 1984

The next morning, I woke up late and I was cranky. I always feel gravelly and uneasy when I eat and drink the wrong things the night before and then sleep too much. Easy was the junk food junkie. Normally, I didn't even like to look at the corn dogs and Twinkies he favored. I had only myself to blame for my mood and an overdose of salt, cholesterol and alcohol.

Besides, Easy had gone all mushy on me. I could have blamed that on the beer too as long as I had it handy. But that wasn't all. It occurred to me now and then that I had no family except my brother, Larry, who lived in Wyoming and whom I rarely saw.

I was determined to put Easy out of my mind. I had a couple of jobs to do and wanted to talk to Aïda again. If I was going to take her case—and it looked like I was going to since I had made hotel and airline reservations—I needed a retainer and I still had a few more questions for her.

I skipped breakfast entirely and took the truck back to the rental agency. I would rather have gone for a walk. I didn't exercise but I liked to walk. I thought a long, brisk walk would have been the perfect thing to brush the cobwebs out of my head. But, that morning, I just didn't have the time.

I delivered the truck, picked up my car then headed to the wholesale florist where I collected my order of three dozen red roses and one white one. When I saw the total cost, I was glad my client had to foot the bill for them.

When I got back, I stowed the roses in the refrigerator. My stomach was making little hungry rumbles so I gave Aïda a call at her hotel, the downtown Westin, and asked her to meet me for lunch.

In the Westin, the restaurants were a choice of moderately expensive, foolishly expensive and the outrageous. I loved them all. I was able to feel elegant at all three, though the moderately expensive one was my favorite, and I knew the waitstaff there. It always impressed the heck out of my clients when I paraded them through the dining room and was greeted by name. There were certain of my clientele that I entertained at "my" table in the bar of the Sun Ya, a shabby Chinese restaurant in the International District. There, I could nurse an orange juice or a diet 7-Up for hours. But I liked to show off to some of my clients and Aïda struck me as one of those.

I drove downtown in a typical Seattle winter day. Sunbursts and rain squalls alternated three or four times during that fifteen-minute drive. The streets never had a chance to dry between one downpour and the next. At least it wasn't snowing, I thought gratefully. The sun had broken through for a moment when I parked and made a dash for the Westin.

Trader Vic's was down a shining pair of escalators from the hotel lobby. A tiny Asian gentleman ushered me into the rattan and wood dining room where I found Aïda ensconced in one of those huge wicker chairs that had often appeared on the TV show, *Hawaiian Eye,* about a hundred years ago. She looked like a queen. When I got there, she was alternately sipping a drink that looked like grapefruit juice and puffing on a slender brown cigarette.

On the phone, Aïda had said she had something for me, and when I spotted her already sitting at the table, she had a large Saks Fifth Avenue bag on the floor next to her.

"Aïda," I said sliding into my chair and nodding a thank you to the host. I saw a few of the nearby patrons giving her covert stares, but not many. The habitués of Trader Vic's were used to celebrity basketball players, screen actors and television personalities in their midst.

"Cheyenne," she said. She gracefully tossed her hair and leaned back. She was wearing a buttery silk blouse that looked as if it would melt into her skin. "I've brought you some things that might help you." She stubbed out the cigarette and put her hand on the shopping bag as if undecided what to do with it. At last, she said, "You must understand that it's very difficult for me to hand these over." She reached under the table and lifted the Saks shopping bag that was seemingly crammed with small, cloth bound books. She set it on the table ceremoniously. "These were my mother's diaries and there are some photographs and a home movie here too. I want you to read through them and see if there is anything that will give you a clue to the whereabouts of my father."

"You have read these, of course," I said, picking one of the books out of the bag. I thumbed through it noting small, neat handwriting. Not too difficult to read, thank God. The book was bound in pale blue cotton with tiny white and yellow flowers.

Aïda shook her head. "I started to but it was too hard. I...couldn't get through them. Maybe someday..." She trailed off and took a big gulp of her water.

The waiter arrived and looked disapprovingly at the bag on the table. I lifted it off and we ordered. She took the Sunflower Salad and I went for the

Green Goddess. She played with another cigarette but didn't light it, while I paged through the diary. A delicate pressed forget-me-not fell out from between two pages. I carefully replaced it then set the book aside.

"Aïda, I'd like to hear about your childhood," I said. "Would you say it was a happy one?"

"Oh, yes." Her eyes sparkled like she was on the verge of tears. "My parents were wonderful. I wasn't one of those spoiled children who had everything, you know." I doubted that but didn't say so. "I was more fortunate than a lot of musicians' kid, though," she said. "I saw more of my folks than they did theirs. My dad, when he was on road tours, took my mother and me with him most of the time. My mother loved the tours. I think she loved him more than anything else."

More than her little girl? I wondered. "And your mother has been gone how long?"

"Ten years now. She died a year after my father... left. She got pneumonia." She looked beyond the present for a moment. "She was so unhappy," she said finally. "It was almost as if she willed it to happen. I was raised by her people. She died when I was eleven. I still miss her terribly." She blinked a few times and looked at me. "You said you had lost your mother, too, I think."

"Yes," I said, almost sorry now that I had brought it up. "She died more than six years ago. She had pneumonia as well." My mother had died of pneumonia but she had had cancer too. I didn't tell Aïda that. "We were very close. Like you and your mother."

She nodded as if she knew exactly what I was talking about. "It's the hardest thing in the world for a child to lose her mother. I don't care how old she is."

In that moment, I liked Aïda better than I ever had. To me she had seemed the spoiled child that she said she wasn't; the child of a rock star who had never known anything but fun and clothes and plenty. I thought she was having a normal reaction to losing her parents—denying that one of them was dead. And perhaps she was, but at least she and I shared a common grief that drew us together. For the first time, I felt I could be her friend. I smiled at her and she smiled back, surprised.

"What about other relatives? Have you anyone you're close to?" I asked.

She shook her head slowly. "Not now. My mother's people, the ones who raised me, are gone. All I have now is Jon-Paul."

"Jon-Paul?"

"My fiancé."

The waiter brought our salads and the delicious flat bread for which Trader Vic's is famous.

I broke off a small piece of bread. "This is going to

be a tough question," I said. "Do you know, or do you suspect that your father might have been having an affair? I know you were a child, but is there anything you remember that might point to that possibility? Conversations overheard? Arguments between your parents? Anything?"

She looked so affronted, I thought I had lost her.

"From what you've told me, it doesn't seem likely but it's a question I have to ask," I said. "If he was, there's always the possibility that he left your mother for another woman." I suddenly felt ridiculous. We were talking about a dead man.

"No, he wasn't having an affair. He was very much in love with my mother." Her slender fingers fumbled with the clasp on her purse. With shaking hands, she lit the cigarette she had been holding, then put it absently on the ashtray next to her water glass. She looked at her drink and picked it up while her salad sat, uneaten, on her plate.

"Why, if he was in love with her, would he fake his own death, do you think?"

"I don't know." She sighed heavily. "I know you don't believe me. But I know that he was in love with her, was not having an affair and is not dead!" For a moment, it seemed as though she might get up and leave. If she had, I would have made no move to stop her. Then she sighed again and that time it sounded resigned. She shifted in her chair and picked up her fork.

"Did you see him closely at the funeral?" I asked. Of course, I, myself, had seen the prize-winning photograph of little ten-year-old Aïda Blue standing beside her father's casket with a look of utter misery on her small face.

"Yes," she said.

"Aïda, everyone in the world who owned a television saw your father dead in his casket." I tried to be gentle but there was really no gentle way I could discuss this with her.

"It may not have been him," she said. "It could have been someone who looked like him."

"Who?"

"I don't know," she said angrily stubbing out the smoldering cigarette she had not smoked. She took another sip of water and looked around as if to determine who might be listening to her. "That's what you're supposed to find out. You've seen all of the men who look like him. They're called Royal Blue impersonators. Sure, there are a lot who look nothing at all like him, but you have to admit there are a lot who do."

"But you can't walk up to a guy and ask him if he would mind dying so he can impersonate you dead. Besides, even when they look very much like your father, they never look exactly like him and that's what it would take."

She shook her head and I saw tears glitter in her

eyes again. She never allowed them to fall though.

"What about exhuming his remains, Aïda? Have you ever thought of that?"

She gulped. Then nodded. "He was cremated."

Of course, I thought. *He would be.*

"All right, then," I said and sighed. "What did he like to do? What hobbies did he have? Besides music."

"He painted," she said. "And he sang. Those were his favorite things." She made a small gesture at the shopping bag on the floor. "You read those. You'll know him better than you've ever known anyone. You'll see him through my mother's eyes. She knew him best." She returned my look stare for stare. The woman, whatever her reasons, was convinced that her father was still alive.

As if reading my thoughts, she spoke. "He *is* alive."

"If he is, why hasn't he contacted you?"

"I don't know. Maybe he's ill. Maybe he's in trouble. I don't know, but I *am* sure, Cheyenne."

After a moment, I nodded.

When we had finished lunch, she wrote a check for me. It was twice the amount I had quoted her. While

I reached into my briefcase for a standard contract, she moved the bag of diaries nearer to me.

"Of course, you'll want to go to San Francisco to

check out the painting," she said, gesturing at the check, suddenly all business. "You'll need more than five hundred."

I accepted the retainer and put it into my briefcase. "I have reservations for tomorrow morning," I told her. She nodded.

"You have my information on the paperwork I filled out yesterday," she said. "I want you to call me at any time with any information at all."

She signed the contract without even a cursory reading. When she handed me the paper, our fingers touched. She felt warm and healthy. Balanced. And yet, I felt sure she was hiding something. Maybe nothing important, but something nevertheless.

"Aïda, I want you to realize that you may be spending your money for nothing. I still am not entirely convinced, on the strength of a single painting, that your father is alive. I'll try my best to find him, or at least to find out the truth about what happened to him, if anything, but I can guarantee nothing."

"I know. That's all I want," she said as if she had been expecting this final argument from me. She seemed relieved that it was finally over. Even if I had known, I wouldn't have had the heart to tell her that it was just beginning.

SIX

Monday, January 2, 1984

After lunch I stopped at Avenue Art Glass and spent a few hours under Ab's tutelage. We covered the basics and he got me started on a small project that I was immensely proud of. He had found me a pattern with a simple design and taught me about preparing the pattern, selecting the glass and cutting the pieces. The time flew. I had thought I would be joining a regular group class, but Ab told me he would be teaching me himself. He praised everything I did and when I left, I was so pleased with myself, I couldn't stop grinning.

Before I could get on the plane to San Francisco, I had one more job to finish, and this one could only be done at night.

Waller and Dean, an accounting firm in the burg of Kirkland on the other side of Lake Washington, had hired me to check out their new security system. I had gone over there just the once when they had hired me and had taken a look at it. The system itself had been fine. As good, in fact, as you could get. But I knew there were ways to get into a place other than breaking in or disabling the alarm.

Randolf Waller, however, was cocksure about his expensive new system. I got the impression that he was not used to making mistakes. Or at least admitting to making them.

The head office, where Mr. Waller could watch over his brood, was walled in glass. Inside were vertical blinds that he could close if *he* wanted privacy, but his employees were not afforded that luxury. His office was raised a few feet above the level of the work floor so he could oversee his workers. I wondered how it must feel to try to do your job with your boss literally looking over your shoulder. His work area was nicely furnished with a heavy desk, a rich carpet and drop lamps that looked like hand-blown glass. He had a private restroom. His staff, on the other hand, worked in cubicles and everyone shared two bathrooms among the thirty-six drones.

I wondered how a person could get any work done without having a single item on his desk. It was a shining slab of cherry wood that looked as though it had never been touched by a human hand or even a sheet of paper. There was a credenza behind the desk with a computer on it where I suspected Randolf did most of the business part of his job. It seemed the desk was just for show. In fact, when I slid the contract across it for him to sign, he picked it up almost as if he expected the wood underneath to have become discolored in some way from contact with it. He pulled out one of those cutting board things that don't allow you to get into the upper drawer as long as it's out. He laid the contract there and signed.

"I want you to check the system thoroughly," he had said. "Some of the accountants have been complaining about…uh, missing items. I thought it was break-ins but since I got the new system, there have been two additional reports. Only minor things have been taken." He cleared his throat. "They don't amount to much but I would like you to check the system to make sure it is secure." I wondered if his staff considered their belongings as minor as he did.

I was sure he thought I had some kind of electronic gizmo that I would wave over the main box and then declare it fine. Instead, I nodded and left, undoubtedly leaving him nervous about who he had signed to check out his precious alarm.

At six, I watched the employees file from the building. I waited in my car for the cleaning crew to arrive at around seven. My trunk was loaded with the paraphernalia I had bought the day before and that morning.

At random, I had chosen one of the diaries Aïda had given me to read while I waited. I would get into them in order over the next day or two and try to learn what I could about Royal and his family.

The diary was dated 1960, two years before Aïda had been born.

In moments, I was caught up in the spell woven by a woman who had been dead for a decade. Her name was Renata, and the name, Renata Blue, sang of mystery. It sounded lonely and bewildered, like the wind blowing off a distant cliff. That impression wasn't all my imagination. I felt a sense of her as I handled the diaries she had poured her heart into. I thought of her looking like an older version of Aïda. Like, in fact, the woman in the painting. Royal Blue had kept his professional life strictly apart from his family life. There had been no public pictures of his wife and daughter until after his death and, there had been only a few of them since. I remembered the famous photos of Renata from the funeral, her face twisted with grief. It had been impossible to tell what she had actually looked like. Her hair had been dark, like Aïda's and they had had similar body types.

Certainly, Renata's mind had been beautiful. She had filled her diary with thoughts of her husband and her deep desire for a child. She had seemed to believe she was sterile and while the thought had given her infinite sadness, she had balanced it with a strength of spirit and a striving for goodness that would have been remarkable in a woman twice her age. She had been so convinced that she would never conceive a child that for a moment, I wondered if

Aïda had been adopted. But no. Of course not. I remembered the announcement of her birth.

I put the small book on my lap and looked out at the darkened sky. Renata had gotten her wish and I felt a breath of relief for her and, at the same time, a wave of pity that she had not lived to see her daughter grow up and have children of her own.

I was deep into the book when a van rumbled up and stopped in front of the building. I reluctantly set the diary down and climbed out of my car. Then, smiling broadly, I walked over to the van.

"Excuse me," I said. "I wonder if you could help me." I approached one of the two who had climbed out of the van, a woman about my age. The other, a man, looked at me with total disinterest and hefted a vacuum cleaner out of the back. The woman, who wore a badge that said "Jo", threw me a harried look and only slowed her pace a fraction.

"I've got three other stops to hit tonight," she said. "I don't have time to help you. Now, if you want to help me out, that would be just fine."

"Oh, I don't need you to do anything for *me*," I said. "I just need a little permission from you. See, I'm from Granada Florists and I'm supposed to set up a staff appreciation display for..." I consulted an invoice I took from the pocket of my jeans. It was a receipt for a new set of back tires for my car, but she didn't know that. "Waller and Dean. I'm supposed to meet Mr. Waller, but it seems that he's unable to be here. If I could just come in with you, I could have this thing set up and be out before you knew I had been here at all." I smiled at her. She gave me a quick once over, decided I was harmless and nodded.

"Okay, as long as you stay in sight of one of us at all times," she said. "I can't let you go wandering off all alone."

"No problem," I said, smiling guilelessly. "Thanks a million."

I followed her in and watched her disarm the alarm. Then I went to work.

The accounting offices of Waller and Dean were done in utilitarian gray, relieved by a dark red stripe around the molding. The floor was covered with a gray, coarse weave carpet that looked like it would be hell on the knees if you had to crawl around looking for a contact lens. To me the place looked like a car dealership, but probably the color scheme had been carefully designed to calm antsy clients in trouble with the IRS.

Jo seemed to be in charge of the restrooms, while her male counterpart did the vacuuming, dusting and emptying of the trash. I shared the women's room with her while I filled the bud vases, but we didn't speak.

There were thirty-six work stations in all with chest high partitions separating them and giving the illusion of privacy. The whole set-up reminded me of one of those mazes that psychology students run white mice through. Each station had a desk, two chairs and a computer. Some of the work stations had cartoons or photographs taped to the dividers. At one, the optimistic occupant had attempted to decorate the surroundings with a potted fern that probably had to be replaced from time to time when it died from lack of sunlight. Next door to it, I saw a crystal paperweight shaped like a ten thousand carat cut diamond resting on the desk. It was lovely. I picked it up, then had to polish off the fingerprints I had left. Other stations were as sparse as Mr. Randolf Waller's own digs.

I set a red rose in a vase and one of my business cards at each station. On the floor of one cubicle, I spotted an earring that had fallen close to the leg of the desk. It looked like gold to me with a small sparkling stone. I picked it up and put it onto the desktop so the owner could find it in the morning.

I stood back and admired my work. The red roses and the red stripe looked almost good together. I wondered if old Randy would find it attractive.

As I passed one of the stations, I saw the male half of the cleaning crew snooping through the trash basket prior to dumping it into the garbage can. He carefully read a piece of paper, smiled and put it back into the can. I hoped there was nothing on it more important than a telephone message or a grocery list. I was sure Waller and Dean's clients wouldn't have been happy about strangers having access to their private information. A thought struck me and I began to check all of the cubicles. The giant diamond was no longer sitting on the desk next to the one with the fern. I backtracked and looked at the desk where I had found the earring. It too, was gone. The mystery, it seemed, had been solved.

While Jo cleaned Mr. Waller's private bathroom, I carefully dried the bottom of the last vase on my shirt, then put the white rose in the exact center of Mr. Waller's bare desk. It would have been a shame to mar the lovely shining top. I left one of my cards propped against the vase. On the back of it, I had written, "Your alarm system is only as secure as those who have access to it." I also left him an invoice which included the cost of the flowers and vases. I quickly wrote a note on it (not using the cutting board but the actual desk top!) advising him that he would be wise to invest in a different cleaning company and a shredder. I added an invitation to call me if he had further questions. I was sure there would be at least one message on my answering machine when I returned from California.

I hung around for a few minutes, waiting for the pair to finish up. When we were outside, the alarm rearmed and the door locked, I put my hand on Jo's arm while the other worker climbed into the van.

"Thanks for letting me in," I told her. "I would advise you to question your coworker about his habit of snooping through the trash and stealing. Possibly, you could see to it that the stolen items are returned."

She looked at me and apparently had nothing to say, so I left her standing in the parking lot with a bucket in one hand and a mop in the other.

❋ ❋ ❋

I was home by nine. I felt it had been a good evening's work. Mr. Waller would probably quibble about the expense for the roses and bud vases, but I wasn't going to pay for them myself. Besides, it was a small price to pay for the security of his firm.

I packed a small bag for the morning, set out my "briefcase" which was an old lockable doctor's bag that Easy had given me as a gift a few years before. In it, I carried the tools of my trade; binoculars, latex gloves, plastic bags, swabs, flashlight, my little camera and any number of PI toys that I couldn't get along without. I did not pack my gun with me. I had one. I was qualified to use it as well as licensed to carry it, but I knew myself too well. I knew that I was not capable of taking the life of a fellow human being. I also had been wrong enough times to know that I did not wish to make a life or death decision in a matter of a split second. Therefore, my weapon remained locked safely at home and I ventured out armed only with a few self-defense moves.

I brewed a cup of tea and settled down with the rest of the Saks bag of memorabilia. There was a spool of film and an album full of newspaper clippings and photos as well as a large manila envelope.

The album fascinated me. It had obviously been put together by Aïda when she was very young. The articles and photos had been carefully taped to the pages and beneath them, captions had been lettered in block print. "My Daddy in Chicago," or "The Movie My Father Is In."

I dug into the envelope and discovered it was crammed with photographs. Not publicity stills, but candid shots of an ordinary family celebrating birthdays and Christmases and doing everyday things.

I found a photo of Renata and studied her face. It was almost startling in its plainness. I was surprised. I had always thought of her as somewhat glamorous. In the photograph, she had large brown eyes and a small nose. The camera had caught her smiling with her thin lips stretched across teeth too small for beauty. But she had a shine in her huge eyes and a smile that would light up the world. The few pictures of her which had appeared in magazines had not only been doctored, Renata had been wearing make-up and styled hair as well. I supposed anyone could look beautiful with a little help.

I peered at each photo, trying to get a sense of

Royal Blue as husband and father rather than the voice and the face the world knew.

He was a handsome man. I had always thought so, but in his family pictures, he looked different. Less handsome and more neighborly. He didn't look like the man who wore flashy sequined jackets and his hair a-fly. This man wore his long hair tied into a conservative pony tail. With the absence of make-up and glitzy clothing, the man himself showed through. On his left little finger, the heart-shaped sapphire ring that was his trademark, flashed. I set the picture aside and picked up another. Aïda, her mouth sparkling with braces, grinned into the camera lens.

I found a photo of Royal with his arm across the shoulders of a heavy man several inches shorter. The legend on the back read "Roy and Mickey." Mickey's arm reached around Royal's waist. Both men were dressed in tuxes with rings twinkling on their hands and their shoes shining like mirrors.

I selected another photo and leaned back in my recliner. I closed my eyes and focused on the memory of the snapshot—Aïda sitting on her father's lap—and let my mind wander. In a moment I felt a surge of warmth and pictures began to flash before my closed eyes. Muted colors swam before me and snatches of music I didn't recognize. Faster and faster the images swirled until I unconsciously clutched the chair arms for support. It was like riding a roller coaster in my own living room. Except that I was no longer in my home but in a strange world where sounds and colors were the same. I gasped and breathed in a lungful of smoke then I opened my eyes. Every image disappeared as well as the sense of smoke and noise. I was alone and the house was quiet. I didn't know what it was that I had experienced, but it didn't seem to be any image of death, whatever that might be.

With my hands trembling, I picked up the photograph of Aïda and her father again and stared into his eyes. What madness had driven this man to suicide?

"Are you alive?" I whispered. He stared back at me, silent, and after a moment I put the picture back.

I called Georgina at the big house and told her I was coming in to use the projector and screen in the ballroom for a few minutes. She assured me that I didn't need her permission and that I was welcome anytime. I flung a jacket across my shoulders and, clutching the reel of film, stepped through the adjoining yards to the house. In moments, I was watching the jerky, silent antics of a family at Thanksgiving.

The camera tilted crazily, then caught Royal preparing to carve a turkey. He flourished the knife with much waving of his elbows then set to work. An Irish setter pressed her nose to his thigh and was shooed away. The camera followed the dog to a fireplace where she joined another. Both dogs kept their eyes on the carver of the turkey.

The scene shifted and a young Aïda, perhaps two or three years old, stood on a chair belting out a silent song. Her dress, a flouncy pink organdy over a stiff petticoat, danced while she flung her arms about like an opera singer. When she finished, she curtsied, nearly upsetting the chair. A hand reached out from beyond the picture to steady her.

The next scene was Royal and Aïda, singing a duet. I heartily wished the film had been equipped with sound. Royal sat in a huge leather winged chair and strummed a guitar. Aïda leaned against his knee and together they sang through an unknown, unheard song.

I watched the film to its finish, then watched it again. It left me feeling vaguely envious and very sad. I left the screen up and snapped off the light, knowing I would want to come back and see it again.

Back in my own house, I selected a diary and began to read.

SEVEN

Monday, January 2, 1984

Renata Hollingsworth and Royal Blue had met on a rainy evening in Cincinnati, when their umbrellas had locked on a downtown street. Afterward, every meaningful look, every sigh, every precious word had been recorded in the diary in which Renata had written faithfully.

"I'd never heard of Royal Blue until tonight," she exulted in one of the small, cloth-bound books. *"But, apparently, he's a famous man. I suddenly love a whole new kind of music."*

I counted up the years and realized that Renata had been only sixteen when she had literally run into Royal on the street and thereby changed her life forever.

They had met while Royal was on tour. Renata, rushing from a late music lesson, had collided with him then had rehashed it again and again in her diary.

"He's so good looking! I love the way his eyes are so blue. He thinks he's ugly, the way he's tall and his hair is so wild, but he's beautiful! He's wonderful! Everything about him is. I think I'm in love! His name is really Roy Bluestone. Of course, he changed it for professional reasons. He seems more like Royal Blue than Roy Bluestone anyway."

I returned to the album and compared Royal Blue with Roy Bluestone. The family man, Roy, had an ordinary, guileless face with dark blue eyes. The ends of his light brown hair curled boyishly and when he smiled, he looked something like a kid, enormously pleased with himself. Professionally, he was a different man. He wore make-up that muted his boyishness and his flashy clothes added dash and mystery. For performances, he sprayed his hair with a sparkle that glinted eerily in the spotlights.

I put down the heavy book and wandered into the kitchen for more tea. The wind had come up and was bashing the tree branches against the house. With a fresh cup, I settled again in the living room.

Renata had apparently kept a diary for many years. The first book, numbered with a tiny "6" marked on the binding, detailed thousands of trivial items important only to a teenaged girl in love for the first time; the first kiss, the first flowers, the first hint of anything more permanent than teenaged puppy love. I read it through, captured by the fresh phrases and breathless, exuberant style. She categorized his virtues and glossed over any hint of failure.

Around me, the quiet house settled. The fire died to glowing coals that crashed softly and were still. I fed it another log and it steamed quietly before catching. Far away, I heard the wail of a siren and I read on. At intervals the wind hit the house, then subsided.

The romance had been conducted long distance for the first year or two, Royal taking every chance to meet with Renata. It wasn't long, though, before it had become serious and when Renata turned eighteen, she joined him on tour whenever her music obligations allowed.

"He's asked me to marry him," Renata wrote near the end of the second book. I wondered at the lack of exclamation that had punctuated nearly every sentence up until then. Perhaps she felt the importance of this entry and realized that exclamations would be more useful later.

"We had a serious talk about all the problems that might come up, but I'm sure we can handle anything that happens. I feel that I know so little," she wrote. *"He wants me to fully understand what I'm getting into, but I know that no matter what he says, I want to do this. I know I can learn to be a good wife and I know I'll never find anyone else that I love as much as I do him."*

It sounded so typical, I thought. A young woman, who had no concept of marriage, calmly stating that she could overcome anything that came along.

I continued reading in detail about the wedding and all of Renata's seemingly infinite plans.

After the wedding, the business of life began again. Renata rarely missed more than a day or two of recording the comings and goings of her daily routine.

"Tomorrow, we start the tour," she wrote. *"We'll be gone for four months. I'll be seeing places I never thought I would see and doing things I never dreamed I would do. Roy says I'll get tired of it in a week but I know I won't. He says I can go home if I want, but that he hopes I'll stay to the end. He says he'd be too lonely without me."*

"Roy gave the benefit concert for the children in the hospital today. I cried when I saw all of the sick little boys and girls, but he held them on his lap and talked to them all when the concert was over. One child said he was going to be a rock star when he grew up and Roy gave him his guitar. He knew the little boy would never grow up."

The picture of Royal Blue was becoming clearer. He seemed, according to Renata, almost overwhelmed at his popularity. He rarely gave interviews, disliked being photographed, and yet, if there was a benefit concert to be sung, he was there helping to organize it. He seemed to yearn only to be with his wife and she seemed perfectly happy to give up any career hopes of her own to be with him. Of course, in those days, girls hadn't thought much about careers for themselves, though obviously Renata had had musical promise. The diaries were peppered with comments of awards and achievements.

It was later, in the book numbered with a small "10", that Renata ran headlong into one of the things that she had apparently not foreseen. For several weeks there were few entries. Then came a sudden twist.

"Oh, my God! I'm going to have a baby! I'm so scared."

I set the book aside and rose to stir the fire. The flames flared then settled once again.

"I've decided to throw myself into my music," she wrote after another interval of more than a month with no entry other than a quick line to mention the city where Royal was playing. *"Roy doesn't mind. He says it would be good for me. I've talked to Mr. Jasperson and he's willing to continue my studies. It will mean I can't follow Roy as much as I have, but without my violin I think I would go insane."*

I glanced at the date, wondering if she had miscarried. But the dates coincided with Aïda's conception. Had she feared losing the baby? From the beginning she had thought pregnancy an impossibility. Perhaps she had been misinformed or had misunderstood a doctor when she had been told conception would be difficult. I rejoiced for her nevertheless. Clearly, she had been unprepared.

"Roy is so wonderful," she wrote a few entries later.

"He's wonderful. I'm going to have a baby. I can't believe it. Now I can put my violin away and never think of it again. Roy says that we must never let it get in the way of our happiness. It's over. We'll never think of it again. Ever."

I set the book aside and puzzled over the last few lines. Why would she never want to think of her violin again when only a few lines before it had been the only thing holding off insanity? Did it, for some reason, evoke painful memories? Had an argument over her music developed into a rift between them? Had the coming child given her the excuse she needed to set aside her career hopes and devote herself to her family? I shook my head. There was something in this entry that didn't add up. There was definitely some piece of the puzzle missing.

I resumed reading.

"If it's a girl, I'm going to name her Clementine after my mother and if it's a boy, I'm going to name him Roy after his wonderful, wonderful father. I'm so happy."

I wondered if Aïda had read far enough to realize the fate she had escaped. Roy must have vetoed the name of Clementine in favor of Aïda.

Somewhere outside a dog barked once. I glanced at the clock, knowing I had to get up early for my flight, yet I was caught in the web of Renata's and Royal's lives.

He seemed to be an innocent man for all of his world renown. His wonder and his naïve comments were duly recorded in his wife's diary and lent him a certain charm. I gathered that he had been too busy for women during his early years of fame, for he seemed to find them mysterious.

Eventually, the small books became sprinkled with references to Aïda's baby antics and her parents' delight in her.

When Aïda was four, Renata wrote, *"Roy says that someday we're going, the three of us, to live in a tropical paradise where no one knows us."* I looked at those hopeful lines and sighed for the lost lives. There were still a few diaries yet to read, each one spanning about a year. Then they stopped. The little family had never found their paradise.

"Richard is back," began the next book. Richard? I had heard no mention of a Richard at all. I made a note to ask Aïda who he was. *"I haven't seen him but I heard Roy telling Mickey that he was in town. I'm frightened."* She didn't elaborate. Rather, she went on to a description of little Aïda's part in the school production of "Teeth Health." Seven-year-old Aïda played an incisor.

"It's happened," she wrote in tiny writing completely unlike the looping letters of the earlier books. It was as if she had been frightened into writing small, as if no one would see the admission if she used tiny, fragile letters. *"It's happened again. I think Roy is going to lose his mind. This time it's worse. So much worse. What am I going to do?"*

There began to be long gaps between entries. I thumbed through the final few books and in the middle of the last diary, the end came. Suddenly paradise had vanished. Royal Blue was dead. In pathetically few pages, Renata described the grief and loss that wracked her life for the few more months of it. As if her heart were broken, she set aside her will to live and almost immediately lost the battle. One year after her husband, Renata too had died.

I put down the final book, lost in thought. What had happened that had frightened Renata so badly? I picked up the album and idly turned the stiffened pages. On one of them was a blank space I had previously ignored. The photo had been removed. "Uncle Richard," read the caption beneath it. I thumbed back through the book. No, there were no others with the same name. With misty recollection, I remembered faded rumors from long ago. There had been a minor scandal involving drunkenness and mention of a brother, I thought. He had apparently disappeared quickly and quietly from public view. There, of course, could lie the answer. I had no idea what he had looked like or, indeed, if he had still been living when Royal died. Richard Bluestone's ashes could very well be lying in the grave marked with Royal Blue's name. Had Aïda suspected? Why hadn't she mentioned her uncle before? Had she been taught that Richard was dead? A black sheep in the family was certainly nothing new. Clearly, Renata had been afraid of him. Perhaps he was estranged from his relatives. If he had committed some crime or some other unforgivable act, it seemed a likely possibility.

By my watch it was 2:25. The wind had died and the house had settled into silence. This bit of information put a new light on what I knew of the case so far. Now, I was inclined to agree with Aïda.

EIGHT

Tuesday, January 3, 1984

I stepped off the plane at the San Francisco Airport into one of those afternoons that I always thought of as typical California weather. Everyone thinks it rains constantly in Seattle. That's just as ridiculous as the notion that it's sunny all the time in California. But that day it was beautiful. The sun glinted off the bay and lit up the streets of downtown.

I took an overly air-conditioned shuttle from the airport to the Chancellor, a small, old fashioned hotel on Powell Street. I knew it and liked its quiet hominess, having stayed there once when I had come to San Francisco to look for a runaway. They had a quaint policy of requiring the guests to drop their keys at the desk when they went out and ask for them again upon their return. For some reason, I liked that.

The bellman, Eddy, took my bag from me and

ushered me into the creaky elevator. "Now, you'll like this here room," he said when he was unlocking the door. He entered ahead of me and fussed with the window shades, the lamp, the bedspread, the ice bucket. "Nice room in the back. Streetcar bells won't keep you awake all night with their clangin'." He gave me a broad wink, as if it were somehow risqué of him to mention my being awake at night. His crinkled smile and elaborate pompadour made me think of an old-time movie actor. His eyes sparkled with good humor and his big ceramic-y teeth clinked at the end of each sentence. "You need anything, anything at all, you just give me a holler." He winked again. If he'd been younger, he could easily have become a pain in the ass, but since he was old enough to be everyone's great-grandfather— too old, probably to still be a bellman—I didn't take offense.

By the time I got settled, it was well after lunch and my stomach rumbled uncomfortably. I downed a quick bowl of soup in the dining room downstairs then headed out on foot to look for the antiques dealer from whom Aïda had acquired the painting. I walked up sunny Geary and found the place crammed in between a used-book store and a haberdashery. The sign over the door said "polk street antiques, deer o'connell, prop." The windows were filled with depression glass, faded photographs in oval frames and dust.

A bell over the door tinkled when I pushed

inside. No one answered the ring so I bent over a collection of last century's postcards under the glass on the counter. When I had finished with them, my gaze wandered up the wall to a silver embroidered sombrero of velvety black that Easy would have cheerfully committed a crime for. I dragged my attention away from it and bent to peer at a tiny jade elephant. He wasn't one of the lucky ones with his trunk raised. Instead, he looked belligerent and rather cantankerous. I supposed that was his appeal.

"Can I answer any questions for you?"

I turned to see a woman of about fifty years old emerging from the depths of the dim back of the store. She was plump and dashing in various draperies of purple, pink and red. Her hair was long, nearly to her waist, parted in the middle and hanging free. It was the color of wisteria in full bloom.

"How much is the little green elephant?" I asked, more to start a dialog with her than because I was thinking about buying it.

"He's lovely, isn't he?" She stepped closer to me and I caught the scent of patchouli. When she moved, she jingled like a pair of finger cymbals. Her feet were bare.

"How much?"

"He's one seventy-five," she said proudly, as if she was telling me what a bargain it was. I knew she didn't mean a dollar and three quarters. I hid my wince and reverently replaced the elephant on the shelf.

"My name is Cheyenne Bruce," I said, and handed her one of my cards. "I'm looking for Deer. The owner."

"I'm deer," she said and drew herself up to a full five feet. She pulled a card from somewhere in her voluminous purple skirt and handed it to me. Sure enough, it said her name was deer, printed in small letters.

"I don't use capital letters," she volunteered primly when I mentioned it. She seemed to have recited the speech many times. "I believe that human beings are on the same level as other animals and plants. Capital letters are a human affectation that places more value on people than on animals. I don't believe in that." She had a soft, husky voice that reminded me, for some reason, of wood smoke.

I nodded as if I agreed with her completely.

"I'm a private investigator," I told her and pocketed the card. "I wonder if you could answer a few questions for me?"

"Certainly," she said.

"Do you remember selling this painting to a young woman about a month ago?" I took the photo from my briefcase and slid it across the counter to her.

While I spoke, deer pursed her lips and began nodding. "Yes, I do remember. I sold it to Aïda Blue.

It is lovely, isn't it? We seemed to think it looked something like her. Aïda, I mean. Lovely girl."

"Yes, it does look somewhat like Aïda. Do you recall where you got the painting?"

"Yes, I do. I saw someone running down the alley just as I was leaving the shop one night. He had left that painting leaning against my window." She smiled. "Awfully mysterious," she said in a near whisper.

I didn't even have to touch her. I could tell she was lying. I stared at her but said nothing.

After a moment, she seemed to deflate a bit. "I'm sorry. Aïda asked me the same thing. I really don't like to give my customers too much background on the pieces they buy, unless, of course, there's a good story connected to it. Most of these treasures are cast-offs." She shook her head and again I caught the whiff of patchouli. "Sometimes I cook up a much better background for their purchase." She leaned her head to the side like a dog does when he wants part of your ice cream.

"So, where *did* you get it?" I asked her. "I'm afraid this is important."

"I don't honestly remember," she said. I believed her that time.

"Would you take a look at your records, please. I'd like to know where you got the painting. I'm doing some investigative work regarding art thieves.

I believe that painting may have been stolen."

She looked properly alarmed and scurried away to scramble among her records.

I don't hate lying as much as I should, and sometimes a vague threat accomplishes much more than the straight truth. I assumed that art thievery was sufficient to frighten her into a little cooperation. Besides, she was the one who liked a good story.

I browsed while deer scrounged through a series of loose-leaf notebooks. Apparently record keeping was another thing she thought unimportant along with proper capitalization.

"Aha!" she said after not nearly long enough for me to thoroughly go over her inventory of glass. She carried a sheaf of papers to my side.

"That painting...hmmm," she said, turning one of the pages over. "It seems to have come with a shipment of items from Hawaii. That's odd. My shipments from the islands are usually mostly tropical carvings, bead and coral jewelry. Things like that. I don't get many paintings. Not from there."

"Were there any other paintings in that shipment?" I asked.

"No." She shook her head and glanced through the papers. "That was the only one. It came from a dealer there named Aloyse Kaneko. She has a gift shop in Kailua or Kona. I don't know. I always get those mixed up. She sends me stuff once in a while. But, like I said, it's usually…" She shrugged. "Island stuff. Of course, she may have bought the painting anywhere. She may have thought it would sell better in California than Hawaii."

"Which island was that?" I asked, trying to peer over her shoulder.

"Hawaii," she said. I must have looked blank. Geography was not my strongest subject in school. The only island I knew about first hand was Mercer and only because I had once lived there. "The big island," she was saying.

"When was that, Ms. O'Connell?" I was damned if I was going to call her "deer". It sounded too intimate to me, no matter how it was spelled.

"Let's see." She made little humming noises while she searched and calculated. "I got it last spring and had it for several months before Aïda bought it. I'm surprised it didn't sell much sooner, really. It is quite nice. But then, maybe people who buy nudes want the fronts of them." She smiled and jingled faintly.

I wrote the name and address of Aloyse Kaneko's shop in my notebook and thanked deer. Just before I gave the jade elephant a last longing glance, I asked her how much the sombrero was.

"Now I got that sombrero in a mysterious little shop in Mex…" she started to tell me. Then she thought better of her story and said she had found it in a thrift store. She didn't want as much for it as I had thought but more than I wanted to pay.

I held onto my wallet for dear life. I didn't need any of deer's "treasures". I was living in a charming house, next door to a mansion filled with beautiful artifacts. Even my clientele had classed up a notch. I still wanted the little elephant. As for the sombrero, I hardened my heart and walked away.

I swung back down Polk and passed a pasta place that looked like a possibility for dinner later. I wanted a quick peek into Chinatown, though, so I turned toward Grant Avenue.

While I walked, I couldn't help but wish Easy was with me. If only he hadn't been thinking about that marriage nonsense, I might have asked him to join me. We could have had a wonderful time.

I did want to find a hat for him, nevertheless. After thinking about it for a few blocks, I backtracked to deer's and bought him the wonderful, embroidered sombrero.

Before deer put the hat into a large hat box for me, I ran my hands over the silky fabric and the sparkling silver embroidery and knew that the hat was probably worth much more than she realized. When I paid, I added an extra ten dollars "for the information on Aloyse," I told her.

"Can you tell me one thing?" She asked before I left. "You said that you knew the painting wasn't left by a mysterious stranger. How did you know?"

"I didn't say that I knew. I didn't say anything," I told her, using as innocent a look as I could muster. "I'm psychic."

She laughed and waved and headed toward the back of the store whence she had come.

I walked back toward Grant Avenue to continue with my tour of Chinatown. The hat box was awkward but I was glad I had gotten the hat anyway. I may not want to marry Easy, but I didn't want to lose his friendship either. The very thought of marriage almost put me into a bad mood. Easy, it seemed, had been crowding into too many of my thoughts. He knew that I was a loner and that I liked it that way.

I had actually been engaged more than once, which was one of the reasons I had an aversion to it. The first man I had been going to marry was killed in Vietnam and I would never, ever forget him. Every time I thought about marriage, I thought about David. The second time I got engaged, I went ahead and married the man. But, at one point, he went out to pick up a quart of milk and never came home. He didn't meet with foul play, nor did he suddenly develop amnesia. The next day, while I was at work, he came and got all of his things and I never saw him again. The unfortunate part was that I had still loved him very much. We hadn't been having any marital trouble that I had been aware of. It was a mystery I had never solved.

The day wasn't turning out as well as I had hoped, so I plunged into the color and noise of Chinatown, determined to be all tourist intent on having a good time. It didn't work. After touring Chinatown three times over, I trudged, hot and out of sorts, back up the hill to the Italian restaurant.

There, the light was low and the linguini was piled high. It was cooked with exactly the right amount of garlic (lots) and the wine was perfect, sweet and smooth. At last, I relaxed against the high-backed leather seat and thought of nothing but the excellent food.

I ate enough that I didn't want dessert and walked slowly back to the Chancellor in the dark. The night had cooled considerably and I regretted not having brought a jacket. For some reason I never could remember to wear one when I visited California. But then, I didn't pretend to have a very high degree of sophistication either.

I hadn't gone a block before I heard heavy footsteps behind me and realized I was being followed. I glanced around but saw only shadows. A streetcar labored up the hill, its lights momentarily chasing away the dark. I thought about making a jump for it but the pasta and wine were slowing me down. I turned back and continued, trying to keep my ears open for sounds. When I heard the footsteps again, I stopped and turned, meaning to face any potential enemy.

I saw a man walking in the deepest of the shadows about a half block back. *He's no one*, I thought, and was surprised to find myself shaking. *He's just going home from dinner like I am.* I turned and walked faster, but his step kept pace with mine. I crossed the street and picked up speed. His footfalls disappeared then resumed on my side of the street.

Suddenly, I stopped and faced him again.

"Are you following me?" I asked loudly, trying to sound belligerent. He said nothing. "I asked you a question." He was closer but I still couldn't see his face. By his outline, I could see that he was tall, though not big. "Are you following me?" I asked again, deliberately sounding like a crabby bitch. He blended back into the shadows.

I was still looking for him when an arm snaked around my neck.

"Yes," a voice whispered into my ear.

NINE

Tuesday, January 3-Wednesday, January 4, 1984

I stomped as hard as I could on his instep. He yelped in pain but didn't loosen his grip. Instead, he tightened it.

"I want you," he breathed.

"Shove it, Bozo!" I said and cracked him in the ribs with my elbow.

"Oof," he said and let go, backing off. I was about to offer him a swift goodbye kick when my arms were caught from behind in a vise-like grip.

"Beat it!" a gruff voice said. Bozo took off running as fast as his injured foot and his bruised ribs could carry him.

Obviously, my rescuer wasn't intending to rescue me at all. I struggled against him and he let me. When I stopped, he turned me around and, before I could react, he pasted me in the mouth. I spun backward but didn't fall. He stepped toward me and his fist glanced off my chin. My heel caught in the crack of the sidewalk and I went down like a sack of ripe tomatoes.

"Here, asshole," I said and shoved my wallet toward him. The box holding Easy's hat lay in a dented heap nearby. "Take it home and enjoy yourself." He kicked the wallet out of my hand and it skidded nearer to the hat box. Then he dragged me to my feet by the front of my shirt.

"You keep your nose out of places where it doesn't belong," he said. His breath stank of cigarettes and something else. Bourbon? It was too dark to see his face and he had a baseball hat on that shaded his eyes even further.

Groggy, I wiped my hand across my lips and felt blood mingle with saliva in my mouth. I gathered a load, then spit into his face. I knew when I was doing it that it wasn't the smartest thing to do. I saw his fist coming, then I fell backward into a black hole.

When I awoke, I was half sitting on a sack of garbage and leaning against a soggy carboard box. I turned sideways and vomited linguini and wine all over the pavement. I struggled to all fours then crawled on wobbly arms and legs until I found my wallet and the hatbox. I stood clumsily, clutching them. "Shit," I muttered through my sore lips. I staggered into the street and didn't have the strength to dodge a car that almost hit me. A man leaned out of the window and yelled something about being crazy. Of course, I must have looked like a drunk. Or worse.

I sat down for a moment on the sidewalk with my feet in the gutter. I put my head down between my knees until the street stopped spinning and I could see only one of everything again. I was furious with myself for not reacting quickly enough to fend the guy off. I thought that first clip to the chin had thrown me off my game right from the start. All the same, I didn't consider that a sufficient excuse.

Finally, I put my head up, looked around and realized I wasn't that far from my hotel. I climbed slowly to my feet and gingerly walked, holding onto buildings. The hill before me looked like a sheer cliff, but by stopping every few feet, I made it to the Chancellor and in the door.

Eddy saw me instantly. He clucked and poked at me like I was a dead chicken. "What the hey happened to you?" he asked. "You been in a ax-y-dent or what?"

"No accident, just a little mix-up with the local riff-raff. But I won," I said holding my wallet and the hat box aloft.

"I'll call the cops for you." He made a grab for the phone, but I waved him off.

"Just let me have my key. I want a quick bath and bed."

"No, no. You let me get Clark over there to call

the cops." He started toward the desk clerk who heretofore had not seen me behind the potted plant in the lobby.

I shook my head, almost too weary to argue. "No cops. Just…" I wobbled into him and he hustled me into the elevator.

"You stay here, I'll go get your key."

"No cops," I reiterated.

He mumbled something but nodded.

During the ride up, he didn't stop muttering about the police but he unlocked my room for me and steered me inside.

"I'm gonna clean that there up for you," he said and gestured at my cheek. I sank onto the bed while Eddy headed to the bathroom for a washcloth. He dabbed at the sorest place and clicked his tongue. "You gonna have a scar for sure," he said. "Might not be too bad, though. Gonna be shaped like a star." He stood back and admired his work and the wound as if appraising a piece of art.

I stood stiffly and hobbled to the mirror. Sure enough, a perfect star was cut into my cheekbone.

"Too bad a pretty girl like you got to be scarred," he said, making another dab at it.

"I guess I should be happy it's not on the end of my nose," I said wearily. "If you don't mind, Eddy, I'm going to take a hot bath."

"I'm comin' back with some tea for you." he said. "I'll put it inside your door so don't put on the security latch till after you get out of the tub." He scurried away down the hall. He would have made someone a terrific mother.

I shed my clothes on the way to the bathroom and drew the deepest, hottest bath I could. I don't know why it is, but when I don't feel well, the first thing I want to do is take off my clothes.

I sank into the hot water, gasping as it touched my skin. Nothing has ever felt so wonderful before or since. In a few minutes I heard Eddy call from the door. I called something back to him but I don't remember what.

I must have slept, because when I awoke the water was tepid and horrible. I shivered and drained it out. Goose flesh dotted my body while I ran fresh hot water into the tub and warmed up again.

When at last, I climbed out, I found a tray with a Thermos of tea and a plate of Scottish shortbread sitting on the floor just inside the door. That Eddy was earning himself one hell of a tip.

My one thought was what a wasted trip it had been. I had learned nothing from deer that I couldn't have found out with a ten minute phone call. It seemed that Aïda had paid money only for me to get my poor face shellacked.

The tea and cookies revived me more than I would have thought possible. I drank every drop and ate every crumb. Then I sank into bed and fell asleep immediately.

* * *

"**I** should have gone with you," Easy mourned when he picked me up at the airport the next day. I had called him from San Francisco to warn him about the sorry condition of my face.

"And you would have gotten slapped around too," I told him.

"Did you call the police?" he asked.

"Yes," I lied. If he thought I hadn't, he'd take over like he was my father. I knew they'd never catch the son of a bitch. Never try. There are thousands of incidents like that in every city every day. The police can't be expected to drop everything and look for a guy who knocked me down, but didn't even bother to take my wallet. Of course, that wasn't why he had flattened me. He had told me to mind my own business. Someone wasn't happy that I was looking into Royal Blue's affairs. I didn't tell that part to Easy either.

"Look, Easy," I said, smiling at him and putting my hand on his shoulder. "I just want to get home. I'm tired and I have a lot to do tomorrow."

"You need some help," he muttered.

"Help? What are you talking about?"

"Help. A secretary. An assistant. A...I don't know. A partner."

"No, thank you," I said, too tired to add anything else. Like I could afford a secretary, needed an assistant or wanted a partner.

At home, I stashed the hat box into a closet. I was going to hang onto it until Easy's birthday. By July, he would no longer be inclined to connect it with my trip to California.

On my answering machine was a surprisingly subdued message from Mr. Randolf Waller of Waller and Dean. I called him and explained what I had seen in his office. I told him to make sure that the next cleaning crew he hired was bonded, and to see to it that each of his staff had a shredder and used it. He actually thanked me.

Next, I called Aïda.

"How awful," she said when I told her what had happened. "You shouldn't have gone alone."

"Did you tell anyone I was going to San Francisco to investigate your case?"

"No. Well, only Jon-Paul, but he..."

Oh, yes, the fiancé.

"But you aren't implying that he had anything to do with this, are you?" Her voice frosted over like ice on a sheet of glass. "He doesn't even know who you are."

I doubted that. "I just wondered who might have known. What have you told him about this case?"

"Why, all of it. We're going to be married. He has a right to know."

"Of course, he does." I swallowed a sigh and told her what I had found out.

"Hawaii?" she said, suddenly interested again.

"Deer said she'd gotten the painting in a shipment from a woman who owns a shop on the big island. I could go, but perhaps a phone call…"

"You should go, by all means!" she said, interrupting me and sounding enthusiastic for the first time since I'd met her. "I think you should *go* to Hawaii."

"The trip to San Francisco was completely unnecessary, Aïda," I told her. "A trip to Hawaii may be just as fruitless."

"No," she said. She sounded determined. "I want you to go."

I wasn't going to argue with her. Instead, I switched to another topic. "Aïda, why didn't you tell me that your father had a brother?"

She was silent for so long, I thought she might have quietly hung up. "He hasn't been around for a long, long time," she said finally.

"Where is he? Does he have a wife? Kids? Anyone I

should be talking to?"

"The last I heard he was going to Australia, but that was when I was a child. I wouldn't know if he has a wife. As far as I ever heard, he never married. He hasn't been around for years. I have no idea where he is or if he's even still alive." She sounded uneasy.

"The very fact that your father had a brother could change the whole complexion of this case. Is there anything else you haven't mentioned?"

Again, she didn't answer.

"Look, Aïda," I said, trying not to sigh so she could hear me. "We'll talk again about Hawaii. It may not be necessary for me to go. This is the expensive season. Why don't you think about this for a while?"

She murmured something and we hung up.

One thing bothered me. The "rescuer" who had saved me from the rapist and then whomped the shit out of me had told me to mind my own business. To keep my "nose out of places where it doesn't belong" was how he had put it. He didn't say anything else, though. Maybe he had said more when I was unconscious. I pictured him standing over me not knowing that I was out cold and giving me instructions to leave town and never come back. Perhaps he didn't know that I'd already found out what I had come for. And there was another thing. While the first attacker had given me a distinct psychic impression that he was a thug who liked to dominate women, the second one had surprised me. He hadn't seemed to be the ordinary mugger type, whatever that was. I had gotten an impression of him too, a clearer one. He'd had an aura of entitlement and power around him. And I had gotten the impression that he was vain and spoiled. I frowned and felt a twinge of pain in my cheek. I thought again about Jon-Paul. There was a man I needed to talk to.

I opened the drawer where the packet of photographs lay and dumped them out on my desk. I selected one or two and set them down again, not knowing what I was looking for. Then my gaze fell on the picture of Royal and Mickey Carrol, his agent, standing with their arms around one another. I dug into the bottom drawer and found a magnifying glass. It was a cheap one. I had a better one in my briefcase, but this one proved strong enough to show me that Mickey Carrol was wearing a ring. It was hard to see, but I swear it was shaped like a perfect star.

Before I hopped onto a chance for a caprice to Hawaii, I wanted to have a little talk with Mr. Carrol. I had an interesting star-shaped cut on my cheek that he might like to see and try to explain to me. I also wanted to talk to Aïda's attorney. Maybe he could give me a few more details about Royal Blue's business.

I picked up the phone book and found Mickey Carrol listed. His number rang seven times before I gave up and called Charles Harbor, Aïda's attorney, and made an appointment for the following afternoon. What with beatings by strangers and unknown brothers popping up, who knew what could happen next?

TEN

Thursday, January 5. 1984

Ab was so appalled at the condition of my face that I thought he was going to run me down to the Harborview Hospital ER just to make sure I wasn't in danger of imminent death. I told him I had met with a little altercation when I had been in California.

He put his finger under my chin and tipped my face up to the daylight. "Damn, woman!" he said. "That looks like you ran into a lot more than a 'little altercation.' You're old enough to stay out of bar fights, I would think."

I laughed. "That actually might have been more fun. It was only a mugger, I'm afraid."

He looked at my eyes. "You okay? No head injuries? I guess you got checked out by a doctor, right?"

I told him I had been checked out, and reassured him that I was fine. I *had* been checked out, even if it was only by Doctor Eddy. The bruise was beginning to really bloom into spectacular color, and I saw that it was going to be a big one, centered with that star shaped cut. Ab made *tsk-tsking* noises every time he looked up and saw me.

Nevertheless, I spent some of Thursday morning in Avenue Art Glass and immensely enjoyed myself. I sold a glass cutter to a woman who was far too polite to mention my facial damage and I worked on my first project. The hour and a half I spent there was over way too soon.

* * *

Charles Harbor's secretary had sounded a bit brusque and pre-occupied on the phone but maybe she hadn't wanted to interrupt her normal routine to deal with anything as sordid as a private investigator. I began to wonder why I was working so hard for little Aïda at all. Even she didn't seem as much enthused as driven to find out what had happened, if anything, to her father. Whatever I found out more than likely wouldn't be pleasant.

My back was giving me a bit of a problem when I set out for the posh offices of Slater and Washington, Attorneys at Law. I resolved to consider making an appointment with a doctor if the twinges and pangs didn't go away in a few days. Weeks. Maybe months. I didn't like to go to the doctor if I didn't have to. I firmly believed that almost every disease and discomfort afflicting a person would go away eventually, and those that didn't, the doctor could then remedy. I resolved to go over to see my friend, Molly, and beg her for a massage. Bearing a plate of brownies, I can get Molly to do anything.

I drove my yellow Honda Civic over the Lake Washington Floating Bridge on my way to Bellevue. On my left, the new bridge was nearing completion. Soon the old one would be closed and the new one would be whisking traffic painlessly in both directions. The sun and sky had turned the water a clear shade of cerulean and Mt. Rainier loomed on my right. There's nowhere more lovely than Seattle on a rare sunny day in January.

Bellevue sat like a jewel between Lake Washington and Lake Sammamish. For the past decade or two it had grown like a crystal and was as beautiful. Back then, most of Bellevue's inhabitants were young, urban professionals who liked to keep their living conditions as pristine and well cared for as possible. Consequently, Bellevue was one lovely city.

I parked in the spacious parking area reserved for the clients of Slater and Washington and locked the car. The building was one of those new colored glass jobs that changed depending on how the light hit it. That afternoon it was aqua and quite elegant.

I went up to the twenty-first floor in a posh elevator that was nicer than my old apartment on Mercer Island and just about the same size. A high-brow version of Muzak played through the concealed speaker.

A doll-like receptionist informed me that Mr. Harbor would see me momentarily. She also informed me that she was a "temp" and I should forgive her for not recognizing me. She eyed my face too, but didn't appear to be surprised that a potential client of a lawyer's office had somehow been injured. If she was the same woman I had talked to on the phone, she had a completely different demeanor for people standing before her than she did with the ones she couldn't see. Or maybe she thought I had been in a brawl and she had better be nice to me.

"I'm not a regular client," I assured her. She smiled wisely and I was certain that if I came in again while she was there, she would not only know my name but would greet me by it and probably know my business too. Keeping her smile firmly in place, she turned back to her typing only to stop a moment later and face me. I had perceived no signal at all from Mr. Harbor to announce that he was ready for me, but apparently, she had.

"You may go in, Miss Bruce," she said, standing and showing me the door, which opened as if by magic.

Not magic. Mr. Harbor stood with his hand on the knob and he took over for Ms. Temp with a smile. Maybe she had somehow silently warned him about what to expect because he made a polite little *tut-tut*, but made no further mention of my appearance whatsoever.

"Miss Bruce," he said and ushered me into the room. "I don't know how much I'll be able to help you, but I will sincerely try to do my best." He did look sincere. He was younger than I had thought he would be. In fact, he looked too young to have a law degree. For some reason, I had imagined the lawyer for Royal Blue would have been a faithful old family retainer with kindly eyes and a small, neat beard. The man before me had been the runt of his junior year in high school. He was the skinny kid with thick glasses who carried a briefcase to school and knew how to use a slide rule.

"Mr. Harbor? Mr. Charles Harbor?" I asked him.

He continued to smile. He had wonderful teeth. I almost asked him the name of his orthodontist, but resisted. His brown hair was curly and thick. "You must have been thinking that my father, Charles Harbor, Sr. would be handling this case," he said. Even his voice was that of a prepubescent. I wondered if it ever cracked. "Never fear," he said. "I'm perfectly competent."

"I'm sure you are, but I was rather hoping that I could talk to the man who had known Royal Blue personally. If you'll forgive me for saying so, you look like you were only a child when Mr. Blue died." Hell, he looked like he hadn't even been born.

"In fact," he said. "I was in college. My father passed away shortly after I began working here."

My disappointment must have been apparent because he reassured me again and offered me a chair in his best kindly old family retainer way. It didn't fit him though. He would have appeared more sincere if he'd flung himself onto the floor and offered me some milk and graham crackers.

"What can I help you with, Miss Bruce?" He leaned forward in his chair. I had a crazy impulse to laugh. He looked like a kid playing funeral director; like he knew he had something unpleasant to talk about and was willing to do almost anything to make the ordeal as painless as possible.

"I'm a private investigator, as you know," I said. I went for my credentials. Most people wave them away, but he waited patiently while I fished my license and ID from my wallet. While he studied them, I located the waiver Aïda had signed and took it from my briefcase then slid that across the desk to him as well. I understood. He was an attorney and their primary focus is always covering their own asses.

At last he moved the ID card and license back toward me and took the waiver. After a bit of scrutiny, he looked at me and said, "Now, what is it I can do for you?"

"I would like to see Royal Blue's accounts," I said. "I would like a copy of his will and any other papers you have." I thought he was going to swallow his tie. I didn't really need the will – Aïda had a copy of it and had given me one. I didn't need any other papers either, but I didn't want to let him off the hook too easily.

"I…" He chopped off whatever thought he had been about to express and nodded. "Of course. Where would you like to start?"

"May I see his account books?"

Mr. Harbor looked decidedly uncomfortable. "I didn't realize that Miss Blue meant, well, should I say, such sensitive material. I can certainly provide you with a copy of the will. As for other papers… I'm afraid that's…difficult. Those papers *are* confidential."

"You have the waiver Aïda signed," I said. I leaned over and picked up the telephone receiver and held it out to him. "Call her and verify it."

He took the phone and held it uncertainly to his ear and then told the temp out front to get Miss Aïda Blue for him. I sent up a quick prayer that she was at the hotel. It would spoil the drama of the moment if she wasn't. I fiddled with a metal contraption on his desk that looked like the tool my mother used to pound cheap steak with. I realized it was a book embosser.

In a moment he was talking to Aïda and his gaze kept shifting from me to the shelves of books behind me before he very gently laid the receiver back into the cradle. His ear was red as if she had blistered it.

"Well, Mr. Wing, our accountant, is out of the office at the moment. He had a little surgery yesterday so he won't be here for several weeks." He tapped his chin with his fingers and looked at the ceiling. "I'm not certain…Yes, well," he muttered and the kindly family retainer was back. He even managed to make the skin around his eyes crinkle. "I'll see that you get those files right away. Perhaps you would step into Mr. Wing's office to look them over. You won't be disturbed there."

"That would be fine," I said, thinking that I probably would never become important enough that I could make people do the impossible simply on a whim. I wondered if Aïda realized the power she wielded.

Mr. Wing's office was so similar to Mr. Harbor's that I wondered if the whole floor had been designed by one unimaginative decorator who had merely used a carbon copy of the same room for each office. I sat in Mr. Wing's comfortable leather chair and resisted the temptation to put my feet up on his desk.

My head began to throb with a dull pain after the first hour and by the second the throb had swelled into a roar. The reading was hard for the woman who had been forced to take Senior Arithmetic before she had been allowed to graduate. But even with an elemental math education, I could spot a few unusual items in Mr. Royal Blue's books.

I made a few notes including names and dates. By the time I returned the books to Mr. Harbor, my hands felt dusty, my throat was dry and my head felt like it was full of cotton batting.

"Mr. Harbor," I said before I left. "I ran into references to the Willis Henshaw Company more than once on Royal Blue's accounts. Do you know if Willis and Henshaw are two people's names or one person?"

Charlie shook his head. "No, I'm sorry, I don't. My father may have known, but I don't."

And that had been precisely why I had wished to meet with the elder Mr. Harbor and not the one who had never even met Royal Blue.

"Can you tell me anything about this Willis Henshaw Company?" I asked him. "Anything at all?"

Charles Harbor turned to the computer on his desk and tapped at the keyboard for a while. I watched him and was amazed that he could locate information that way and understand what he was looking at. I had heard rumors that such devices would someday spread to personal, in-home use, but it seemed incredible. I couldn't imagine learning how to use one myself.

At last, he looked up.

He explained to me, or at least tried to, how the whole holdings/corporation/company thing worked. Lots of it was legalese and I mostly didn't understand. It seemed, to me anyway, that one of Royal's companies had paid another of his companies regular payments. According to Charles Harbor, there was nothing unusual about that. The Willis Henshaw company had been paid, quite legally, Charlie assured me, a little over a million dollars over a span of two years."

"What kind of business was it?" I asked.

Charlie tapped again at the keyboard, then shook his head. "I'm afraid there isn't much data from that long ago. It isn't specified here," he said. "Very little of it has been entered. These records are quite old and not likely to be complete. When we transferred data to the computer..." His voice trailed off and he shrugged.

I thanked him then headed back to my car.

I drove slowly back over the floating bridge, ruminating about the case as I went.

I had written a very short list of names that had come up frequently in Royal's dealings. Mickey Carrol was one, of course. It was expected that his manager's name would turn up often. The mysterious Willis Henshaw Company was on it, as well as the other members of his band and household. Aside from the name Willis Henshaw, though, none of it had been surprising or suspicious in any way.

Besides the will, Aïda had given me copies of

the coroner's report and the death certificate. Both documents had stated that Royal's death had been due to a self-administered drug overdose. According to popular gossip, Royal had begun freely using drugs in the early years of his career. I supposed the constant pressures of fame, family and public life had become increasingly more difficult for him to handle. Then, one day, he had taken an amount that proved too much for his poor body to bear. It had looked like suicide to the coroner. That didn't seem like something the Roy Bluestone I had read about in Renata's diaries would have done. There had been a note, however, written in Royal's lyrical style in his own hand.

When I reached home, I debated whether to take the time to shower, but went into my office to see if there was anything that needed my attention. The red light on my telephone answering machine was blinking so I sat on the corner of the desk to listen. The first message was a potential client who didn't leave a number. Smart! Next was a message from Easy to remind me that I'd promised him dinner. I tapped my pencil on the desk while I listened to several hang-ups and then heard a voice that was completely unexpected.

"Cheyenne? This is King. Meet me tonight at the Dragon. There's something you should know." It was King Diamondis, unofficial head of Seattle's shady side. He and I went back a long way. Usually, he wouldn't talk to me in public because he said being seen with him would ruin my reputation. My theory was that he secretly thought it would ruin his.

What could he have to tell me that was so important? I quickly called Easy and arranged for him to meet me, then decided in favor of a shower after all.

ELEVEN

Thursday, January 5, 1984

T he Sun Ya Restaurant was on the edge of Seattle's International District. The *dim sum* lunch crowd was phenomenal, but the dinnertime customers were all but non-existent unless a tour bus had rumbled through. It wasn't because the food wasn't good, but because the owner didn't seem to try very hard. In the evenings, the parking lot was full and the bar was virtually rocking while the dining room almost echoed.

Easy was sitting on the sofa next to the bar when I pushed open the door. He sat leaning against a wall with a Mariner's baseball cap tipped back on his head. He also wore his Burger Planet T-shirt and a sexy looking black leather jacket. I always liked a guy who felt he didn't need to dress for dinner. Not that the Sun Ya was a place you had to worry about that.

He grinned when he saw me and stood up. I steered him into the bar and we sat at one of the small tables so near the ladies' room that you could smell the sickly-sweet air freshener. The bartender, Bill, waved when I raised two fingers. The regular crowd was in their usual seats, some hanging over the bar, staring into their drinks and some ringing the tables, leaning back and calling to each other in raucous voices. On the television over the bar, a rousing game of Wheel of Fortune played to an audience of one.

Easy looked uncomfortable. He was out of his element in a bar and watching him was like finding a polished agate among a bunch of ordinary rocks. Pleasant to see and refreshingly, fascinatingly different. He sat stiffly while Bill brought him a beer and a Perrier for me. Bill good naturedly waved away the five-dollar bill I offered him.

"Hungry?" I asked after Bill had gone.

"Very. We going to have dinner here?" He watched Vanna turn over two Ps.

"Yeah, we are," I said. "I thought I'd like to loosen you up a little first." I winked at him. He grinned and took a sip of his beer as if obliging me.

"I have to meet someone later at the Golden Dragon, but I want to eat first."

Easy's eyebrows elevated. "The Golden Dragon? You hate that place."

I nodded. "I don't want to *eat* there. We can have dinner here first, then I'll go."

"Who are you meeting at the Golden Dragon?" His eyes narrowed and were filled with suspicion.

"I have to meet King Diamondis." I dug into my wallet for a couple of bucks to leave Bill.

Easy took another sip and shook his head slowly. His mouth pursed into that smug look men get when women ask them to do something they consider out of the question. Like clean a toilet.

"King Diamondis?" Easy stared at me over the top of his beer. I stared back, daring him to continue. "Why do you need to talk to him?"

I still didn't say anything, implying that I didn't need to explain my intentions.

"He isn't the kind of man a guy wants his girlfriend talking to," Easy said. My head snapped up and I looked at him. "Okay," he amended. "He isn't the sort you want your *friends* talking to."

"Listen, Easy, King *is* a friend of mine whether you like it or not. He called me and asked me to meet him, which I'm going to do. I don't need your permission and I certainly don't need your presence."

"Can we eat first?" he asked. I took the question as a sign that he might give up if he were properly fed.

We went into the dining room and we ate. We started with fried chicken wings. At the Sun Ya, they put ginger in the batter and they are very nearly the best chicken I've ever eaten. After that we shared an order of cracked crab with lobster sauce. It was messy but that sauce over rice was better than mama's home cooking on the hungriest day of anyone's life. For nutrition's sake we had an order of mixed fresh vegetables with oyster sauce and loads of hot green tea to rinse some of the salt from our systems.

Good as dinner was, I was chomping at the bit for Easy to wipe up that last bit of lobster sauce so I could leave. I was as curious as hell about what King wanted to tell me.

As usual, Easy gave me shit about my paying for dinner, so, for the sake of speed, I conceded. It was hard for me not to snatch the cash out of Easy's hand and simply toss the money at the cashier, but I waited and let him pay like the civilized person I was. After that I was out the door and heading for the Golden Dragon, Easy tagging along behind me.

I never went to the Golden Dragon if I could help it. The only bar I frequented was the Sun Ya's and that was usually for business purposes. I went there to meet contacts or talk to clients. I got in the habit of meeting my clients there when I had my office in my apartment on Mercer Island. Not only was my place all the way down at the southernmost end of the island, it was in the basement of a house and not the most professional looking of places. Not that the Sun Ya bar was professional either, but, for some reason, people expected private detectives to hang out in such surroundings. If I couldn't entertain at one of the posh Westin restaurants where I had met with Aïda, the Sun Ya was a perfect substitute.

The bar at the Golden Dragon was a little seedier and the clientele a little more hostile than that at my usual haunt. Whenever I walked in there, I could feel unpleasantness in the air. The Dragon had been the scene of more than one tragedy and the miasma of all its past agonies lingered.

We walked in over a painfully red, not too clean carpet and sat down at a small black lacquered table. The bar maid slapped two napkins down in front of us and said something that sounded like "Wadyahav?"

"Perrier," I said and raised my eyebrow at Easy.

"Iced tea," he said, his voice morose. I saw him watching the barmaid's rump as she walked away from us. She was wearing a pair of shiny, flesh pink Spandex leggings. From a distance, when she leaned against the bar, it looked as if she was wearing nothing more than a short tee shirt that said, "Damn, I'm good!" across her breasts.

Easy tore his gaze from her shiny butt and let it sweep over the room. He sighed with some satisfaction and said, "Well, I guess he's not here."

"He'll be here," I said.

He glanced at me but said nothing.

"Easy, you really don't need to be here. He said he wanted to talk to me. I think I should talk to him alone. If you're here, he might suddenly forget what he wanted to say."

I could see a glint of anger spark in his eyes.

"Chey, King Diamondis is a dangerous man. I don't like this at all." Suddenly he stood up. "Come on," he said, "let's go. This isn't a good idea."

I barely glanced at him. "Go ahead. I'm staying."

He hesitated a moment, but didn't sit back down.

The barmaid brought our drinks and set a small bowl of little pretzels between us.

"Cheyenne, King Diamondis is dangerous," he said after she had gone.

"You already said that."

"I'm not going to leave you here alone to talk to him. No way." He put his hand on my arm and pulled gently. I felt the steam starting to build.

"Let go," I said quietly, but I put steel into my voice and frost into my eyes. He didn't release my arm and I yanked it away and stood up. "I'll move to another table if you don't stop."

The regulars were all gaping unashamedly by then. A guy down at the end of the bar smirked, evidently hoping we'd get down to fists and chairs.

"Look," I said, sitting down again. After a glance around, he sat down too. I lowered my voice and forced a smile onto my mouth. "I don't want to start anything in here." Disappointed, the crowd started to lose interest. "I'm going to talk to King. You can stay or you can go. Or, if you feel you really can't trust me, you can sit at another table and watch. Frankly, if you're going to act like a nursemaid, I'd prefer it if you went." I knew that Easy wasn't being macho, nor was he bullying. That wasn't him at all. He was frightened. He didn't know King like I did. He only knew him by reputation, which, admittedly wasn't a good one.

Easy's beeper squealed suddenly and the bar maid giggled. Several of the clientele swung languidly around on their stools for another look, then turned back to their drinks. Apparently, we weren't providing the entertainment they'd hoped for but they weren't ready to give up too soon.

"Aren't you going to answer that?" I asked when Easy had cut off the noise.

"Later," he said and took a long swallow of his tea. "I'm not going anywhere until you're through talking to King."

"Oh, Easy, really! Besides," I said, waving at his pager. "It could be something important. It probably is. I think you should call in. You're on call. It's your job."

He knew I was right. Reluctantly, he pulled himself up, threw me a suspicious glance and moved toward the phone. He kept his eyes on me all the time he wasn't scouting the door for King. I saw him speak into the receiver, frown and hang up. He was back in under a minute.

"We have to go," he said. He picked up my jacket off the neighboring chair and threw a dollar bill on the table. He held my jacket out to me. I made no move to take it.

"You go on," I said. "I'll stay."

"I'm not leaving you here."

"Easy, do you have a call?" Of course he did. The Seattle Police didn't page him for no reason.

He nodded. "They want me in Greenwood right away. Domestic disturbance."

"Then go. I'll wait here another five minutes and if King doesn't show, then I'll leave," I said, having no intention of leaving until I had spoken to King.

Easy stood before me oozing uncertainty. He was well aware that he was creating the beginnings of another scene holding my jacket the way he was. At last, he draped it back over the seat of the chair and sighed. "All right. But I don't want you to hang around here very long," he said in that patronizing way I hate.

"I won't," I promised and gave him the most guileless smile I could come up with. It wasn't the first time I'd been rescued by Easy's pager.

"I'll have another Perrier," I told the waitress when he was gone. "And when Mr. Diamondis arrives, will you show him where I'm sitting?"

TWELVE

Thursday January 5, 1984

Even if I hadn't known him for almost two decades, I could have picked King Diamondis out of a crowd of thousands. Aside from the brilliant dome that lacked even the lowliest hair follicle, there was something shiny about him that set him apart from everyone else. He was famous for wearing diamonds which added to his brilliance, but that wasn't all of it. He exuded a smoothness that you rarely find in ordinary people. He wore a well-cut, expensive looking suit of gray silk. His tie, upstaged by the large diamond stud, was a muted splash of blue and mauve. I was sure it was the finest Italian tiemakers could craft. His brown skin was flawless, his manicured nails, immaculate. It was hard to imagine him doing mundane tasks like wiping egg yolk off his chin or putting on a pair of socks. He was too perfect. Too polished.

I watched him stop inside the door and survey the room. The barmaid gestured to me and he nodded at her without saying a word. I gave him the briefest of nods and he started toward me.

"Cheyenne," he said. He slid into the chair opposite me and gave my face some serious scrutiny while he straightened his impeccable tie, his hand lingering at the monstrous tie tack. His fingers were very long and slender. He wore another large diamond on his pinkie finger and it glittered with a hard, cold light. I was near enough to him to feel a heat emanating from his big body. He exuded an aura that was almost visible. The man had secrets. Sexual secrets. I liked him.

"I was surprised to hear from you," I said. "I thought your image couldn't tolerate being seen with me."

His smile was nothing more than a faint wrinkling around his eyes. "Being seen with *me* will get *you* talked about," he said. He let his gaze wander to the cocktail waitress' sleek behind. When she turned, he signaled for two drinks.

"This must be pretty important then, for you to put my reputation at risk."

He watched me. His depthless black eyes didn't blink. He was known for his lack of expression. Rumor had it that he could kiss or kill with the same cold bloodedness and I believed it.

"Word is out that you are snooping around in someone else's business."

"Snooping *is* my business," I said. "Who's talking about me now?"

The waitress set another water in front of me and something with ice in front of King, her gaze never leaving his face.

"I don't know. I haven't been able to find out yet," he said after she had gone. One long finger wiped a line of condensation from his glass.

"It must be more than that, King," I said, watching him carefully. "You wouldn't have had me come all the way down here just to tell me that I'm stepping on someone's toes."

"There's a contract out on you," he said.

"Me!?" I laughed.

"I should clarify. It isn't a contract yet. Just talk of one. Word is going around."

"But, why me?"

"I don't know that either. I think you should be careful though. What are you working on? You aren't mixed up in labor troubles, are you? Gambling?"

"No. I am working on a case but I'm not yet sure how big it really is. Ever heard of Royal Blue?"

"A baseball player?"

I laughed again. He had said it with his customary completely poker face. It was sometimes hard to tell when he was kidding, but I knew he was that time.

He'd heard. Everyone had. Finally, he nodded.

"Okay, I know who Royal Blue is. Was. What about him?"

"His daughter thinks he's alive. Has me looking for him."

He dismissed the case with a wave of his hand.

"He didn't contact you for help in getting a new identity, did he?" I asked. Might as well hit all the bases while I was in the ball park.

"It's my understanding that the man is dead," he said. "You are, I trust, referring to a time prior to his death?"

"Yes," I said with exaggerated patience. "Before he died, did he contact you for help? To set up a new identity?"

He shook his head. "I have never spoken to Royal Blue," he said. "I'm sorry I can't help you. The man never came to me."

"I don't know that he acquired a new identity," I said and shrugged. "But if he had wanted to, he would have come to you. Royal was a man who would have wanted the best."

He nodded. "What have you been stirring up, Cheyenne?" His mouth smirked into the tiniest of smiles. "This Royal Blue case doesn't seem big enough to be muddying anyone's waters. Unless you have been digging a little too close to a secret someone would do anything to keep hidden."

"What you mean is, if someone connected with Royal Blue wants me dead, the chances of him being alive just rose by several hundred percent. Why would anyone care if I was snooping around the affairs of a dead man?"

"Dead men have secrets too."

"But they can't put contracts out on people. Especially small fish like me."

"I may be an alarmist."

"You're not the alarmist type," I said.

He took a long swallow of his drink. "I'll find out a name for you," he said, "and give you a call. The deal hasn't yet been struck." He kept one hand in his lap and one on his glass, otherwise he didn't move. I fiddled with my napkin, folding it and refolding it into unrecognizable origami shapes.

"Well, I don't want to wait around until it has," I said. "I have plans for the next fifty or sixty years."

"You aren't doing any loan sharking on the side, anything like that?"

The idea made me laugh. "I swear. I'm into nothing controversial. I didn't think this case was, anyway, until now."

"What do you have?"

"Not too much. She—his daughter, that is—has a painting she's convinced he painted."

He shrugged. "I understood that he painted."

"She insists that it's a recent work. And, she says she doesn't 'feel' that he's dead."

"Do you?"

I chewed on that for a moment. "I have to admit that I don't 'feel' it either. I've gotten a few flashes, but nothing much."

He nodded. He was well familiar with my psychic ability.

"At first, I thought that she simply had a crazy idea, but when I was in San Francisco, I was warned to butt out. Maybe it was the same guy." I fingered the healing star on my cheek.

"I was wondering if that was a new and colorful make-up trend or perhaps a tattoo, but I was too polite to ask," he said.

"I'm inclined to agree with Aïda that he's alive. I think the man may be hiding in Hawaii."

"You going?"

I nodded.

"Good work if you can get it," he said. "My advice is to leave the man alone. If Royal Blue has carved himself a new identity, he more than likely had his reasons. Respect them."

I swallowed the last of my water. "I would, but his daughter doesn't see it that way."

He shrugged and drained his glass. I pulled my jacket off the seat of the neighboring chair. "If you'll see what you can find out for me, I'd appreciate it."

"I'll give you a call. If you need anything, you know how you can get in touch with me."

"I do need one thing, King," I said. "A name. I need a driver's license."

"I'm assuming you are referring to an *additional* driver's license," he said.

"Yes. I did have a guy, but, uh…he's spending a little time in jail right now."

He nodded, reached into his inside jacket pocket and extracted a small silver case. It was engraved with an ornate KD and I was pretty sure it was sterling silver. The case housed a little note pad and a matching silver pen that all but disappeared in King's big hand. He jotted a name and address on the top sheet, tore it off and handed it to me. I tucked it away without looking at it.

"Thanks, King." He grasped my hand and I felt a pulse of electric energy pass between us.

"I trust you know enough to be careful without my having to mention it," he said. His eyebrows raised a fraction of a millimeter. I wouldn't have noticed it at all except I was in the habit of looking for subtle facial movements.

He eased his bulk out of the chair and threw a pair of tens on the table next to the dollar that Easy had left. Then he waved at the waitress. She laughed as if he had said something hilarious.

I sat alone for a few minutes thinking hard about what King had told me.

THIRTEEN

Friday, January 6, 1984

The next morning, I was outdoors before the birds were awake. It was misty and quiet in the West Seattle neighborhood and I liked it that way. I walked down California Way and back toward the marina. The wind blew off the water in a fine spray. I welcomed its chill and quickened my pace hoping to generate a little warmth into my joints. I liked to go for "thinking walks". They were absolutely *not* for exercise, which I strongly objected to. I considered them part of my work but didn't bill anyone for them.

While I walked, I puzzled over what I knew so far. Someone obviously was not happy that I was looking into Royal's death. I wondered why. Money had to be an issue. It usually was. Aïda had seemed to believe the will had been on the up and up. She had provided me with a copy and I had agreed. Her father had left some money to his household staff and his manager and band members. He had left enough for his wife and daughter to live well on for the rest of their lives. Aïda had recently received the first portion of her inheritance and would get more as the years passed. Of course, if Royal Blue was found to be alive, Aïda's inheritance could be in jeopardy, but I thought she would rather have had her father back than be wealthy. Her potential wealth brought to mind her fiancé. I was pretty sure that old Jon-Paul had a hand in this somehow.

Then there was the million plus dollars Royal had paid the Henshaw Company, which was a subsidiary to Royal Blue Holdings. Essentially, he was paying money to his own company. Transferring accounts, as Charlie Harbor had said. At least, that had been the way I had interpreted what Charlie had told me and the almost indecipherable account books I had perused the day before. So, who was Willis Henshaw of the Willis Henshaw Company?

A dirty yellow dog followed me for half a block sniffing at my heels and growling half-heartedly until he lost interest and stopped to investigate a clump of grass by the roadside. Then, before my legs started shaking from dehydration and lack of food, I headed back home.

At the house, I toasted an onion bagel and poured a large glass of juice. Then I phoned Mickey Carrol, Royal's manager.

He sounded none too happy to hear from me, and interrupted our conversation with several deep, rumbling coughs. Reluctantly, he agreed to see me about noon

I puttered around in my office during the morning putting away books and files and finishing unpacking. My office was finally beginning to look like one. I displayed my business and PI licenses and pushed a couple of plants over to flank the French doors that opened to the front of the house. The plants had been a welcoming gift from Magda. They classed up the place very well.

I put my teak bookshelf together, and slid it over to rest against the far wall and arranged my collection of how-tos, reference books and equipment catalogs there. A smaller shelf held several dozen paperback mysteries to which I am addicted and my collection of Richard Bach's new age stuff. I had met him once and he had impressed me as being a genuinely soulful guy. I liked him and I liked his easy, affable narration.

❊ ❊ ❊

After a quick mug of tomato soup and a handful of oyster crackers, I nabbed a banana and made for my car. The roads were damp from the mist and I headed carefully over the West Seattle bridge. It's known to be slippery in the rain.

Mickey Carrol's condo was downtown, in one of

the new buildings near the Pike Place Market. He must have made a bundle from Royal, I thought, even before his inheritance. The sumptuous lobby, complete with a doorman, had a grand view of Elliot Bay. Its floors were, apparently, all named for artists. The doorman informed me that Mr. Carrol lived in Pollock B. He eyed the rainbow hues of my face, made his own judgements and held the elevator door open for me.

The apartment door was answered almost immediately by Mickey Carrol himself. The last time I had seen him, he had been on television. Some photographer had caught him close up standing near Royal's casket with his face done up in mourning. Before that I had often seen photos of his bulldog jaw and mop of unruly graying hair standing nearby when Royal dealt with autograph seekers and photographers. I had expected to come face to face with the same man; possibly the burly tough who had assaulted me in San Francisco.

If Mickey Carrol had been the man who had attacked me, he had worked some sort of magic. The man who stood before me, scowling, was shrunken and sick. His hair was now completely gray and beginning to recede. He wore a yellow chamois shirt several sizes too large, and a pair of gray slacks, obviously left over from a time when his body was sturdy and well-muscled. On his feet were a pair of leather scuffs. He wore no star shaped ring.

He didn't attempt even a pretense of a smile,

clearly not pleased that I had come. He looked at me, though, and probably thought that private investigators routinely get into physical altercations and that the bruises were normal. He didn't say anything, but I saw him taking it in.

"Mr. Carrol," I said, and smiled as charmingly as I could. "I'm Cheyenne Bruce." I held out my hand for him to shake and discovered that he was one of those men who were uncomfortable shaking hands with a woman. He flushed and recovered, but too slowly for me to touch him. I had dropped my hand.

He ushered me into a spacious living room done in shades of sand and pale blue. His decorator had not only been talented, but obviously expensive.

"You're investigating Royal's death," he said as a statement. His voice was gritty, like sand, abraded by too much booze and cigarettes. At the end of his sentence, his breath wheezed out in a tiny whistling cough. He shook his head. "Hasn't it been kicked around enough?" he continued. "I don't know why you people won't leave it alone. Saw a headline in the store the other day. Said he'd been spotted alligator hunting in the Everglades." He shook his head again. "Royal wouldn't have killed a spider let alone an alligator. Crazy!"

I nodded and let him wind down. "Actually," I said when he had finished, "Aïda asked me to look into it. You'll have to believe me when I tell you I'm not one of those crazy fans. Neither am I a reporter. I like his music very much, but I too am convinced Royal is dead. I'm looking into this because Aïda hired me to do it. She wants to be sure."

"She was there," he said frowning. "She saw the funeral first hand. How could she think…?" His question dissolved into a cough from which he had trouble catching his breath.

"She was a child, Mr. Carrol. It's difficult enough for a child to accept a parent's death. It must be doubly hard when he lives on and on in his music. I suppose it doesn't help that there are so many rumors about him being alive."

He turned away and walked to the coffee table where he fumbled with a cigarette and lighter. "What do you want from me?" He turned a tormented face to me. Could it be that the rumors got to him more than he cared to admit? More even than they got to Aïda?

"I'd like to hear about his death," I said softly. "I realize it's difficult for you to talk about, but if you don't mind, I think it might help."

"I don't want to talk about his death, young lady. I don't want to talk about anything. I want to be left alone."

"I know that, sir. But Aïda needs help. I won't take up much of your time."

"Well, that's good, because I don't happen to have much of it left." He sighed wetly and leaned back. "Royal Blue," he said, looking at the space between us. "Did you know that his name was Roy Bluestone?"

I nodded. I didn't mention the diaries Aïda had given me. I wanted his version untainted.

"He was one of the handsomest men around." He glanced at me for affirmation. "He was... those blue eyes..." He shook his head again.

"You must have loved him very much," I said. Renata's diaries had hinted at a strong father-son bond. I sat back and let him talk.

His mouth worked but it was several seconds before he spoke again. "I knew him before he was even Royal Blue. I knew those boys when they were nothing but skinny runts playing on rubber bands and shoeboxes. I brought Roy up to be what he was." He pleaded with his eyes. "Did you know they used to say that I made Royal Blue what he was? It's true, I did."

I nodded.

"He was scared to sing. Yep. He was scared. Both of 'em were. You wouldn't have known it though. His wildness was all an act to cover up the fact that he was so shy he could hardly talk to people. He talked to me, though, and then after he met Renata, he talked to her. Then, until Aïda came along, he hardly said a word to anyone else. Unless he was on stage."

"What do you remember about Royal just before

he died?" I asked him keeping my voice soft.

"A few days before he died, Roy took Aïda on a picnic. I mostly went along wherever he went, unless he was with Renata too, but that day he said he had some errands to run and before I knew it, they were gone. He drove her up into the foothills of the San Gabriels and took along some sausages and cheese and bread. It looked like..." He cleared his throat. "Later, it looked like maybe he was saying goodbye to her."

"Then you are convinced his death was a suicide?" I expected him to vehemently deny the suggestion of suicide. Most people reject that notion in connection with relatives or close friends. He stared at me a moment as though thinking over my suggestion, as if the possibility of anything else had never occurred to him. Then he slowly nodded his head.

"It was the drugs. He took too much on purpose. Yes. The coroner called it 'self-administered overdose.' Self-administered, young lady." He took a deep drag and stubbed out the cigarette then immediately lit another.

"Did he take drugs often?"

Another cough caught him and he had to nod his head. "His drug and alcohol use was famous."

"Had you noticed him using drugs more before he died?"

He shrugged and chewed his upper lip with his heavy lower jaw. "He didn't always use in front of me," he said. "But I saw him do it once or twice. Then, the day he died, he took a handful of pills and washed it down with a tumbler full of Chivas Regal. They said there was enough in his system to kill five men. That didn't happen accidentally. Richard said Roy had been depressed but maybe I didn't want to see it."

"Mr. Carrol," I said. "Do you have any pictures of Richard? I see that you have some of Royal, but I wondered if Richard looked anything like him."

He started shaking his head before I had finished. "You don't need to see a picture of Richard to see what he looked like. They were twins. Identical twins."

Ah, I thought. "Did you ever consider that Richard might have been the one who died? That Royal could still be alive?"

His coughing fit almost sent me to the phone to call the paramedics. His face purpled and I thought he was choking. At last, he gasped and with tears streaming, he said, "No. I've never considered that he's alive. I saw him after he was dead. I'm the one who found him. I'll never believe that he's alive. Never." His voice strangled when he tried to shout.

"Okay, Mr. Carrol," I said. I stood and tried to lay a comforting hand on his arm, but he jerked himself away. *Fine*, I thought. If he wanted to believe that

Royal Blue was carted away by a giant eagle, it was all right with me. More than anything, I wanted to get a good look around the place. A quick check through the desk drawer would suffice probably, or even a riffle through his dresser. "May I use your bathroom?" I asked. He looked taken aback and nodded, maybe somewhat ashamed of his outburst.

He showed me through the bedroom then retreated to the living room. I shut the door to the bathroom, staying outside it. His room was large and clean. A huge blond wood dresser stood near the bathroom door. On it was a lamp, a small wooden box and a photograph of a young man. I eased open a drawer and saw nothing but stacks of neatly folded underwear. Another drawer revealed nothing more startling than shirts. I didn't have much time. I opened the little jewel box quickly and scanned the interior. Nothing but tie tacks, cuff links and a couple of old coins. I found no star-shaped ring.

I quietly opened the bathroom door and studied the contents of the medicine cabinet, then flushed the toilet and left.

"Mr. Carrol, I believe you own a ring that's in the shape of a star. Would you mind showing it to me please?"

He stared at me.

"You do have such a ring, don't you?" I asked when he didn't answer.

"I used to have one. Shaped like a star with little

diamonds in between each point. Roy gave it to me."

"Where is it now?"

"I don't know. Lost." He shrugged his shoulders, clearly and honestly bewildered. "I lost it several years ago. How...How did you know about that ring?" Then he seemed to see the scabbed cut on my cheek for the first time. Perhaps he had been too involved in his own pain to notice before, or maybe he had been too distracted by the colors surrounding it to pay attention. As he studied it, a dull flush rose up his neck.

"I saw it in some old photos. You have no idea what happened to it?"

"No."

"One more thing, sir. The photograph on your dresser of the young man? Who is that?"

"What? Oh, that's my nephew, Jon-Paul. Why?" He bit off the last word in order to cough.

"You should see a doctor about that cough, sir," I said, smiling at him.

"Have an appointment this afternoon," he said, gasping into a handkerchief that he had dragged from his hip pocket. "In fact, it's in about an hour. But the doctor isn't going to tell my anything I don't already know."

"Mr. Carrol," I asked. "Do you know anyone named Willis? Willis Henshaw?"

He looked startled. "No," he said, shaking his head. "No, I don't."

I didn't believe him for a second. Nevertheless, I put my hand out for him to shake. "I want to thank you for your time, Mr. Carrol." This time he shook it and my mind was flooded with the essence of him. There was a deep and throbbing sadness, fear over his health and more. I knew, too, that there was nothing a thousand doctors could do for his cough. There was something else as well. I was convinced that Mickey Carrol had something he desperately wanted to keep hidden.

FOURTEEN

Friday, January 6, 1984

On the way out of the building, I made a quick perusal of the names listed on the mailboxes. The doorman stood nearby so I pretended to fumble in my briefcase until he turned away to help an elderly woman with her walker. Then I jotted two of the names on the back of an envelope. When the doorman had turned to me again and was just about to ask me what I was doing loitering in his lobby, I shoved the envelope into my pocket. Then I confidently walked out the door and into the afternoon drizzle, thinking hard. I wanted a better look at Mickey's life.

I was somehow not surprised to discover that Aïda's Jon-Paul was Mickey's nephew. It answered a lot of questions. It seemed obvious to me; the boy had stolen his uncle's ring and was "engaged" to Aïda solely for the purpose of getting her money. I had threatened him by investigating the death of her father. If her father was discovered to be alive, she may not be coming into the amounts of money Jon-Paul had been counting on. I wondered how much Jon-Paul knew about Royal Blue.

At some point, I would have to tell Aïda about my suspicions, but, after considerable thought, I decided I would wait. I wouldn't be astonished, though, if King called me in the next day or two to report that Jon-Paul was the one who so desperately wanted me to meet with a fatal accident. If that proved to be the case, I would tell her then.

Before I talked to Jon-Paul, I wanted to find out more about Mr. Mickey Carrol. I was getting very different vibes from the man than I had expected. There was a guilty aura about him as well as something secret. I was determined to get into his apartment alone and do a thorough search. Of course, that was as illegal as hell and I was risking prison if I did it and was caught, but that had never deterred me. I didn't think it would be that difficult to get past the doorman and back in to Mickey's place.

I stopped at the coffee shop across the street from Mickey's condo to think. It was warm and dry and quiet, the lunch crowd having gone back to work. It was a good place to cogitate my next move. I hauled the envelope back out of my pocket and studied the names. I needed a woman, a single woman or a widow, for this job. A.L. Andersen was probably a woman. Anyone with a name as common as Andersen would want their first name listed, unless, of course, she didn't want the world at large to know there was an Alice Louise Andersen living alone. I found a phone booth about a half a block down First Avenue. I looked the number up in the phone book and made a quick call to make sure.

A.L. Andersen told me regretfully that her husband was deceased. I spoke to her for a moment. She was friendly and open to my quickly cooked up story.

I returned to the coffee shop and settled in for a wait. I ordered a cup of coffee and a piece of rhubarb pie, both of which I dislike and knew it would take me a long time to finish.

I hadn't gotten quite halfway through the piece of pie and the coffee had long since gone cold when I saw Mickey nod to the doorman and head up First Avenue. I abandoned the pie and, dodging cars, made it across the street.

"Mrs. Anna Andersen," I said to the doorman. His suspicious frown said that he obviously recognized me and he reached for the phone to call Mrs. Andersen to see if she actually expected me. After a moment, he scowled wholeheartedly and let me proceed into the elevator.

I found apartment D, on Monet. I knocked and Mrs. Andersen presented me with a whole bouquet of smiles.

"Miss Bruce," she said. Her grin couldn't have gotten any bigger. She had carefully done up her face with a palette of make-up. Her eyes flashed with lavender shadow and she had painted her small mouth with scarlet. "Please come in."

She opened the door wider and I stepped into a room full of antiques. She obviously had kept much of the furniture from her early marriage on. The room was crammed as full as possible, leaving very little space to maneuver at all. She was a small woman who seemed able to slither around the fragile bric-a-brac covered tables and antimacassar draped chairs. I suddenly felt all elbows and knees.

In the living room, she seemed to take a better look at me.

"Oh, my!" she said. "What on Earth happened to your poor face?" She began to flutter around and I half expected her to produce Mercurochrome and bandages.

"It's nothing, really," I said modestly. "I do part time work as a stunt woman."

"Dear, dear," she muttered, seeming to believe me. "Please sit down. I've always wanted to discover my genealogy," she said, pleased again. "I do hope you find something worthwhile."

"Well," I said, launching into another lie and hating myself for it. "I have found a connection to Hans Christian Andersen that you might find interesting."

"Oh, yes, indeed!" she said and wriggled in her

chair as if settling in for a long siege. "Andersen, of course, was my husband's name, but I'm very interested in his genealogy too."

"Oh, my gosh!" I said suddenly, making a great show of rifling through my briefcase. "I seem to have left my notebook in the car. Will you excuse me? I'll just run down and get it. I won't be a minute." I leapt to my feet and was out the door before the startled look had time to settle on her face. I waved at her from the elevator and was sure to take it down a floor, to Klee, before getting off and catching another to Pollock.

I slipped the lock on Mickey's door easily. The tenants apparently had placed all of their trust in the doorman for they had secured their front doors with nothing but cheap, insubstantial locks. I already knew Mickey didn't have a burglar alarm. I automatically checked every home I ever entered.

Inside, I carefully shut the door leaving it unlocked. In case I had to make a quick getaway, I wanted the easiest way out. I had no desire to dangle from the ledge waiting for Mr. Carrol to go to bed that night.

I did not like snooping through other people's homes and belongings, but it *was* my job. I had learned long before not to feel guilty about it. People often did not tell the truth and even if they did, they often didn't tell the whole truth. I was an investigator and it was my job to investigate, unpleasant as it may sometimes have been.

I didn't know what I was looking for. Sometimes, I didn't find anything. Sometimes all I found was a feeling or two, and often, that seemed to be enough.

I moved to the bookcase and pulled out several hard bound volumes to make sure nothing was hidden behind them. They had all been pushed flush against the back of the case. Mickey Carrol owned a copy of *John Winston Lennon* by Ray Coleman that looked like something Easy might have liked. He also had a book called *Elvis: What Happened*, that was autographed by its three authors. I wanted to flip through the pages but reverently replaced it on the shelf.

Behind a wall of polished built-in cabinet doors, I found rows and rows of shelves. I was astounded and envious at the number of videos the man had collected. Popular films and classics were mixed with obscure foreign films. He had hundreds of record albums, too, ranging from Bix Beiderbecke to Yma Sumac and everything imaginable in between. *Easy would be in heaven here*, I thought. I opened one door of the armoire and sure enough, there was his stereo system. From what I knew about stereos, it could have been made by Fisher-Price, but if lights and switches were an indication of quality, his was top flight.

Next, I went to his desk and quickly searched each drawer. The man was incredibly neat. It made me more than usually careful while I looked through his things. I knew that I wouldn't be able to put everything back exactly as it had been and I knew he would know the difference if I failed.

I found a flat folder with a picture of Royal and Mickey holding aloft a Grammy. It was marked, "Thanks, Mick. I couldn't have done it without you. Royal." I slid my hand under the picture but nothing was there.

Frustrated, I frowned, concentrating. Where? There had to be something. I stopped thinking and moved to the center of the room where I closed my eyes and began to turn slowly. When I felt a tug, I opened my eyes and I was facing the bookshelf.

"No, no," I said impatiently. "I already looked there." I walked to it, letting my eyes graze over the titles. A large medical text that I hadn't noticed before, caught my eye. The spine of the book next to it was indigo blue with gold lettering. I peered at the title. *Moby Dick*. It seemed out of place among the books of music and medicine that flanked it. Mickey Carrol's interest in fiction was satisfied at the television screen. I slid the book from its place and opened the gold-edged pages. Instead of falling open at the place where the white whale has lunch, the cover opened to reveal a secret hiding place. Some people put their valuables in the freezer, some in a safe deposit box. I shook my head and *tsked* my tongue at Mickey's naiveté in thinking this feeble attempt would foil any robber.

Inside the "book" were three folded papers, and a box containing a gold chain, an inexpensive looking tie clasp and a lock of hair. The hair, dark, fine and silky appeared to be a baby's and not something that the aging bachelor agent would keep secreted away.

I unfolded one of the pieces of paper. It was an ordinary enough letter from someone telling Mickey that he had arrived safely and would soon be moving. There was no return address but it was signed "Willis". as if Willis was uncomfortable using that name and felt the need to bracket it in quotation marks.

A second letter was signed the same way. That letter seemed to have preceded the other one and appeared to be a letter of farewell. The third, dated the following year asked Mickey if he would care for the few items contained in the box until he could again retrieve them.

The phone rang in the quiet room and startled me so much that I almost dropped the book and box. After two rings it stopped. The switchboard operator had probably picked it up downstairs for a message. At any rate, it reminded me of my other duties and I shut the book and pushed it back into its place.

In moments I was out the door and running down the stairs to Anna's apartment.

"My, you took so long, I thought you'd forgotten all about me," she said. Her red mouth pouted.

"No, I.... There was a ticket on my car so I had to move it." I was getting to be an accomplished liar, I thought, not proudly. Though I don't really mind lying, sometimes it simply has to be done. I pulled my notebook from my briefcase where it had been all along and waved it triumphantly at her.

"Now," I said. "Where were we?"

I listened to Mrs. Andersen's voice chittering in the background while I went over the details of the case so far.

Willis Henshaw had come up more than once in Royal Blue's accounts. The painting could have been done by someone with the initials of WH, although, to be fair, the signature could also could have been WW, HH, or any combination of the two. I would take a closer look at the photo when I got home.

I knew I had to find Willis Henshaw. The man may have had something to do with Royal's death, may have been blackmailing him or may actually *be* him. If it *were* blackmail, however, it hardly seemed likely that he would have killed his cash cow.

And what was the significance of the hair, the chain and the tie clasp? The chain seemed to be the only item that had any monetary value at all. The tie clasp was obviously inexpensive so it and the hair must have some sentimental value to the mysterious Willis.

"Mrs. Andersen," I said suddenly, the moment there was a break in her chatter. "Do you know Mr.

Carrol upstairs?"

"Why, yes, I do," she said. Her doll-like eyes opened wide in surprise. The heavily mascaraed lashes stabbed at her upper lid. "He's a quiet young man, but he seems quite nice. Are you doing genealogical work for him too?"

"I'm doing some investigating involving him, yes," I said in all truthfulness. "How long have you known him?"

"Oh, since he moved in here. Let's see, that was about ten or twelve years ago now. He's a shy one, he is, but I have my ways of getting to know the other tenants." She nodded and winked and held up a cookie. "He's a famous man, you know."

"Really?"

"Oh, my, yes. He used to manage that singer, Royal Blue. Isn't that the loveliest name you've ever heard? He died, you know. I'll tell Mr. Carrol I met you."

"I'd really rather you didn't," I said. "I shouldn't be discussing my clients with each other if you know what I mean." I leaned over conspiratorially. I caught the faint aroma of nutmeg and dusty roses when she nodded understandingly.

"He must have been quite distressed over Royal Blue's death, I suppose," I said as if thinking aloud.

"Oh my, yes indeed. He moved in here right after that happened, as a matter of fact. It was fortunate he had the place. My, my, they were very hard to get back then."

"Had the place?"

"Oh, yes. This building had just opened when my husband, Dwight, and I bought our apartment, but Mr. Carrol owned his apartment already. He had purchased it before the building was even finished, I guess. He had it furnished and everything. It stood vacant for only a month or two before that poor boy died and Mr. Carrol moved in. I was awfully sorry for him. He was so broken up over it."

So, Mickey Carrol had bought his condo in Seattle before Royal had died. How, I wondered, had he known that he was going to want to retire in Seattle before his client was even dead? Of course, he could have bought it as an investment I supposed.

I stood up, crumpled the sugar cookie crumbs into my napkin and held my hand out to Mrs. Andersen. "Ma'am, you've been very helpful," I said. It was the truth. Without her, I wouldn't have been able to get into Mickey's apartment, nor would I have had a half hour to chew on the details of the case.

"The pleasure was all mine," she said, smiling. "I don't know when I've enjoyed a visit so much. Now, when you find out more details, please let me know. I'm awfully curious about my lineage."

"Oh, certainly!" I told her, not without a little twinge of guilt. I resolved to come and see her again.

FIFTEEN

Whe I got home, there was an ominous message from Ab on my machine. He said to come over to the shop right away and he sounded serious. I couldn't imagine what could possibly be so urgent.

Coming home, I had had to bypass Fauntleroy. The street had been closed but I had assumed it was for repair work. I was wrong. It had been a crime scene.

The front of the shop looked as though a bomb had detonated and the inside was in chaos. The floor of the showroom was littered with shards of glass. Ab was using a broom to sweep up the mess. But that was only part of the devastation.

"You just missed the police," he said, dumping a dustpan full of glass into the bin. "They've been here all morning."

He looked like he was in shock. I have to admit I was as well. All around us was the wreckage of what had once been lovely and valuable works of art. A lamp that had been in the showroom window was nothing but a twisted pile of metal and glass. A window had been smashed and another had been bent almost double. The racks in the sample window which had held hundreds of small square examples of every color of glass Ab had in the shop, had been pulled down. The floor was littered with what looked like the contents of a giant overturned jewel box. Most of the pieces were broken and would have to be recut.

"Ab, what happened? Were you robbed?"

"No, that's just it. Nothing was taken. Only smashed." He reluctantly turned back to the wreckage and shook his head. "Who would want to do this?" he asked. "He could have come in and taken anything. He didn't have to smash up the place."

I picked up the broken lamp and set it onto a work table. I thought it unrepairable, but knew Ab would have to decide that. I lifted a small window from the floor. It had been one of my favorites; a gorgeous thing of green leaves and tiny yellow flowers. I thought it could be fixed and reverently set it on the work table too.

"Ab, I'm so sorry," I said. "Do the police have any ideas?"

He shook his head. "I opened up as usual, but then I got a call to go out and look at a repair job. I was only gone a couple of hours. When I came back, they must have just smashed the front window before leaving. We're pretty visible here. If it had been done first, there wouldn't have been time for all this damage. Someone would have alerted the police. As it was, he threw a chair through the front window. It hit a car and landed in the street. They had to close off Fauntleroy for a while. They think he left by the back door during all the commotion." He looked at me then. "I hate to tell you this, but your project was one of the casualties."

"I don't care about that so much," I said, but an icy little start of regret formed in my stomach. "I can start over. Don't worry about *that*. It's all...this..." I waved my hand over the rest of the destroyed treasures. "This is what I care about. I'm glad you weren't here. You may have been hurt."

"I don't think it would have happened if I had been here. I think it was a crime of opportunity." He sat down on the floor of the display window and his shoulders slumped. He had leaned a huge piece of plywood against the supports of the smashed display window. It blocked out the light and made the shop look dismal and dim

I wasn't at all sure that it had been a crime of opportunity. "Ab," I said. "I've been working on a case. It seems to be getting more and more serious." I sat down next to him. "I only hope that this didn't happen because of me."

"Naaawww," he said, drawing out the word. "I

don't see how this could be connected to anything you're doing. Why do you say that?"

"I told you that I had been mugged in California, but that wasn't entirely true. I got attacked by someone who told me to mind my own business. He had to have been someone who would seriously lose if I kept investigating the case I'm working on."

He looked at me and started to protest again.

I interrupted him. "That isn't all. I have a friend… a friend who knows lots of unsavory characters, let's say. He says that someone is looking to have me… killed." I couldn't think of a softer way of phrasing it.

"My God!" he said. "You've got to get into a safer line of work."

"You sound like Easy," I said, smiling.

"Well, he's right, and I'm serious. You need to get a different job."

"It usually isn't this dangerous. But I'm afraid that whoever it is, may have been following me and knows that I work here. This…" I swept my hand over the scene of devastation again. "This could be a warning. To me."

"Do you have any idea at all who it might be?" he asked.

"I think I may," I said, but my suspicions were still too uncertain to tell him or anyone else yet.

"You should let the police know," he said.

"Ab, If the police roust him, he will know that I suspect him and it could undermine the case." I looked at him. "If it's okay with you, I'd like to wait until after I've spoken to this guy. Then I could give some real information to the authorities."

He nodded. "Well, it's fine with me, but I don't like the idea of you talking to someone who would do this. You be careful."

"Now you *do* sound like Easy," I said, then changed the subject to a different aspect of the problem. "We have to think about what to do here. I can't allow you to put your livelihood and maybe even your life in danger because of me. Maybe I should stay away from the shop until this is over."

"Uh-uh," he said, shaking his head. He stood up. "You help me get this cleaned up. I'll put up this plywood. We'll go over the damage and I'll contact the insurance agent. You look into a good burglar alarm system for me and we'll go on as before. I'm not changing my life because of some cowardly hood, and I don't think you should either."

"I'm going to make some calls right now," I told him "I think we can get an alarm installed for you right away."

In twenty minutes, I had set up an appointment for the smashed window to be replaced and another with a security company for the next morning. We spent the next few hours sweeping and making lists. "Do you know how they got in?" I asked while we were taking a break.

He looked shamefaced. "I do. The lock on the back door is—was pretty flimsy. He just had to push a bit and it gave. I need to call a locksmith too, I guess."

I shook my head. "The security company will take care of your locks as well. I gave them a strong hint that they weren't all that secure."

"Aw, thanks, babe." He sounded genuinely grateful.

I nodded. "But no money was taken?"

He laughed then, though it sounded pretty thin. "I have made it a habit to put all the money in the register into my pocket before I leave." He rubbed his hand over his gray head and down to his grizzled beard. "I guess I wasn't a complete idiot about security, huh?" He looked so hopeful, I had to smile.

"Did anything happen to your contest entry?" I asked.

"Oh, jeez! I haven't even looked." We took the two steps up to the work room at a run and hurried through the door into a smaller workspace. The piece, a magnificent window done in a Tiffany style, depicted blooming wisteria along the top and sides. In the center, a peacock turned his head upward while a fountain flowed behind him. Ab had cut most of the pieces and they, thankfully, lay unharmed on the table. We both began breathing again.

"It might be a good idea to keep this door locked," I told him. He nodded and we went back out to the main work area.

One of the tables held the projects of Ab's students in various stages of completion. Beside each, was a name crayoned on the butcher paper that covered the table.

I moved down the length of the table and looked at the pitiful pile of twisted metal and glass shards that had been my project. "See this?" I said, gesturing at the other unharmed pieces. "Mine is the only student's work that was damaged. I was right. This *is* because of my investigation."

"I'm so sorry, babe," Ab said. "It was coming along beautifully too."

"Well, I'm the one who is sorry. All this devastation is my fault. I'm terribly sorry, Ab."

"It's not your fault at all!" he said. "It's mine for having a crappy lock on my back door. I don't want you to blame yourself. We could argue about it all day, but it won't get any of the work done."

"I'm going to start over and do an even better job," I said thinking of the joy that piece had given me and the pride I had taken in it.

"Atta girl," he said. "You've been doing a terrific job. I'd hate to see you give it up."

"Oh, I won't give it up," I said. "Let's look at this damage as simply one of those things that happens.

It's like a flood or a fire. It's part of life."

He nodded. "Shit happens all the time. Insurance is going to cover most of this. We'll be fixed up in no time. I don't plan to leave until there's a new lock on that back door and a burglar alarm is in place."

"When you're here by yourself, you keep your wits about you," I said. "The new front window should be installed later today. I'll be back in the morning to help you. I can cut squares for the sample window while the security company works."

Before I left, I gave him a quick hug and a pat or two on the back.

After leaving Mickey Carrol's, I had been relatively sure that Jon-Paul was mixed up in this whole business. After leaving Ab's, of course, I was convinced that the damage at Avenue Art Glass was the work of Jon-Paul too. Whether he had done it himself or hired someone, it made no difference. I knew I was going to have to have a talk with him and a talk with Aïda as well. Up to then, I hadn't been completely sure about any of it. I hadn't wanted to ruin anyone else's relationship because of my speculations, no matter how sure about them I felt. Now, though. I *was* certain.

SIXTEEN

Saturday, January 7, 1984

I awoke the next morning to a bank of fog smothering West Seattle. In the distance, I could hear fog-horns calling back and forth over Puget Sound. Otherwise, the world was silent, stifled in the mist.

The face I encountered in the mirror looked way more colorful than it had the day before. An aurora borealis surrounded my little star-shaped scab. I rummaged around until I found an old jar of foundation make-up that was probably older than many of my clothes and tried smoothing it over the bruise. I never wear makeup and I honestly have no memory of where I had obtained the jar. It may have belonged to my mother. In any case it did an adequate job of disguising the worst of the damage.

After a quick breakfast of raisin bran and a banana, I headed back to Avenue Art Glass to see if the security company had arrived. They had. Ab was supervising and getting an education in proper security habits. I got to work cutting the little three by four inch rectangles of every color we offered for sale in the store. They would go back onto the sample rack and into the window.

At lunchtime, I headed downtown. I had some slightly illegal details to see to there. On the way, I kept checking my rear view mirror to see if I was being followed, but I saw nothing unusual.

By noon, watery sun was just beginning to break through the remaining tufts of fog. The sidewalks steamed softly making the city look like the left-over set from an urban horror movie.

I walked up Pike to Fourth, then turned right and walked slowly, gazing into shop windows. I stopped at a corner vendor to buy a bag of popcorn for lunch, then continued walking.

If Aïda's father was alive, I had to assume that he had acquired a new identity. When I had worked for Gale Siddens, at the agency where I had gotten my private investigation training, before I got my license and my own agency, I had learned the rudiments of acquiring a new identity. I had never had occasion to use the information. Now seemed like an excellent time for it. If someone was looking for me with malice aforethought, my having a different identity in my pocket wouldn't make it the slightest bit tougher to find me unless I changed everything else about my life. But I *would* need a good solid cover for the case that was coming up in the spring. It was an undercover job that I was very much looking forward to. Plus, I wanted to try this identity thing for myself. There were a couple of ways to go about it.

If I were Royal Blue and planning to become someone else, I would need a birth certificate and a driver's license. My first task would be to decide who I was going to become. Of course, I would choose a person who had already passed on to the great beyond, since I wouldn't want to run into her at a cocktail party here below. How did one find out who had died and when? You could look in the obits in the newspaper or you could check the birth and death records at the courthouse. Find someone who was born about the same year as you were and had died shortly thereafter and you could get yourself a new name.

Since it was Saturday, the courthouse was closed. But I was near the Seattle Public Library, so I decided to make a stop there. I walked down Fourth to the library then rode the escalator to the newspaper section. I found a huge rack of small boxes, each holding microfilm of approximately a month's worth of The Seattle Times and The Seattle Post Intelligencers. The years went back to when Seattle's newspaper had been called The Seattle Star and the pictures were drawings rather than photographs.

I chose 1954, eight years after I was born. Might as well shave a few years off of my age as long as I had the opportunity. I put the film into the viewer, then quickly realized that it would be possible to be completely amused all day doing nothing but reading old newspapers. I had, at random, chosen July. The headlines were amazingly similar to those in the paper I had thrown out the previous night. Food was cheaper, and so were cars, houses and everything else. A wedding ring set with eleven diamonds cost $249.50 and a gallon of gas was 25 cents. But prices were on the rise even then. People were doing crazy things, just like they have always done. Hunger strikes were being staged and people were mad at the government. Crime seemed rampant. Telephone numbers were two letters and four digits. Eisenhower was President. I quickly read an article about a guy in Germany who had committed suicide by walking into a lion's den at the zoo. Was that any weirder than drive-by shootings?

I scanned the table of contents and found the obituaries. I needed someone who had died as a child. A quick look at the deaths showed me no one under the age of forty-three had died within the previous few days. I went on to the next day and the next until I abandoned 1954 and selected another year. I pulled the microfilm for a paper from 1948.

I found three names. The last one was tailor-made for my needs. A little girl named Sarah Noble Augustine had been born in Portland, Oregon on April 22, 1946, which happened to be just a few days after the day I was born. According to the listing, she and her family had moved to Medford, Oregon two years later, where she had died. Her obituary was a lovely, sad little drama written by people who had loved her dearly. Apparently, she'd had several relatives in the Seattle area or space in the local papers most likely wouldn't have been purchased. I wrote down her mother's maiden name, father's name and appropriate dates. I sighed a little over the pathetically short amount of time between poor little Sarah's birth and her death.

Back in my car I thought about my next move. Sarah had been born in Portland. Her birth records would be there. What I needed next was an address, and since I was choosing a new one, I wanted it to be ritzy. I chose Mercer Island—just right for someone of the caliber I intended to become. Besides, I knew one of the postal workers at the Mercer Island office. It would be good to see her again.

Luckily, Hilary Painter wasn't out to lunch or on vacation. She beamed at me when I pushed through the door. We exchanged small talk for a few minutes then I made my request.

"What are you up to now, Cheyenne?" she asked in a whisper. She leaned over the counter and breathed her excitement into my face. She acted as if I were a jewel thief planning to ship my loot to the Orient. In reality, anyone can rent a post office box. I was doing nothing underhanded at all.

"Just checking out a theory," I told her.

"Yeah?" She cocked her head to one side. "Well, I'd bet you're up to no good." She gave the application a decisive stamp of approval anyway and slid a key across the counter to me.

"I never saw you before in my life," she whispered and threw me a broad wink.

My new address was 3040 78th Ave SE, the street address of the Mercer Island Post Office. When I added my box number as an apartment number, it was complete.

I headed back downtown and parked in the first spot I could find. I had an errand farther up First Avenue.

I walked past a "theater" with a marquee that said "50 Girls, All Nude!" and a specialty shop that sold nothing but scanty undies and bizarre looking equipment of indeterminate purpose.

I found King Diamondis' acquaintance in a sleazy looking tattoo place just down from the Market and connected to "The Blue Lady." The poster stuck to the window of "The Blue Lady" suggested that the women therein were neither blue nor ladies.

King's friend was amiable enough. We chatted for a few minutes, long enough, I guessed, to prove that I really did know King and could be trusted. He had a way of asking probing questions that seemed innocuous enough, but were aimed at ferreting out the details. I had often used the same tactics and answered him as honestly as I felt necessary.

Apparently, I passed his test because he cheerfully provided me with exactly what I needed. My new driver's license, or I should say, Sarah Augustine's, looked damned good. I held it up next to my own and thought it looked legit. I wasn't an expert, but neither was anyone else who might have occasion to look at it.

Armed with my new address and my new driver's license, I stopped by my favorite Sodo print shop where I knew the manager.

"Look, Evan," I said, sidling up close to him and shamelessly using his attraction to me. "I need a little favor." There's nothing illegal about buying business cards with someone else's name on them either, but I thought Evan could use a little excitement in his life.

Evan's Adam's apple jumped when he swallowed. "Anything," he said.

He always said that. I sometimes wondered what he would do if I asked him for a thousand bucks or a quick, kinky lay. His grin exposed teeth that deviated to the right and lots of gum. "I'm still waiting for my invitation to run away to Mexico," he said. "Is this it?"

"Not yet," I said. "I need a few business cards printed. Not a whole box, though I'll pay for the whole thing. I need about a dozen this time."

"Sure." He said, punctuating the word with a nod.

"I want them to read 'Sarah Noble Augustine, Freelance Writer.'" I gave him my new address and my own telephone number. At the last minute, I amended the order with a request for another dozen cards that said "Sarah N. Augustine, Real Estate." Same address but with a made up telephone number with a Mercer Island prefix.

Evan's response was a single raised eyebrow followed by a wink. I promised him everlasting heaven with my eyes.

We talked about color and script. I got him to promise to have them ready for me the next day, then I wrote him a check.

"So," he said, "Got a hot date for tonight? If not, I could make myself available." He said 'available' with an eyebrow wag that was loaded with alternative meaning.

"Sure do," I said sweetly.

From Sodo I drove up I-5, then veered off to the Greenwood district where my friend, Molly, lived. She had been the mother figure in my life ever since my mother died. She coddled me when I needed it, kicked my ass when I needed that, but mainly she was around and full of good advice whether I wanted any or not. As usual, she was delighted to see me.

"Come in!" she said just before she smothered me in a hug. "It's wonderful to see you." She pressed me back for a better look.

"What happened to you?!" She almost screamed the words. The make-up I had so carefully applied to my bruised face that morning must have worn away. I could never remember to keep my hands off of my face. No one else had mentioned it. Hilary hadn't said anything and neither had Evan. Leave it to Molly to ferret it out.

"I had a little run in with a disgruntled door," I said, brushing her concern aside.

"A door didn't put a star shaped scab on your cheek," she said. She made little *oohing* sounds as she folded me into another hug.

"Tell me," she whispered into my ear, but I shook my head and she knew I meant it. "Don't worry," she said. "You're just as gorgeous as ever."

"You always make me feel good, Molly," I said, escaping her grasp. She laughed and headed for the kitchen with me in tow. Molly loved any excuse for food. Well, so did I. She was the one person in the world who thought I was too thin and she was constantly trying to remedy that.

"I have some chocolate cheesecake left over from last night," she said from the depths of the refrigerator. "Let's have some."

"If there's one thing in the universe of food I won't resist, it's an offer of cheesecake," I said. I snuggled into the bentwood rocker she kept in her kitchen and felt myself sink into comfort.

Being inside Molly's home was like being inside a pillow. She had drapes and curtains over every window. Doilies and tablecloths rode on every surface. Even the sofa and chairs were decorated with bits of crochet. The kitchen and the dining room were separated by a ruffled curtain in the doorway. She had scorned the hard surfaces of doors and floors in favor of soft fabrics, carpets and rugs. Perhaps that's why her house was so comforting. I felt that even if I fell down, I would sink into the floor as if it were a feather mattress. Molly kept the temperature at a level that was just under too warm. She had wrapped herself in a cocoon of comfort.

"Anything interesting going on in the spy business?" she asked when we had sampled the cheesecake with accompanying groans of pleasure.

"I'm working on a case for Aïda Blue," I told her shamelessly.

She gasped and her hand flew to her chest. "Royal Blue's daughter?" Her eyes opened as wide as they would permit.

"She lives in Los Angeles, but she came all the way to Seattle to hire me." I knew Molly would jump right in on that one.

"First it was Magda St. Martin and now Aïda Blue. Chey, your clientele is getting to be very high class. I'm impressed." She chewed another bite of cheesecake thoughtfully. "I don't suppose you can tell me about the case," she said, feigning complete disinterest.

"Actually, I can't right now. I know you understand."

"I do," she said with a resigned sigh. "Sometime, though, I'll be able to catch you off guard."

"You might, at that," I told her."

We savored the cheesecake for a few more minutes.

"Molly, do you want to go to Portland on Monday?" I asked. "I have an errand to run down there." I didn't really need to go. I could have accomplished my errand by mail, but going there would get it done faster and I knew I could do something for Molly at the same time.

Her eyes stared into mine. "Thank you," she said. "Yes, I'd love to." She hadn't forgotten.

"It's not a glamorous errand, I'm afraid," I told her. "I have to check on some records. And Monday *is* the ninth."

Her gaze slid toward a pair of photographs sitting on the plate rail that ran around the kitchen. She nodded.

More than six years before, Molly's children had been killed in a car accident. At the time, I had been worn out from grief at my mother's death and together we had dragged each other out of hell. Since then, Molly had found solace where she could, in making her house insulated against the world and in food. I had found mine in work. Each year as the anniversary of those two deaths neared, I tried to drop in and take Molly to visit her children's graves. She had taken them back to their home town of Portland to be buried. Someday, I knew, she expected to be buried there too.

"Remember that wonderful *dim sum* restaurant we found last year?" she asked, having forgotten about the cheesecake on the fork that was a scant inch from her mouth. "Maybe we could go there."

I laughed and nodded.

"So, tell me more. What are you doing for Aïda Blue?" she asked.

I laughed again and shook my head. "Nice try."

"Oh, phooey! Forget client privilege. I won't tell anyone. Who would I tell?"

"Sorry, Molly, not this time." Usually, I didn't mind telling Molly about my cases, even though they were confidential. She generally had good advice for me and often offered valuable insight. Besides, she was the most honest person in the world and my clients' secrets were absolutely safe with her. That time, though, I hadn't wanted to drag her into the sleazy world of Jon-Paul.

She nodded. "I understand," she said and I knew she did.

"I have to go home and make a phone call," I said. I needed to check on Aïda. I was becoming increasingly concerned about her ignorance regarding Jon-Paul. I wasn't ready to warn her yet, but I felt responsible for her safety.

"You can use mine." Her face lit up.

"Not a chance."

✳ ✳ ✳

On the way back to West Seattle, I again carefully monitored my rear view mirror but still noticed no one following me.

When I got home, there was a large box on my front porch and three messages on the recorder.

I shoved the box into the entry hall—it was way too heavy for me to lift – then went to the answering machine. With a sinking heart, I listened.

"Cheyenne. King. The young man in question is named Jon-Paul LaCross. He's willing to pay. The only trouble is, he's having difficulty coming up with the money. Not that I think you will, but don't panic yet."

A second message was from my newest client. He explained that he had left the box on my porch and had packed instructions inside. I would deal with that later.

The third was from Aïda, informing me that she had moved from the Westin into an apartment.

She proceeded to recite her new phone number and address.

I immediately dialed her new number. "Are you alone, Aïda?" I asked her when she'd answered and we had exchanged hellos.

"Yes." She instantly sounded suspicious. "Why?"

"Is Jon-Paul's last name LaCross?"

"Yes." That time I could hear her voice icing up.

"He's Mickey Carrol's nephew, isn't he, Aïda?" She didn't say anything. She didn't have to. "Does he have a ring shaped like a star?"

She hesitated only a second. "Yes."

I took a deep breath and let it out slowly. "Aïda, if I'm going to help you, you are going to have to be straight with me. First, you fail to mention an identical twin your father had and then don't happen to mention that you are engaged to your father's agent's nephew. Do you want me to drop this whole thing, or what?"

"No, Cheyenne. I don't want you to drop it." I could have sworn her voice quavered and I felt a sudden rush of pity for her which I tried to shake off.

"I have to talk to you," I said. "Could we meet? I can come to you."

"No. I'll come to your place." She hung up before I had a chance to say another word.

✳ ✳ ✳

"Your boyfriend is the one who knocked the living soup out of me in San Francisco. Were you aware of that?" I had settled Aïda in my living room. She sat on the sofa and I took a small chair nearby. Her face blanched at my words but she kept her composure.

"No. That's not possible. He's…" She stopped, giving my damaged face a hard look.

"I have a sweet looking star permanently engraved on my cheek, Aïda," I said, fingering my scab. "It was your Jon-Paul who gave it to me. And that isn't all." I scrutinized her face. *Is she strong enough to hear what else I have to tell her?* I wondered. "I've been told by someone, a person who is absolutely reliable, that Jon-Paul has been trying to scrape together the money to have me killed."

Understanding flooded her face and an unattractive hot looking red crept up her neck. I wondered if he had asked her for a loan. And, if he had, how she had responded.

"I'm sorry to have to tell you these things," I said. "But I think you should look at this rationally and know what is going on. I believe he's after your money, Aïda." She looked at me for what seemed like a long time. "Did you lend or give him money, recently?" I asked.

"No. I..." She hesitated for so long, I wondered if she was going to continue. Finally, she cleared her throat, took a deep breath and seemed to gather her resources. "He asked me if he could borrow ten thousand dollars. He didn't want to say what it was for at first. Then he said that he needed it for a business deal." She licked her lips. "I...It didn't feel right, so I said I would think about it. We left it at that." She looked down into her lap. I could feel a wave of deep regret rolling off of her.

"I also believe that Jon-Paul is behind the break in at Avenue Art Glass yesterday. He definitely has me targeted. I've been working there part time. Yesterday someone broke in and vandalized the store. He created quite a lot of damage and destroyed the project I was working on but left the other students' work alone."

She looked stunned.

"I'm so sorry, Aïda," I said. "This is serious. I think that man is not only a danger to me but to you as well."

She swallowed once and lifted her chin. "Of course, I won't let him have any money. I...don't think I would have anyway. I'm sorry this has happened."

"It isn't your fault," I said. "None of it is your fault."

"What do you want me to do?"

"That's where the hard part comes in," I told her. "I thought at first that I would want to have a discussion with him, but for now, I don't want him to know that I'm onto him."

"You want me to act as if I know nothing about it."

I nodded. "I *am* sorry, Aïda. I know this is very difficult for you and it will probably get even harder. Are you going to be all right?"

"Oh, yes," she said. Her clear brown gaze burrowed into mine.

I realized then that Aïda may have put up walls of her own that were even higher than mine.

"I've been through worse," she added.

I knew she meant it.

SEVENTEEN

Sunday, January 8, 1984

I spent the next morning cleaning my new house. For some reason, I didn't mind doing the chores that I normally hated. Mopping a new floor or swabbing out a new toilet is way more enjoyable that doing the very same things with an old floor and an old toilet. I felt downright virtuous when I finished and thought I would treat myself to an afternoon in Avenue Art Glass. It was Sunday after all. My time.

I opened the box that had been left at my doorstep the day before. I glanced through it and stored it in my coat closet for later. The case wouldn't begin until spring. There would be lots of preparation involved but this was no time to start it. I would get into it when I had finished with Aïda's case.

Before I left for the glass shop, I called Easy. When I had last spoken to him, late Thursday night, I had been well aware that he was checking up on me after my meeting with King. I had called him on it. Neither one of us had been happy with the outcome of the discussion we had had over the incident.

"So, you aren't mad at me anymore?" he asked getting right into it. Normally, I would have danced around the subject for a minute to scope out the battlefield.

"I'm not mad at you, Easy," I said. "I just don't like it when you go all overprotective on me. You know I don't like that."

He didn't say anything so I pressed on. "I'm going to Portland tomorrow and then I'll be going to Hawaii. I thought we could have dinner together tonight since I won't be seeing you for a little while."

"Sure," he said. It wasn't his usual enthusiastic I-can't-wait-to-see-you attitude and I wondered, not for the first time, if his feelings for me were changing.

"If I bring the groceries, could I meet you at your place and we could cook? I promise it won't be leek casserole or anything you won't like."

His voice had softened when he agreed and I knew he could see that I was waving a white flag.

Actually, I had an ulterior motive for wanting to meet at Easy's apartment rather than mine. If I was going to conduct a successful search for Royal Blue, I needed to know the man. I thought that a good way to accomplish that would be to listen to some of his music. I knew that Easy owned at least one of his albums and probably more. We talked for a little while longer, then I headed down to the shop to see if I could help Ab with some of the repairs necessitated by the break-in.

* * *

I was unpacking the groceries I had brought when Easy said, "I think we have a little problem here."

"Really? What problem?" I asked, trying to sound casually interested, but my heart had started to thud. Easy's words sounded like the beginning of a *talk*.

"I can't help worrying about you," he said, "and it seems you are resenting me because of it."

I looked at his wonderful blue eyes. They looked genuinely sad and a little frightened. "I don't resent *you*," I told him. "I just don't need you to worry."

"Cheyenne, when you go to San Francisco and get beat up," he said, holding his hand up to stop my interruption. "And when you have meetings with a man like King Diamondis, you are getting into dangerous territory. How can I not worry about you?"

I was glad he didn't know about the contract on my life. Well, the tentative contract, anyway.

"In November you had a death threat and you

will always have a scar on your arm from getting attacked because you were involved in the same case. I can't think of a reason to *not* worry about you." He looked so patient, and so dear.

"Being a private investigator is what I do, Easy," I told him. "I have chosen to do this work because I love it. What are you asking? For me to stop being a private investigator? There isn't anything else that I want to do."

"I can't ask you to change jobs," he said. "And I won't." He gave me a long appraising look as if carefully considering his next question. "Have you thought about carrying your weapon?"

"No, and you know the reasons why and you agree with them," I said. "I'm surprised you would even suggest it."

"I know." He looked defeated. I wanted to gather him into my arms. He had taken the job of Police Chaplain because he had wanted to work in law enforcement but didn't want to carry a weapon any more than I did. He had admitted to me once that he had been secretly disappointed that his false eye had kept him out of the military during Vietnam. He had, he had said, wanted to be a conscientious objector and go to prison for it.

"I know it's pointless to ask you not to worry about me," I said. "And when you do worry, it's pointless for me to resent it. Do you think we can agree that if I promise to be more careful, to brush up on my self-defense skills, that you won't be so vocal about your disapproval of what I do?" I had known already that I needed to hone my defensive skills. The set-to in San Francisco had taught me that.

"I guess I can't ask for more than that," he said.

I stepped into his arms then and he gave me one of his warm, generous hugs. There was an almost overwhelming sense of relief, affection, gratitude, and, yes, love coming from him. I felt waves and waves of it but I did not step away from it. I was grateful for his goodness and even the fear that I also felt under it all. The feelings he had were for *me*. How could I ever hope to deserve such a man?

After that, we enjoyed a delightful and relaxed dinner. It was as if we had cleared up something heavy and dark that had risen between us. In actuality, we had spoken only a few words and neither of us had conceded anything. But that was how it was with Ezekial Zachary Radford. In that way, he truly was easy.

❉ ❉ ❉

"You have some Royal Blue in this collection, yes?" I asked him when the dishes had been put in the dishwasher. We were in his music room so he could change out the record that had been playing on the turntable.

He went to one wall of record albums and selected a few. "I have all of them, but these three are my favorites. 'Living in the Rain,' 'Dissatisfaction of the Different' and 'Afterthought'. Anything in particular you'd like to hear?"

"I really don't know much about his music at all. I've heard some of his songs on the radio, of course. I like "Sounds From Tomorrow" and I like that song, 'Sign Your Life Away'." I shrugged. "You pick something."

He put one of the records on the turntable and we sat in the living room and listened. I held the album cover and looked at the photos of the man, Royal Blue, on the back. The camera had caught him in the middle of a concert with his hair flying and his face twisted into a grimace.

"What's the name of this one?" I asked Easy. "It's hard to understand the words."

He pointed to the selection on the cover. "When We Were Young and Stupid," it read. I tried to listen carefully but much of it was indecipherable.

"I wish I could catch the words," I said.

He got up, headed back into the music room and came out to hand me a folded sheet of paper. It was a list of the songs and their lyrics. I scanned them until I found the song I was looking for and followed along with the words. Suddenly, Royal Blue's music seemed to come into sharper focus in my mind. We listened to several more songs and chatted quietly during the instrumentals.

"Do you have these lyric sheets for all of his albums?" I asked. "I didn't know record companies did this kind of thing."

"Lots of them don't. And certainly not for every artist. Royal's company was probably willing to invest more money in his albums than they would for other artists. They knew they would be making it all back and a lot more," Easy told me. "I have lyric sheets for all of his albums. Do you want to see them?"

"Could I borrow them?"

He looked doubtful. I was well aware that Easy never lent his records to anyone. I imagined the same applied to the lyric sheets.

"I promise I'll get them copied and bring them all back safely," I added.

"I trust you," he said, but he still looked like he didn't.

"I would like to take them with me to Hawaii. I'm going to Portland tomorrow and Hawaii the day after that. I think studying the lyrics of his songs, particularly since he's the song writer *and* lyricist, would be the best way of getting into the mind of Royal Blue."

"Tell you what," he said. "I'll have them copied tomorrow and bring them with me when I pick you up to take you to the airport on Tuesday."

I reached over and gave him a soft peck on the mouth, then leaned to whisper in his ear, "I knew you didn't trust me."

EIGHTEEN

Monday, January 9, 1984

The next morning, it started raining just after my alarm went off at five-thirty. I had ignored Molly's grumbles about the early hour and told her I would pick her up at seven-thirty.

I dragged myself out of bed, dressed, then sat down with an oat bran muffin and a cup of tea to scan my notes.

Okay. I was willing to concede that Royal Blue could be alive and had changed his identity. *Who*, *where* and *why* seemed like reasonable questions at this point, with the *where* more important right now than the *why*. Another good question was whose ashes were lying in Royal Blue's grave if Roy, himself was still alive? Hawaii would be an intelligent place to begin trying to figure out some of the answers.

* * *

I picked Molly up under a charcoal gray sky, essentially still night. A fine mist was in the air that covered my hair with tiny glistening beads of moisture.

Molly brought along an overnight bag.

"We aren't staying the night," I told her, knowing that she didn't have clothing packed in the bag.

"It's a little lunch," she said, unruffled. "I thought it would be easier if we didn't have to stop to eat."

I knew we would reach Portland well before lunch, but knowing Molly's cooking skills, I wasn't about to turn down whatever delicacies she had brought along.

Driving to Portland on I-5 on a rainy winter morning is like spending a couple of hours in hell. If it's raining hard enough, you can't see anything on either side of the freeway, even if there was anything to see. All I could do was slog through and try not to let trucks pass me, for, when they did, it was a full ten seconds until my windshield wipers could cope with the spray. Ten seconds is a long time when you're speeding down a crowded freeway at 70 miles per hour.

At least twenty-five trucks passed me that morning. Molly sat ramrod straight beside me uttering panicky little gasps each time a truck blistered my windshield with dirty water. She did admirably well, considering that the two people she had loved most in the world had been killed on a rainy stretch of highway one winter night. At intervals, she offered me some of the tea she had brought in a large Thermos. It was all I could do to keep the car on the road and in my own lane. I didn't need any caffeine or sugar to push me over the edge. My own adrenaline was doing fine.

We pulled into a soggy downtown Portland at ten-thirty-five. I headed straight for the Oregon equivalent of the building in Seattle where one acquires birth and death certificates. The parking was abysmal and I circled the block three times, then parked in a passenger load zone. Molly looked at me with suspicious eyes.

"You can't park here," she said.

"It's okay," I told her. "I will only be gone a few minutes. You won't let me get towed, will you? Just jump behind the wheel and act like you are going to drive away."

"I can't drive," she said. Her voice scaled up several notes. "What do I do if a policeman comes?"

"No one will bother you. We're allowed to park here for a few minutes. If I'm gone longer than that, and anyone comes, offer him something from our lunch bag. I know you have some cookies in there." I shut the door against her indignant face. I believed she would be safe from any encounter with the law.

The elevator whisked me to the third floor where the directory indicated the birth certificates were.

I marched up to the counter as confidently as if it actually was my own birth certificate I was requesting.

It was surprisingly simple. Almost shockingly so. Easier than it should have been, really. I filled out one of the forms to request a birth certificate, using Sarah's mother's maiden name and other information gleaned from the death notice in the newspaper, and presented it.

"I'll need to see identification," the clerk said in a monotone. Poor thing probably had to say those words a thousand times a day.

I produced my phony driver's license. King's friend had done a surprisingly good job on it. It may not have passed scrutiny by a police officer in Washington, but it may have. Anyway, what did the Oregon clerk know from Washington driver's licenses?

Since Sarah had been born in Multnomah County and had died in Jackson County, I was reasonably certain that the two events would not be connected in her records. Even so, there was an uncomfortable two or three minutes while the clerk perused her computer monitor.

"I'll also need something else with your address," she said finally. "A utility bill or an envelope from a piece of mail you have received."

I offered that I didn't usually carry around utility bills or envelopes from discarded mail but how about a business card? I gave her one of the Sarah Augustine, Real Estate cards that I had picked up from the ever reliable Evan the day before. She barely glanced at it, only long enough to verify the address and name. I paid in cash while the clerk copied the certificate then I slipped it into my briefcase with a grateful smile.

I got back to the car just as Molly was launching into a one-sided verbal boxing match with the driver of a car who wanted to use the loading zone.

"Don't holler, Molly," I said when I was in the car and had pulled on the seat belt. She kept telling the driver of the tan Toyota to keep moving. He was patiently ignoring her. "He wants to park here."

"I was afraid he was going to block us in," she said with her mouth prim.

I gave the driver of the Toyota a wave and mouthed "sorry" to him. He scowled.

"Shall we find a good spot to have our lunch? Or would you rather do the restaurant and save our lunch for dinner?" she asked when we had pulled into the late morning traffic.

"If the lunch will keep, let's find that restaurant," I said, suddenly famished.

I drove past an unfamiliar pet groomer and a florist I had never seen before, but otherwise Portland hadn't changed much since the previous year when we had made our last pilgrimage. I turned left on Sandy and found The China Garden still painted the same shade of nasty green on the outside

Inside the *dim sum* were as delightful as we had remembered. The *shumai* were hot little bundles of garlic and pork that tasted like heaven. The fried *won ton* were light and crisp and the sesame buns were, as usual, wonderful.

"So how are things going with Easy?" Molly asked me between a fried *won ton* and a bamboo roll. I had known she was going to ask me sooner or later, but I had been hoping to get her back into the car and asleep before it had occurred to her.

"Fine."

It didn't work. She stopped chewing and looked at me. "Okay. I know there's a lot more to it when your answer to a question is 'fine'."

I still didn't say anything and her eyes narrowed.

"He proposed, didn't he?"

"No, he didn't propose," I said. After another moment, I offered, "but, he was going to." Her eyes went round and I was afraid she was going to choke.

"How do you..." she started to ask then caught herself.

"I *am* psychic."

"Marriage? He wants to get married? What did you say?"

"Since he never actually asked the question, I didn't say anything. I changed the subject before he could ask. I can't talk to him rationally when he gets like that. It was only lust talking anyway. You know Easy can't think of sex without thinking of marriage. It makes the sex act acceptable to him for some reason." I swallowed a too hot mouthful of tea and burned the heck out of my tongue. Talking about marriage was making me more uncomfortable by the second.

"That's because he's a good, honest man and wants to marry you. Your mother would have wanted you to get married," she said. She took a bite of a *hom bao*.

"My mother would want me to be happy, not marry if I wasn't inclined to," I said, sorry that I hadn't lied to her. Unfortunately, I didn't lie well to Molly. She was too much the mother figure to me, even though she was not old enough to have given birth to me. She knew when I was keeping back something just as easily as I know when someone isn't being straight with me.

"Chey, think of it. You could have children." With that thought, her eyes clouded and I was indeed sorry that the subject had come up. "Don't you want children?" Her chin trembled and her eyes turned to liquid.

I dropped my gaze to my plate. I did and did not want children. Someday or never. Seeing my meager load of possessions when I had moved, I had come face to face with how little there was of me in the world. I envied writers and artists who left something of themselves behind for future generations. Writers, artists and mothers, that was. The thing was, I couldn't tolerate the thought of loving someone so very much. I had done that and...Out of nowhere, a memory struck me from behind. I remembered a rainy afternoon many years before. David and I had walked home from an afternoon movie. We had talked of children, though we ourselves were still kids. I felt a residual warmth from that long ago conversation followed by the usual thrill of dread. I pushed the thought of David from me. He was as dead as Molly's children and there was no use dwelling on him. I moved my plate aside, physically shoving the thought of David out of my mind.

Molly watched me, but said nothing more. She had sat with me and cried with me enough times to know almost exactly what I was feeling and, as far as I knew, she didn't possess a shred of psychic ability.

"You okay?" she asked after a moment. "Honey, I'm so sorry."

I smiled at her. "You have nothing to be sorry for."

"I am the one who made you think of marriage and children and that always makes you think of David. I'm sorry for that."

"It isn't that I cannot love," I said. "I love you. And I love Easy too. I *love*. Just not too much." I stopped, then added, "if I can help it." Neither one of us said anything for a moment. "I loved my mother," I continued at last. "I loved David and I loved Cam. Loving people hurts, Molly."

She didn't add anything. She well knew that love hurt, probably more than most people did. She just watched me silently while we finished up our lunch.

* * *

Afterward, we drove to the cemetery where Molly's boy and girl were buried. I stayed in the car and waited for her. She preferred it that way, but I always felt guilty watching her plod slowly to the pitiful little graves under the dripping trees. We did it every year, but I never got used to it and I know she never did either.

While I waited, I thought about our conversation. Molly was the most loving person I knew. She knew better than anyone how much love hurt, yet she was still able to believe in it. I had to admire her. She seemed to have conquered love's awesome and terrifying power.

At last, she returned to the car and we decided to make a quick stop at Powell's Books before heading home.

Inside the huge store, I browsed among the new releases. I picked up a couple of paperback mysteries and looked at a display of a new science fiction novel. It looked fascinating, and I had heard of the author, but I put it back. Brand new hardbacks seemed like too much of an extravagance. Molly, however, bought four cookbooks.

The weather had cleared by the time we rolled past Centralia and it was smooth driving from there on. At last, we rounded the curve on I-5 just south of Spokane Street where Seattle looms in the distance. It's a weary traveler's first sight of home and no matter how many times I see it, I always get a lump in my throat.

When we got to Molly's, we ate the onion bagel and cream cheese with smoked salmon sandwiches and yes, chocolate hunk cookies she had hauled all the way to Portland and back. I was glad to be back at her place and it was so snug and comfortable that I wasn't looking forward to the trip home.

"What do you need it for, anyway?" she asked when I had told her about my shenanigans with the birth certificate.

I actually didn't really *need* a birth certificate. I had the fake driver's license and that was probably enough for my purposes. But I had wanted the whole package. Who knew? There was always the chance that I would someday need it. "This has to be kept absolutely quiet," I told her. "I have a case coming up in the spring where I'm going to be going undercover. I need a new identity for it."

She was thrilled, and wanted details but I didn't indulge her. Not all of the plans had been made yet and the contract had not been signed. Instead, I told her how shamefully easy it had been to get the birth certificate.

"Isn't it illegal?" she asked, laughing at my outrage.

"Sure. But in my defense, I won't use it to escape the law or swindle anyone," I told her. "You know, someday, it will be a lot more difficult to get other people's personal information. If computers really do become common and everyone has them, it will be almost impossible to do what I did today. Not only that, there will be laws to protect everybody's privacy."

"Count your blessings, then," she said, "that it's so easy right now."

* * *

Aïda had said she wanted to speak to me before I went to Hawaii, so, on the way home from Molly's, I stopped downtown at her new apartment. I hadn't called her and risked her being out.

"It's Cheyenne," I said into the speaker in the lobby of her building. I was impressed. Of course, I'd known the girl had money, but how often do you rent a condo for a couple of weeks' stay out of town just on a whim? Me? Never. She buzzed me up and the lavish, silent elevator delivered me to the top floor.

Aïda met me at her polished oak door and held it open for me. She was barefoot and wearing a pair of skin tight designer jeans and an oversized silk shirt of soft coral. Her fine hair was tied into a shining pony tail. Funny, when I was in the sixth grade, my pony tail never looked that good. She wore no make-up, but her skin was fine and clear without it. Her eyes' warm chocolate brown gave her the look of a fresh child. And actually, I supposed, that was what she was. Hers was a face that had never known the sting of a snowball or the feel of baseball diamond dust ground into it. Her pillowcases had been made of linens, her nighties of silk. Her fingernails had never been chipped or broken short in the course of a fight. For a moment, I envied her, then felt pity take its turn.

"I tried calling you this morning," she said. She padded back into the living room. I followed and tried to take it all in at once without seeming to gape.

The rug was a sumptuous dusty green, thick enough to bounce on. Surrounding it was a border of gleaming oak flooring. Aïda settled into a huge recliner of honey gold, then tucked her feet under her. Feeling cloddish and somewhat grimy, I sat on the cream sofa. It offered perfect support and the arm was exactly the right height for mine. I felt myself relaxing into it. A panoramic view of the city swept before me through a sparkling window.

"Are you all right, Aïda?" I asked.

She set her mouth into a firm line and nodded.

"I'm sorry," she said, suddenly placing her feet back on the carpet. Her toenails were a shining coral, pale and clear. "Would you like something to drink?"

"No. Nothing, thanks." I waved her back to her seat. "I was out of town for the morning."

"Did you find out anything about my father?" she asked. Her gaze darted to mine and held there.

"It was business of my own," I told her and brought her up to date on what I had found out so far, which didn't seem like a lot. I didn't mention Jon-Paul.

"Do you think this Willis...this Henshaw person could be my father?" she asked. Her eyes glittered with hope.

"I don't know. It's possible."

"But you *do* think he's in Hawaii?"

We had had this conversation before. It was as if she needed constant reassurance. She had arranged my flight and my hotel and my rental car on Hawaii, yet she was still asking me the same questions.

I shook my head. "I believe he's in Hawaii, but I can't be sure."

She rose and, with a graceful sweep she moved to

an exquisite rosewood desk and unlocked it.

I stood and followed her. "Aïda, if your father is there, you should be the one to go. If you found him you would be right there on the spot and it would satisfy you once and for all."

"You're the detective. I wouldn't know how to go about finding him. Besides," she glanced at me. A bleakness was visible in her face that carried more power than any amount of pleading. "Besides, I don't know what I'd do if I couldn't find him."

"You'd do nothing. You would come back knowing that your father was dead and then you would let the matter rest and go on with the rest of your own life."

"And if he *is* alive?"

"Then you would have a lot to talk about, wouldn't you?"

She turned silently back to the desk and wrote out a check.

"Aïda, you've already paid me enough to cover the trip," I said. "You—"

"Nonsense." She tore the check from the book and held it out to me. "Here's some money for expenses. Your flight is tomorrow, right? Will you call me the minute you have any information?"

I nodded, wondering how it would feel to write checks for a thousand here and a thousand there.

"You will most likely be getting all of this back after I return, Aïda. I won't be spending anywhere close to this much."

Her pony tail swished back and forth as she shook her head. "I want you to consider this a flat fee," she said. "Even if you don't find him. Even if you discover that he really is dead. Then, I will feel that I had done all I could."

I wondered then what it was that was driving her. Perhaps it was none of my business. Perhaps she didn't even know, herself.

I still had most of the money she had given me in the first place. More than enough to take a trip to Hawaii. I considered leaving the check lying on the coffee table, but didn't. I decided not to refuse Aïda's extravagance and would add the check to my account. I had been on a shoestring budget for a long time. While I was paying off my mother's medical bills, every penny had gone toward that. That second check would at least allow me a cushion for when business slowed and that was something I had never had before. It would also help to give Aïda the closure that she craved.

NINETEEN

Tuesday and Wednesday, January 10 and 11, 1984

I hated flying. No, the flying wasn't what I hated so much as the take-offs and landings. For the second time in a week, I had climbed aboard a huge metal machine and expected it to lift into the sky. I gathered my stuff together and found my seat. I tended to dig in and read during the scary parts, but even when I got myself completely immersed in a book, I found my knuckles white and my teeth clenched. It didn't help that my seat mate looked even more scared than I and actually took a rosary out of her purse during the take-off. I heard the beads clicking over the roar of the engines.

When she finally put it away, I had to assume we were safe so I could look around at my fellow travelers.

Across the aisle from me a father was busy with a little girl. She was being delightful in that way kids have when they act like angels, making me almost want to have one of my own. They were playing one of those games where the cards have pictures instead of numbers. I watched as Dad hid his eyes so the child could set out her cards. Her little hands were so small, she couldn't hold all of the cards in one hand. I watched her for a few moments and marveled at the trust she had in her father. She won the game, and when her dad pretended to be hurt, she dug her head into his arm. I found a lump in my throat that made me angry and I turned away.

I took out the lyric sheets Easy had copied for me and began to immerse myself in the creative mind of Royal Blue. He was a talented writer. In some of the songs there were charming double *entendre* and clever word play. In others, the words evoked deep emotion. The man seemed to have put his soul into his music. After a while, I came to the conclusion that a truly good songwriter creates lyrics that are worthy of the melody and vice versa. Melody alone is only half of the song and even though it may be pleasing by itself, bad lyrics can ruin it. I studied his lyrics for at least an hour until I thought I began to see a pattern emerging, but was not yet sure of its meaning.

He had written,

> *"Like darkness invading the glory of light,*
>
> *dreaming your death disturbs my night."*

Was he simply making a convenient rhyme or did the words mean something more to him? I made several notes on the sheets Easy had copied for me.

Eventually, I fell asleep. I never considered napping the smartest thing in the world to do while flying. Asleep, I wouldn't have been ready to grab my life vest.

I awoke stiff and feeling rumpled. My seatmate had sprawled out and nearly crowded me into the aisle. Her arm was touching mine on the mutual armrest. I couldn't help it. I had just awakened and wasn't able to filter out the feeling that was coming from her. There was deep despair, some anger and quite a lot of guilt. I realized that she was facing the imminent death of a parent. Mother, I thought. Briefly, I considered offering her a word or two of encouragement, but it seemed rude to intrude on her private thoughts. Besides, I knew the pain she was facing and that no words would help at that point even if I had some to offer her.

When we landed in Honolulu, the air was stifling and it wasn't yet deep afternoon. The airport was open -air and surrounded by flowers and trees that swayed in the trade winds. The scents of unfamiliar flowers were everywhere. For a moment I was sorry I hadn't thought to try to persuade Easy to come along. It wouldn't have worked out well, though, I knew. Being together in paradise would have made it too difficult for him to rein in his feelings. I, myself, didn't feel I had the strength.

After a rather long, hot bus ride to another part of

the airport, we took off in a second, smaller plane. That flight wasn't as scary as the first. My brain went through some weird thought processes that convinced me it wasn't as dangerous if I was only going a short way. In my mind, apparently, it didn't matter that it was just as far to fall.

We passed the Waikiki coastline on the left. I watched until my neck hurt. A rainbow stretched over the city of Honolulu and ended at Pearl Harbor.

I picked up the rental car Aïda had reserved and drove down the coast to my hotel in Kona. It was surrounded by tropical trees, bushes and flowers and a million birds sang among the fronds. I felt as limp as a piece of cooked lettuce.

As listless as I felt, I was excited too. I was aware that Willis Henshaw could be there on that island, and he knew something about Royal Blue. I had been blundering close to a secret that someone wanted me to stay away from and that made me as curious as hell.

The hotel room was chilly from overactive air-conditioning. I switched it down and at the same time realized that I was far from home in a place where I didn't know anyone. Sometimes I didn't mind that feeling, but on that day, it hit me harder than usual. I briefly wondered why.

I showered and changed into a white jumpsuit and a pair of sandals, then went down to the bar. My nerves were still dancing from the day-long stress of flying.

For a little while I looked at the world through the bottom of a Mai Tai glass, and, even though I only drank two, I began to feel like one of those lonely barflies who spend their days getting slowly anesthetized. A couple sat down near me and we chatted for a few minutes until I felt a little less alone. We laughed and exchanged stories. I wondered if theirs were as fabricated as mine was.

At ten, my new friends headed out to look for a place to dance and graciously asked me to join them. I declined. I was ready to get some sleep. The locals close down the world at nine and it's only the tourists who cavort until morning.

I went back to my room feeling a little tipsier than I've felt in a long time and the cold stark loneliness had returned. The hall was empty and where it turned into the main building, I thought I heard a voice behind me.

I whirled, thinking I had heard my name, but no one was there. "Hmm. Too much Mai Tai," I muttered and tried to ignore the nagging feeling that had been chasing me all day. I *had* heard a voice. In my Mai Tai fogged mind it had been David's voice and he had said my name. Once there had been a time when David had been on my mind so constantly, I thought I would go insane. It was like one of those songs that spin around and around in your head until you can't think of anything else. I had dreamed of him during my flight. It seemed he wasn't planning to leave me to myself that night.

* * *

The next morning, after a heavy, dream-filled sleep, I awoke to find the Hawaiian sun pouring through the drapes. The heat pooled into the room like hot honey. Though I heard birds and the shouts of happy people playing hard, I wasn't cheered. The cold mood of the evening remained.

I yanked on a pair of shorts and a T-shirt, then slathered on some heavy-duty sun block.

The hall was quiet, empty but for a maid's cart two doors down. I stepped around it and headed for the lobby to sweat some of the foul mood out of my system. In the heat, I thought, a brisk walk should do it.

By the time I had walked up Alii Drive and back, my body was drenched and I felt much better. More virtuous anyway. I quickly showered, grabbed a fast breakfast and went out to search for my rental car.

I wanted to look up the dealer who had sold Aïda's painting to deer o'connell in San Francisco. Deer had given me the address and I had verified it by looking it up in the phone book in my room.

Menehune Gifts was in one of the more run-down blocks of old Kailua-Kona between a fruit stand and a fishing charter. A handsome young man, a native, ignored me from behind the counter. His hair was cut short and he wore just enough jewelry to look like an imitation of a rich *haole* from the mainland. His shirt was made from a brilliant print of bright green philodendron leaves and blood red pineapples. He stabbed frantically at a hand-held electronic game.

I browsed a minute until the boy's rudeness began to scrape too sharply against my nerves. I idly flipped through a stack of post cards, then sprayed some of them over the counter and the young man. He raised his head and his startled gaze found me.

"Oops," I said.

He frowned.

"Cheyenne Bruce," I said and held out my hand.

"Rainier Kaneko," he said. He looked confused and didn't offer to shake.

"Were you named after the mountain or the beer?" I asked.

He grinned suddenly. "Neither. I was named after some prince dude."

"Pronounced differently, though," I said.

"Huh?"

"The prince's name is pronounced "Ren-yay," I told him.

He stared at me in surprise for a moment, then

shrugged. It must be a blow to find out you've been mispronouncing your own name all of your life.

"Is Aloyse here?" I picked up a fearsome god carved from black wood.

"Nope."

"Do you know when to expect her?"

"Nope. Later." He had gone back to his game.

"I wonder if you could help me with something, then." I pulled the photo of Aïda's painting from my pocket. "I'm looking for the artist who painted this picture. Would you know who he is and where I could find him?" He snatched the photograph out of my hand and studied it with almost trembling intensity, then thrust it back at me.

"Nice," he said.

I waited.

"Can you tell me anything more than that?" My exasperation was beginning to leak into my voice.

He shook his head. He reminded me of a squirrel, using great economy of motion and making every movement quickly. Also, apparently, he was a man of few words.

"Sorry, I don't know anything about it." He shook his head and began to gather in the cards I had scattered. I reached out to help him.

"Aloyse sold this painting to a woman named deer o'connell in San Francisco. I believe this was painted here on the island." I was trying to sound patient, but I wasn't feeling that way.

"Sorry," he said again. "Can't help you." He started to turn away. I could have reached out and grabbed his arm, but I could tell, without even touching him, that he was lying.

He sullenly collected a couple of the cards that had fallen to the floor and returned them to the counter.

"This your place?" I asked. Of course, I knew it wasn't. It belonged to Aloyse, deer had said. Probably his mother.

"Don't even suggest it," he said, grinning tentatively again, though with more relief than friendliness. "My mother owns it. She wants me to stay here for the rest of my life and work here. No way." While he spoke, he relaxed and his voice took on a native lilt.

"Your mother is going to be here at some point today, yes?"

Instantly he was on the alert again. "Why?" he asked.

I stared at him. "I would like to talk to her."

He looked suspicious. I could see I wasn't going to get anything out of him.

"She be back later," he said abruptly, dropping into pidgin. Then he returned to his stool behind the counter and took up the game. In a second, he was deep into its intricacies.

I wasn't quite finished with him yet. I passed him a photo of Royal along with a folded up ten dollar bill. "Do you recognize this man?"

He let me wait while he played, then set aside the game and took the picture from my hand.

"Sure. He's a big shot singer back on the mainland. Name is Royal Blue." He handed me back the photo and pushed the money down into the waistband of his shorts. Suddenly, he grinned. "We don't have him for sale neither."

"Have you seen him around?"

"He dead, man. You don't keep up with the news." He smirked and turned back to his game.

"Do you know anyone named Willis Henshaw?" Instantly, I saw in his eyes that he did.

"Never heard of the dude."

I stood at the counter and stared at him long enough for him to get nervous. But instead of being intimidated, he went back to his game. I left him there.

Outside the sun beat into the street like a solid mass. The air was damp and thick.

I visited the fruit stand next door and seriously considered an interesting looking cherimoya and a perfect pineapple. They looked so tempting I almost couldn't resist buying them, though I had no idea how I could ever use them. I knew I couldn't take them home, nor could I cut them up in my hotel room. But that was one of the things the islands did to you; convinced you to buy things you couldn't possibly use.

Next, I moved over to the fish charter and peered at the photos tacked to the bulletin board. I spotted a bookstore across the street so I headed over there to get out of the sun and to find some reading material for the evening.

First, I perused the mystery section. I love a good mystery. I made my selections. One was *The Dark Place* by Aaron Elkins. I knew he was from my neck of the woods in the Pacific Northwest. I thought he lived on one of the San Juan islands. The other was a private eye tale by a female author named Sue Grafton. The PI, it seemed was female as well. Would wonders never cease?! I asked the clerk if she knew of any other mysteries written by that author. She told me that rumor had it Grafton had a second book coming out either that year or the next, one with "B" in the title. She said she hoped it would be soon. *A is for Alibi* was so good, she told me, she hoped the author would make it all the way to "Z".

On my way out the door, I saw a display of the new science fiction hardback that I had seen in Portland. The book, *Still Life: Earth*, was written by Guy Loring. I had heard the name but had never read any of his work. On impulse, I picked up a copy and went back to the clerk.

As she rang it up for me, she told me I had missed

a book signing by only two days.

"He was here giving a little talk and signing books on Tuesday night," she said. "He lives right here on the island. He's famous for being kind of a recluse and doesn't go out too much. We were lucky to get him."

I wasn't paying much attention. I don't care if my books are signed, scribbled on or fished out of the trash bin. Besides, I had spotted Rainier Kaneko loping down the street, released, apparently. I thanked the clerk and headed back to the gift shop.

In Rainier's former place behind the front counter stood a large, smiling woman. *Now, maybe I can get somewhere*, I thought.

"*Aloha*," she said. "Welcome to Menehune." Her voice was melodious and fruity. She was as brown as a polished nut and wore a brilliant yellow and orange *muumuu*. Her eyes were dark, round and brimming with good will.

"*Aloha*," I said. "My name is Cheyenne Bruce. Are you the owner?"

"Yes, I am," she said. I imagined that her singing voice was magnificent. "I'm Aloyse Kaneko."

"Would you mind if I asked you a few questions?" I showed her my ID. She barely glanced at it, but nodded, smiling.

"Not at all," she said.

I slipped the photo from my pocket and showed it

to her. "Did you sell this painting to deer o'connell in San Francisco?"

She took the picture and tapped the edge with a strong, healthy looking nail. She looked at it only a second then nodded. "Nice, isn't it? One of my son's friends sold it to me."

"I'm trying to find the artist. Would you happen to know his or her name?"

"Well, I believe his name is Willis," she said, staring past me at nothing "I'm not sure of his last name. Henry... or...Harry...I'm sorry, that's all I know."

"Could it be Henshaw?"

"Why, yes. It *could* be. I can ask my son when he comes back if you like. He just left, I'm afraid."

"Please do," I said. "If you could find out what his full name is and where he lives, it would be very helpful." I pressed a ten dollar bill into her hand, knowing the other ten had been wasted. "If you wouldn't mind, I'd like to be discreet about this. Please don't tell anyone that I was asking." I knew there was little hope that no one would find out I was looking for Willis Henshaw now. I realized that it had been a huge mistake pursuing my questioning of Rainier.

I handed her my card with the hotel number written on it. She nodded and glanced at the card. Her kind face looked bewildered.

I stopped at a phone booth and leafed through the directory. No Henshaws at all. Of course, there was no law saying a man had to have a phone listing or even a phone. It was reasonable too, that he might want to remain unlisted especially if he were in hiding.

I went back to my hotel. While I waited for Aloyse to call, I engrossed myself in one of the mystery novels I had bought.

* * *

It was after five when Aloyse finally phoned. She told me that the mysterious Willis lived in Puako, a little town up the coast. Rainier, she said, either didn't know or simply wasn't telling Willis' last name, but that she was quite sure it was Henshaw. I thanked her, hung up and headed for the rental car. Puako sounded like a wonderful place to have dinner.

The evening was still warm, but a breeze was blowing off the ocean. I turned off the car's air conditioner and rolled down all the windows.

I drove north on Highway 19, a two-lane route. Bougainvillea lined the road but there were no signs of civilization other than the names and messages written in white rock against the dark earth. Peace signs and other whimsey had been spelled out in rock for travelers to read. The ocean, to the left, sparkled in refreshing contrast to the dry, desolate landscape of lava rock and grass around me.

According to my map, Puako was a tiny town, a mere dot near the northern part of the island. I turned off at Puako Road and followed it into town, my hopes for dinner dimming.

On one corner stood a shabby general store. I stopped in a cloud of dust and went in to buy a Diet 7-Up.

"Aloha," I said to the clerk, a very old Asian man. He peered at me, then seeing me as a paying customer, eased down from his stool and grinned. A younger man sat nearby and picked at his nails with a pen-knife. A pregnant young woman stocked shelves near the door.

"Aloha," the Asian man said. "Fitty-fi cen."

"Would you know where Willis Henshaw lives?" I asked when I handed him the money along with yet another ten.

"Sorry. No English," he said. He peered at someone over my shoulder. I turned to see a lady about his age. She rocked in a chair as ancient as she was and chewed on a pipe. The young man snapped his knife shut and slid off of the stool. In a second a back door banged and he was gone.

"No English. Sorry," he said again and turned away from me. I walked slowly back to my car and when I turned, I saw both of the old people peering at me from the doorway.

I drove a few yards then parked at the edge of the main residential street and walked toward the ocean. Each house had a mailbox at the side of the street with peeling house numbers painted on it. At the end of the street was a huge dead tree that guarded the path through to the beach. There was a sign forbidding use of the access, but I suspected it had been put there by the locals to keep the tourists out.

The sun was sinking rapidly toward the horizon when I heard the rustle of leaves and turned around. No one was there. In fact, *no* one was there. It was surprising that at that hour there wasn't a dog or a cat or a kid playing in the road. There didn't seem to be a soul around.

Darkness falls quickly in the tropics, offering little twilight to bridge the gap between day and night. It's as though a black curtain drops over the earth. One minute it's light and the next, not. I really wasn't eager to be out there in the middle of nowhere in the dark.

I walked past a sign painted with an arrow and the word "Petroglyphs." I tried to remember what I had read in Fodor's about them. They were ancient carvings in the rocks that warriors had made in ages gone by. According to the book, the petroglyphs depict facets of Hawaiian life; birds, fish, warriors and battles. Standing among them, I could feel the presence of ancient Hawaii around me. The air felt filled with the mystery of Hawaii's past and the mood of old things that wait. I felt like an intruder, which, of course, I was.

Suddenly, I realized I wasn't the only one walking along the road. Someone, it seemed *was* following me. Someone who knew the area far better than I did. On impulse, I turned down the lane where the faded sign pointed.

In the quickly falling darkness, the faint lines of arrows pointed the way to the rock carvings. I followed them across a scrubby field and onto a massive slab of lava rock. I heard the scrabble of footsteps on loose rock behind me and I slipped behind a tree to wait.

After a moment of silence broken only by the dull roar of the ocean, I stepped out. Before me was a huge Hawaiian almost invisible in the starlight. He brandished a machete as long as my arm. I stumbled over a rock, recovered and began to run.

TWENTY

Wednesday, January 11, 1984

I scraped my hand badly on the sharp lava when I went down on one knee and felt a warm, sticky dampness on my palm. My pursuer could either see in the dark, or he had chased people in that area before. He brandished the machete and uttered an unearthly growl.

I tripped and fell with a thud onto a relatively flat bed of rock. Beneath my fingers, I felt the grooves in the lava rock that must have been one of the petroglyphs. I shivered and hoped the ancient warriors were not watching me desecrate their art with my blood. And, if they were, I hoped they would forgive me.

The Hawaiian seemed to have lost me for a moment. He trampled the brush on the other side of the clearing allowing me time to scramble to my feet and try to slip away as quietly as I could. I jumped over a fallen trunk and quickly rounded another tree then stopped and tried to hold my breath so he wouldn't hear me.

He crashed into the brush on the other side of the clearing, slashing with his machete. I shivered again. The air was warm and damp, like breath. It smelled faintly of decaying vegetation. If I had chosen to hide on the other side, I would have been hamburger by then.

He came closer with the machete and I again stepped out and made a dash for the way I had entered. I hadn't gone three steps before I ran smack into a man standing in the blackness who had seemingly been waiting for me.

He grabbed my arms and held them down beside my body. I tried everything I knew, kicking and twisting, but he held me tight. In seconds, the Hawaiian had put the blade of his machete between his teeth and grabbed me by the ankles. My first captor clasped his arms around my upper body. I continued trying to squirm but I was helpless between their combined strengths.

They carried me without speaking back the way we had come. At last, in a clearing, they sat me on a rock and I decided against running when I saw the Hawaiian take the machete from between his teeth and thought I saw the glint of a gun or a knife in the other man's hand.

"Okay," he said. He wasn't even breathless after carrying my struggling body for several yards.

"What are you doing here?" The Hawaiian stood mute, but I could see his eyes and his machete glittering in the dark.

"I came out here to see the petroglyphs," I said. "Do you treat all tourists this way? Send somebody after them with a machete? The sign says the beach access is forbidden, not the petroglyphs."

"You came to see the petroglyphs in the dark?"

"Well, I probably would have turned around and gone home except for your henchman here." I tried to give him a scornful sneer, but I doubted he could see it in the dark. Besides, I was too shaky for a really successful one.

"I heard you have been looking for Willis. What do you want with him?" His voice was deep and smooth, like melted chocolate with a hint of spice. I got the impression he wasn't a native. I tried to see him through the gloom.

"Are you Willis?" I asked.

"I asked you what you want with him?"

"It's personal. Between him and me." I was trying to sound tough, but I didn't think I was succeeding.

"He doesn't know you."

"How the hell do you know? Unless *you* are Willis."

"If I was Willis, what would you want from me?" he asked. His voice was suddenly a little less threatening, almost as if he were smiling. I refused his friendly overture. His thug had been trying to kill me. And together they had literally manhandled me.

"If you were Willis Henshaw, you would call off your dog and sit down and talk to me like a civilized person. For all you know, I'm an attorney, come to bring you an enormous inheritance."

He was quiet for a moment, but I thought I felt a lessening of tension in the air around us.

"Harry, go on," he said. "Harry" did. He, without a single word, turned and headed to the opening of the clearing. Against the sky I could barely see his silhouette. He was as big as a tree trunk and looked just as hard.

I turned back to my companion. "*Are* you Willis Henshaw?"

He nodded, then apparently realizing I could barely see him, he added a soft, "yes."

"Why did you try to kill me?"

"I didn't try to kill you," he said, sounding genuinely surprised.

"Your Harry did. He was all set to chop me up into cat food. And, you're carrying a gun."

"No, he wasn't. And I'm not." He smiled then and I saw his teeth gleam in the dark. "He wasn't even on the right side of the clearing. Don't you think he knew where you were? Listen now. Why don't you come back with me to my place? I've got some friends arriving soon and we're going to have a little gathering. I'll talk to you there."

"Are you fucking kidding me?! Your toady threatened me with a machete, then you picked me up and hauled me here and now you want me to go to a party at your place?" I was so angry the words were actually coming out with spit. I did manage a quality scornful laugh.

"Come on," he said, still sounding calm and slightly amused. His humor only made me more furious.

I had no intention of staying for his party, but I let him lead me over the rock and through the bushes.

His house was three up from the opening into the hedge. It was a neat house, a little better kept than the others in the neighborhood. It was painted a fresh white and trimmed with some slightly darker color that I couldn't see in the dark. I thought light blue. It's best feature, since it was really nothing more than a box, was a huge front porch. It extended all the way across the width of the house and was ringed with comfortable looking chairs and small tables. It looked as though Willis Henshaw was used to throwing parties. Light spilled out of the front room like caramel sauce.

"Come on in," he said and held out his hand to me. I thought about slapping it away or spitting in it but neither of those things seemed disdainful enough to adequately express my contempt. Instead, I ignored it and went into the house. I wanted a better look at the guy.

The interior was stifling. I couldn't help but think that if the lights were dimmed and some of the clutter cleared away, the place would have at least seemed cooler.

As if reading my thoughts, Willis started a ceiling fan, snapped lights off and dimmed others. Though he didn't gather scattered magazines or clothing from the furniture, nor make any of the moves people typically make when confronted by unexpected visitors, the heat did seem less oppressive.

"My God!" he said, suddenly. "Did you get that tonight?" He was scrutinizing my face. The bruise was fading but was nowhere near gone. I had covered it again with the make-up that morning but I was sure it had long ago worn off.

"No," I told him. "Not that you didn't try."

He looked a moment longer then shook his head.

"I did, however, get this thanks to your Harry." I held up my bleeding palm. It had begun to throb a bit now that the initial surge of adrenaline was dissipating. Blood was still oozing slowly from two long cuts and some had dribbled down my fingers.

"Oh!" he said and winced. "Let me fix that up for you. Come in here," he said, giving me a little nudge toward the bathroom. He sat me on the edge of the tub and turned toward a cabinet over the sink. When he turned around again, he had Band Aids, cotton and peroxide. I watched the top of his head as he leaned over and, in moments, he had cleaned, disinfected and bandaged my hand. His touch was light and gentle.

"Now," he said when we had returned to the living room. "What did you want to see me about so badly that you were willing to risk getting killed to say it?"

I got a good look at his face for the first time.

He didn't look any more like Royal Blue than I did. His hair was black with streaks of gray that ran through his black beard as well. He had a rather large, not unbecoming space between his front teeth that Royal did not have and his eyes were warm brown. Royal's eyes were, according to legend and pictures I had seen, a spectacular shade of blue.

Willis' face was open and seemingly guileless. His voice had held a ring of concern. He gestured toward the sofa, but I sat instead on a chair which faced the door and the interior. Aside from the fact that I was in his house after he had tried to have me killed, I was taking no more chances.

"I want to know if you know Aïda Blue?" I thought if I got right to the heart of the matter, I could blindside him into some kind of revealing response.

He didn't react at all. Easy has a glass eye in which the pupil never changes. The other pupil widens when Easy is excited or interested. I saw no change whatsoever in Willis' eyes.

"I don't know Aïda Blue," he said. His mouth had formed a curious, tight line which could have been confusion or distress or simply his habitual expression. He was either telling the truth, crazy, or such an accomplished liar that he could convince even himself.

"Have you ever heard of Royal Blue or Mickey Carrol?"

He stared at me a moment and I thought he wasn't going to answer. Then he nodded. "Of course," he said. "Everyone has."

"I believe you know them personally," I said.

He shook his head slowly, as if he had searched his memory and come up empty.

I stared at his eyes and didn't say anything. I wanted him to feel uncomfortable and try to fill the gap in the conversation.

Unfortunately, he was almost as good at that as I was.

Finally, he said. "Who are you, anyway?"

"Fair enough question. My name is Cheyenne Bruce. I'm working for Aïda Blue."

His dark eyebrows lifted.

"What does this have to do with me?"

"Miss Blue has a painting, done by you, which she thinks was done by her father. After his death. She thinks her father is still alive. It's a very strange situation."

He nodded, almost as if he was fully aware of all the details. "I can imagine. What is the painting of?"

"It's a nude. We think it is a portrait of Aïda. The model's back is to the viewer and she has a pendant hanging down her back. You *do* paint, don't you, Mr. Henshaw? The villagers say you do." That was a shot in the dark. The only "villagers", besides Aloyse Kaneko and her son I had spoken to was the old Asian man who hadn't understood my English.

"I have done a little painting but I gave it up. I've never sold any of them. I threw them all away long ago." He put out his hands as if to show me that there were no paintings in the house.

"Nevertheless, a painting of yours turned up in San Francisco where it was purchased by Aïda Blue. I traced it to a gift store in Kailua and then to you."

His face gave away nothing. He drew his hands down his thighs as if wiping something from his palms. "I don't understand why you think I have anything to do with Royal Blue." I watched him talk. He seemed honestly puzzled. "Surely you know that an artist draws images out of his mind and puts them on canvas," he was saying. "If you think this painting looks like Aïda Blue, couldn't it be simply that I saw her picture or the pendant or both in a magazine and they became imprinted on my subconscious? Do you believe those things happen?"

Of course, I did. I stood up.

"I'm sorry to have caused you so much trouble, Mr. Henshaw," I said. Right in the middle of this little speech, I realized that there was no reason for *me* to be sorry. "Actually, I'm not sorry at all," I said. "You ordered your friend to scare me to death, if not actually threaten my life. No, I'm not sorry."

He looked at me a moment and I swear I saw amusement flit across his face. "I had hoped you would stay and join me and some of my friends," he said finally. "I have some people coming over this evening. He glanced at his watch. "They should be starting to drift into the yard. I wish you would join us. I would be pleased if you would."

If I left then, I knew there would be scant chance for me to learn more about this man. What was his connection to Royal Blue? And why was he hiding it? From him I felt nothing but bewilderment at my appearance in his town and my questions. In his home, I felt contentment and was comforted by that, yet, there was something more. A past of sorrow. I caught glimpses of it, like a lingering unpleasant perfume. I made a decision then and forced down the anger. There was more investigating to be done.

I nodded. I did want to join him. I wanted answers. Why had Royal Blue paid him a million dollars? Why had he painted a portrait of Aïda? And why lie about it? Was it true that he had seen her picture in a magazine? Certainly not in the nude.

I watched as Willis puttered in the kitchen mixing fruit juice and various alcoholic beverages to make something he called Power Punch. He held a blue paper cup out to me and I sipped. It was delicious and did pack power. I tried to sip it but it was quite delectable. There were flavors of unfamiliar fruits that invited me to sip and sip again. After a few moments, we chatted easily about the islands in general and Puako in particular. I was surprised at how comfortable I felt with him, but thought the punch may have had something to do with that. Halfway through the third cup, I was feeling that the whole investigation didn't matter much.

When people started drifting into the yard, I moved out to the front porch and sat in a wicker chair watching the palms sway and feeling the trade winds touch my skin. Men and women lounged around me on the porch and in the yard talking in low voices. Occasionally, a voice would be raised in pidgin and then a shouted laugh. We seemed to be waiting for something to begin.

Willis' neighbors were a friendly bunch. Many of them stopped by my chair to welcome me and offer me delectable tidbits of the food they had brought. At times, I wandered among them chatting easily as though we had known each other for years. I learned that Willis was, if not actually beloved, then certainly well regarded in his community. I was introduced to a little boy of about two or three whom, they told me, had been delivered by Willis during a hurricane. Apparently, aside from delivering their children in emergency situations, Willis lent them money, helped out with chores and, in general, made himself a favorite brother to everyone.

The heat, heavy with stars, settled around us. A high male voice broke into a sad, melodic song and was joined by other voices. Willis appeared next to me with a guitar and began to strum softly. Gradually, in a voice blended with the low thrum of the surf, he began to sing. His friends and I willingly joined in and soon we were swaying and singing soft melodies in English and sometimes in a language that transcended meaning. Some of them were popular songs of the day, such as "Sweet Caroline" and "Hey, Jude", others, familiar and comfortable hymns.

Somewhere in the depths of my mind, I tried to reconcile the man who relaxed beside me sweetly singing the songs of the islands with the Royal Blue whose music had become legend for its occasionally harsh discordant notes and sometimes unintelligible words. It didn't work.

Someone passed me a joint. I took it and inhaled deeply. The soft breezes wandered among the palms and perfumed air kissed me again and again. I leaned back and closed my eyes. Crickets hummed in the grass at the side of the yard. The small boy of the hurricane legend who had flirted off and on with me all evening, eventually climbed into my lap and fell asleep with his thin legs curled under him. His hair smelled of sand and sunshine.

I remember nothing of lying down on Willis' sofa and crashing headlong into a mountain of sleep.

* * *

My dreams caught me by surprise. In sleep, I was again with David. Twenty years had somehow vanished. I was eighteen and in love. In my dream he was sitting by a window watching for me. I came to him and put my hand on his shoulder. Under my hand still beat the love that he used to feel for me together with a longing to make things right. In my sleep, I called out to him, "Don't leave me again."

In my dream he said something I couldn't hear then began to fade.

I awoke feeling as if I had been sobbing, but my face was dry. Only the lump in my throat remained and the wish that David was nearby.

TWENTY-ONE

Thursday, January 12, 1984

I n the morning, clouds pressed the air with a heavy hot stickiness. I sat up on Willis' sofa and my head swam. I tentatively planted my feet on the floor and waited to see if it would stay level enough for me to rise. Remains of my dream echoed through my fuzzy mind. I wondered why it had felt like so much more than just a dream.

In sleep, it hadn't seemed odd to be thinking of David for the third time in 24 hours. There had been a time when I had thought about him constantly. For a very long time, I hadn't known what had happened to him. The Army had given me scant information. There had been an explosion, they had told me. Of David's remains, only his dog-tags had been found. I had had to ferret this information out on my own. David's parents were gone and the Army had more important things to do than notify a little friend of one more death in Vietnam. But, by clumsy amateur detecting, long before I had been trained, I came to know that he indeed had been killed.

As I sat on the strange sofa in the eerie early morning, the sense of loss was particularly keen. I stayed still a moment, waiting to see if it would dull. If it did, I would know that it was a leftover, a residual from the stresses of the past few days. But the feeling persisted, pushing at me, pricking my skin like a sharp knife cutting just deep enough to draw a thin line of pain.

No one else in the house stirred. There were people sleeping on the floor and a young woman was curled at the other end of the sofa where I had spent the night. Soft mutterings and easy breaths were the only sounds. I quietly slipped out of the house and took a lungful of Hawaiian morning. It cleared my head enough for me to find my car.

Though my stomach was making bizarre noises, I didn't stop until I was out of Puako and heading south on Highway 19. There I found a roadside store where I bought a bran muffin and a plastic container of guava juice which I ate and drank leaning against the fender while I watched the ocean far below.

Back in Kona, I cranked up the AC in my hotel room and threw myself onto the bed. The dreams returned almost instantly. A triumvirate confronted me. David, Easy and Willis stood before me and seemed to be accusing me, of what, I had no idea. It came as a relief to awaken.

I glanced at my wrist and with a start, realized

that I had lost my watch. It had probably slipped off my arm sometime during that disturbed night at Willis'. The watch had been a gift from my mother and I was not about to abandon it.

After a shower and a change of clothes, I climbed back into my car and headed first to downtown. I spent an hour at the Public Records Department in the Kailua-Kona Courthouse searching, researching and doing some general snooping.

Willis Henshaw had arrived in Hawaii eleven years before, I noted, just three months after Royal Blue had died. At least, that was when he had bought his house. Before that, there seemed to be no record of him at all. I thought the state courthouse in Honolulu, or perhaps the courthouse in Hilo might have more records. I could easily make a trip to Hilo, but, If I had not learned enough by the time I left Hawaii, I would make a stop on Oahu a priority.

After my sojourn in the courthouse, I got back into the car and once again headed north.

Judging from the people he had partied with the night before, Willis seemingly had lots of friends. He had plenty of money, of course. He had gotten a million from Royal. I knew how easily one could change his or her identity. I had done it myself. Simply get yourself a new birth certificate and, like the Royal Blue song said, sign your life away. New name, new birthday, new life.

But Willis Henshaw and Royal Blue, though they

had seemed to have similar personalities, didn't look enough alike to be the same man. Of course, I knew there were many ways to change one's appearance. My confusion came more from the lack of any feeling from Willis that would indicate dishonesty. Naturally, I felt a bit of hiddenness from him. Everyone hides facets of their personality whether they realize it or not. But, to me, it seemed that if Willis really were Royal Blue, he would have a pretty big secret to keep and I doubted that he could have hidden it from me. I would have felt the enormity of it at least, if not what the secret actually was. I wondered if my own emotions weren't getting in the way. I had an uneasy feeling that I wasn't sorry to have an excuse to return to Puako and Willis.

I turned down his street and drove slowly to Willis' house. The yard was baked and barren in the late morning heat. The neighborhood children were likely in school and the animals were indoors, escaping the scorching equatorial sunshine.

I climbed the porch and knocked. Willis startled me by opening the door at once.

"Cheyenne!" he said. His pleasure was evident and I was surprised and a little disconcerted at how much it pleased me.

"I think I left my watch," I said.

"Indeed, you did." He ushered me into the house and produced the watch from the coffee table. "I found it about to slide down the sofa cushion. I was going to have to call all of the major hotels to find you and I wasn't looking forward to it." He smiled. "The calling, that is. I was eager to see *you*." His imperfect teeth gave his face an appealing, impish charm.

"Thank you," I muttered. I felt bruised, sore and tired. All of it, I was sure, could be blamed on too much Power Punch, weed and having slept on Willis' sofa. Not only that, I felt almost dazed from the onslaught of images that had peopled my dreams. Seeing Willis again so soon brought them uncomfortably back.

"Are you all right?" Willis asked me suddenly, peering into my face.

"Yes," I said, trying to shake off a vast feeling of malaise that seemed to be overwhelming me. I was confused to exhaustion and tired to the point of pain. "Too much party, I think."

He smiled, slipped a supporting hand under my elbow and guided me to the sofa where he sat next to me. Grateful, I let myself lean back. "You know what I think?" he asked, his brown eyes crinkled, kind and friendly. "I think you need a picnic. Would you care to join me in a bite of lunch? I know some lovely spots around here."

My instincts told me to say no, but when did I ever listen to my instincts? Besides, he was right. I did need food.

"You need a little Power Tea and one of Willis'

industrial strength sandwiches." He pushed himself off of the sofa and in two steps was in the kitchen. Soon, I heard the refrigerator door slam and the quick *chup, chup, chup* of a knife.

"Wait. Does Power Tea have the same 'power' as Power Punch? If so, I'll pass. You do have water, I hope," I said.

"We'll bring water too," he called.

I pulled myself from the sofa and followed him. He was chopping a mound of chicken meat. Beside him, a stalk of celery and a smooth onion awaited the blade.

I made myself useful fetching plastic wrap and fishing dill pickles from a jar of brine. In minutes we had packed chicken salad sandwiches, pickles, some of the remains of the previous night's chips and a Thermos of Power Tea into a cardboard box. Power Tea, I had discovered, was the same recipe as the punch but with a base of cold tea. I made sure more than a few bottles of water made it into our supplies as well.

It seemed we had enough food to feed the entire town, but when Willis stowed the box into the trunk of a Porsche parked in the back of the house, I realized this party was just for two.

I cocked an eyebrow at the little red car. "Did you have a rich uncle who died or just lots of generous friends?" I asked.

"What? Oh!" He laughed comfortably and said no more, but folded himself into the car and turned the key.

He drove fast, using his sleek car like a swift red bullet. He took chances, passing recklessly. The wind through the open windows pounded our faces and whipped our hair. At the old Upolu Airport, he turned left and we entered a narrow, one lane road. Dust rose around us in a red-brown cloud. We jounced and ricocheted over the bumps and ruts for several miles. He tossed me a wide grin and threw a wild howl of pure pleasure out the window.

The end of the road brought us to a huge, grassy meadow that overlooked the sea, where Willis finally brought us to a stop. A *heiau*, the ancient ruin of a Hawaiian temple guarded the site from everyone but the most dauntless explorers. I imagined that few tourists knew the place existed. Those who did, lost heart on the long, teeth-jarring ride to reach it.

We left the car and carried our lunch over the lush grass. The sky stretched overhead, cloudless and almost white in its intensity. The grass grew startlingly brilliant and thick. The sea continually tried to climb the rocks to bathe us in a spray of cooling mist.

Willis stopped near the cliff edge. He set down the box and spread his arms to the wind. "This is the birthplace of Kamehameha," he said grandly. He spread a blanket from his trunk on the grass. Below us, the sea foamed into a white fury and its crash was so loud we sometimes had to wait to speak.

Willis handed me a paper cup of Power Tea and I sipped it carefully. After that one cup, water would be my drink of choice for the afternoon, I promised myself. The beautiful day pushed thoughts of David, Easy and the whole trip that had been my life so far, into shadow.

"King Kamehameha was called 'The Lonely One,'" Willis said suddenly, "because he rarely laughed and had a great sadness in his eyes."

"You sound like you knew him personally," I said, smiling.

His delightful laugh sounded small in the expanse of sky and sea. "He was one of the greatest kings the islands ever had. Did you know he taught the people conservation of food? He trained medical *kahunas* too, and saw to it that all trees that were cut, were replaced."

"Sounds like he was a real ecology-minded guy. There was more than one Kamehameha, though," I said, uncertain.

"There were five, but the first one was the greatest. He was seven feet tall, it's said. A giant. He had a great love, too. Her name was Kaahumanu and she was six feet tall and weighed over three hundred pounds."

Willis' voice went on, drawing pictures of fierce Hawaiian warriors and lovely island women. I found myself enjoying watching him as much as I enjoyed listening to his melodic voice.

"The only legend I know about is Pele," I said. I was lying on my back and gazing into the blue-white sky. "They used to send young males to sacrificial death in her honor."

"Pele was a dangerous woman, all right," he said. "The goddess of the volcano. Legend has it that she danced with the natives as a beautiful, muscular woman with red hair. Some said her arms and legs would glow and her eyes would flash with fire. But her breath was supposed to be made of heat and poisonous vapors." As he spoke, he bent over me and breathed his own warmth into my face.

I felt the island's pull. It tempted me to make reckless choices. What did I have keeping me in Seattle? I wondered suddenly. Was it so important to be a private investigator? Brief glimpses of Easy, my mother and my brother flashed into my sore mind and I let them all fly away into the breeze. The only thing that mattered was the soft, fragrant trade wind and the deep calm that seeped into my soul. I closed my eyes and let it take me.

After a moment, Willis pressed the back of my head into the blanket and kissed me. I opened my eyes, and breathlessly watched him.

"It's beautiful up here, isn't it?" he asked, still

looking at me.

"Wonderful. I was just thinking about staying."

"We can stay as long as you like."

"I meant 'staying' as in never going back home."

"The islands do that to everyone," he said. "Pretty soon, though, you would get island fever and couldn't wait to get back to the mainland."

"Not me."

"That's what they all say." He moved closer and I could feel his breath on my cheek. This time I moved away and laughed.

"Did you?" I asked. "Get island fever?"

He shook his head, 'no,' then said, "Well, yes, a little. But surely you have something to go back to." He stared at me lazily. "Someone?"

I again thought of Easy. His strange denim blue eyes seemed to accuse me and the David from my dreams haunted me.

"Tell me, Willis, what did you do before you came here? You aren't a native, obviously," I said instead of addressing his implied questions.

He pulled back and looked at me in false surprise. "Why 'obviously'? How do you know?"

"Well, you said you got island fever. And you don't seem like a native, for all the history that you know," I said.

He settled back onto the blanket and took a deep bite of a sandwich. Breadcrumbs sprinkled down the front of his shirt and he idly brushed them away. "You're right. What are you, a psychic or something?" He laughed when I nodded. "I came from Washington State. Seattle." I must have raised my eyebrows because he peered at me. "What?" He asked.

"Nothing. I'm from Washington State too," I said, and took a bite of my own sandwich. *Interesting*, I thought. *So was Royal.*

"Really? Where?" I could see his mind working almost as if it had suddenly gone transparent. He seemed to have so many synapses firing, they almost lit up the inside of his head. I placed my hand gently on his arm and caught a glimpse of his soul. A great, yawning emptiness swept me and shook me with a chill. I felt a longing and saw bits of bleak pictures, some so formless they shifted like wisps of smoke. I still got no impression that he had once been a famous man, nor that he had had any life elsewhere before the here and now. Nevertheless, the starkness of his innermost self rocked me and I drew my hand away from his hot skin, startled at what I had seen, then plunged ahead so he wouldn't notice.

"I live in Seattle," I said. "I didn't tell you that last night?" I had no idea what I had said or done, and little of what I was saying now, I was so shaken by the images his touch had given me.

"Yeah?" he said and bit into a shining, dripping pickle. "For some reason, I had the impression you were a Californian. I was born in Seattle, but moved away when I was a baby." He rummaged in a bag for a handful of potato chips.

For a moment, I thought he looked guilty. I got powerful reflections from him, but my lie detection system didn't seem to be working. It was as if it had gotten scrambled by all of the Power Punch I had consumed the night before. And, though I had gone much lighter on the Power Tea, it was no doubt adding its dulling effects as well.

Willis, it seemed, was somehow adept at hiding himself from me. Either that or he simply had nothing to hide. But from the images I had seen, I knew there was more to him than he was allowing to the surface. I was determined to discover what secrets he was hiding. Yet, there still was no indication that he was anyone other than Willis Henshaw of the easy friendships and fast car.

"Where did you move to?" I asked between bites. His sandwiches were delightful and I was hungry.

"Ever heard of Woodburn, Oregon?"

I had the feeling he had picked the name out of the air. At least he had pronounced Oregon correctly. Those not from the Pacific Northwest tended to say "Ory-gone." I nodded. I could play his game too. "Sure," I said. "My mother was born there." She was not. She was born in Cheyenne, Wyoming. Hence, my name.

"Let's not talk about me," he said then. "Let's talk about you."

I had been right. He was getting uncomfortable with details. I sat back and didn't say anything.

We ate in comfortable silence for a few minutes then we made occasional comments about ourselves. I surprised myself by telling him nothing but what was absolutely true. I normally add fiction to my interactions with strangers. But then, for some reason, he didn't seem a stranger at all.

When we had finished eating, I turned to the sun and let the wind sweep my bangs off my face.

"Got to be careful with that sun," he said. "Here, let me put some of this on you." He pulled a bottle of sun block lotion from the depths of the lunch box and I allowed him to spread it onto my face. His fingers were hot and he let them linger in the hollows of my cheeks and jaw. He brushed my lips with his and let them travel to my throat. I could hear myself breathing harder. He kissed me again and I wondered if he was deliberately distracting me from our conversation. *Well, okay*, I thought. *There is more than one way to get to know your fellow man.*

We pushed aside the crumpled wrappers and cups and laid down side by side on the blanket. His hand slid up my bare arm and I shivered in the heat. His fingers, strong and sure, traced the outlines of my body. His eyes, inches from mine, glittered with a warm, gold light. I pressed my body to his and heard his quick intake of breath. My hand traveled down his chest and moved over his hipbone and toward the center of him. Suddenly, he clutched my wrist and stopped my hand. I looked at him in surprise.

"What is it?"

"Someone might come along and see us," he said, breathing hard. No one had arrived in the hour we had been there, and acres of sugar cane surrounded the meadow, screening us from the world.

"Willis," I said, breathing the word softly into his ear. "Let me."

He struggled to his feet and strode to the edge of the cliff. His hands, jammed into his pockets, were balled into fists. He looked out over the ocean.

"I'm sorry," he said, turning to me.

"Hey," I said. "That's okay. If you don't want to, you don't want to." I had certainly been turned down by Easy plenty of times, but this was a little different. I could understand, although it would be just my luck to run into yet another guy who was a fanatic about abstinence prior to marriage.

"It isn't that I don't want to," he said, coming back to the blanket.

I waited. Surely I didn't have to actually ask the unspoken question.

"I can't. I…I had an accident as a child and I'm unable to…um…function. The uh…" he laughed uncomfortably. "The equipment isn't complete."

He abruptly began to gather the litter, chip bag and Thermos. He stuffed it all into the box, then hefted it and went down the hill to the car. I gathered the blanket, slowly shook it out and folded it. A wadded piece of plastic wrap danced across the grass like a space age tumbleweed.

I wondered why he had begun when he knew he couldn't follow through. Did he think that if he chose a semi-public area, he would have sufficient excuse to cut any potential session short? Or had the power of the tea and the beautiful day along with the ocean and fragrant air overcome him and swept away his good intentions as it had mine?

I snagged the piece of plastic. When I joined him, we silently put the blanket and box back into the trunk and took our places in the car. He said nothing, but when I glanced at his face, he looked neither embarrassed nor apologetic. In fact, I thought he looked rather pleased with himself.

TWENTY-TWO

Thursday, January 12, 1984

The drive back was filled with laughter and great spaces of silence and, when we reached Puako, Willis leaned to place a kiss on my forehead.

"Willis, I had a lovely time," I said.

"I'd very much like to see you again," he said. He brushed a wisp of hair from my eyes and let his fingers linger on my temple.

I wanted to see him as well. I was conducting an investigation, wasn't I?

"Why don't I give you a call tomorrow?" he asked. "We can have dinner."

I told him dinner would be fine. I had plans for that young man.

Before I climbed into my stifling car, I scribbled my hotel name on one of my cards and handed it to him. Not one of the regular cards, printed on stock. My special ones.

"Oops," I said, holding out my hand. "I think I gave you two."

He handed back one and I slipped it carefully into my pocket.

I switched on the car's air conditioner and relaxed on the way back to my hotel. It seemed days since I had been there, when, in reality, I had been away just the afternoon. The light was fading and the wonderful Hawaiian sunset wasn't going to be disappointing. I turned the radio on and sang along with the Beach Boys. I realized I was looking forward to seeing Willis the next day.

It was full dark when I pulled into the Kona Surf parking lot. I found a place under a tree so I'd be parked in the shade the next morning and, still humming, I locked the car.

At the desk I asked for an envelope and put the card with Willis' finger prints into it then addressed it to myself. The desk clerk graciously agreed to put it into the mail for me. Of course, it was possible that Willis' prints weren't on file anywhere, but it was certainly worth a shot.

It was 7:00pm in Kona which meant it was 9:00 in Seattle. Not too late to give Aïda a call. I wanted to talk to Easy too, if only to stabilize myself. The past two days with Willis had unsettled me more than I had realized. His was a striking personality and he had affected me more than I wanted to admit. And, always, in the background, for some reason, was the image of David. *Except*, I thought, *David is not in the background. David is not anywhere. David is dead.*

Easy was an anchor for me to hang on to. He reminded me of home.

He answered the phone on the first ring. I had the uncomfortably guilty feeling that he had been waiting for my call.

"Easy!" I said, genuinely delighted to hear his voice.

"Hey, Chey," he said. "How is the case going?"

"I think I'm at a dead end, otherwise fine."

"Didn't find that Henshaw fellow, huh?"

"Oh, yes, I found him all right, but the situation gets curiouser and curiouser. I'm certain there's a connection but I don't know what the connection is. I'm going to call Aïda after I've finished talking to you, but I honestly don't have anything concrete to tell her."

"I tried calling you earlier," he said. "You were out." Did it sound accusatory or was my conscience affecting my hearing?

"I was investigating," I said. "That's what I'm here for."

"Have you had a chance to get any sun? See any sights? We had some snow last night just to make you a little homesick."

"A little snow sounds lovely. You can't get away from the sun here, I'm afraid. Even when it rains it's a passing shower that's warm and falls while the sun is still shining. I think I'm a little burned as a matter of fact." My face did feel hot. "There's sun and heat until you get tired of it."

"I wouldn't get tired of it," he said.

"I miss you, Easy."

"If I didn't have to work, I would join you for a few days," he said.

"You just want to check up on me." I swallowed down the instant discomfort his suggestion gave me.

"I miss you, too, Chey," he said, his voice grown husky. He didn't say, but I heard–or maybe felt–the "I love you" embedded in it.

"Listen, Easy, I'm going to call Aïda and I haven't had any dinner yet," I said.

"You okay?" His voice was right there, in my ear, but he sounded so very far away. And so infinitely dear. Suddenly I was almost unbearably homesick.

"Yes, I'm fine," I told him but I felt a ridiculous urge to cry. I shook it off and told him I had had a long day.

We chatted for a few more minutes about nothing, then I gently hung up and sat for a moment with my hand on the receiver. My poor beaten brain simply wasn't up to trying to explain Willis to Aïda so I opted to wait until after dinner.

I wouldn't have thought I needed any food. Not after that lunch. But, yes, I was hungry again.

The next decision was where to eat. I wanted to avoid the buffet downstairs. When my eyes saw great quantities of food, my stomach didn't know when to quit. Besides, the lunch had been much more substantial than I was used to and I wanted something light.

I retraced my steps to the car and wandered down Alii Drive. I chose a nice, popular restaurant in Kona Village, put my name on the waiting list, then ventured out along the wharf peering into shops and boutiques. I bought a T-shirt for Easy that said something in Japanese. The tag said it meant, "I got lei'd, Hawaiian style." The Japanese characters, *katakana*, the sales clerk had told me, made the sentiment look several notches classier than if it had been in English. Besides, I didn't think Easy would wear a shirt that said such a thing. In another shop, I found a perfect, blue-green glass conch shell for Molly.

After a thoroughly delightful crab salad and glass of crisp white wine, I drove back to my hotel pleasantly relaxed and rested.

I drove slowly, going over the details of the case. So many things didn't make sense.

I was going to assume that Royal was alive. Maybe that Willis himself was Royal. It was a big maybe. He didn't look anything like the man. But I was willing to concede that a person can drastically change his looks with the right motivation. Willis was lying when he had indicated he didn't know Royal or Mickey Carrol. Royal had paid him a million bucks and Mickey had three letters from him. Why did he get the million dollars? And why did he lie? I decided the best thing to do would be to ask him point blank. Maybe that would get some sort of reaction from him.

And where was Richard? One of the twins, I thought, was most definitely lying in Royal Blue's grave. If Royal and Willis were the same person, then Richard must be the one who was dead. If not, someone had died at a supremely opportune moment, just happening, of course, to look exactly like Royal. That was so unlikely that I wasn't going to consider it. There was no other way to look at it. It had to be either Roy or Richard who was dead.

I could understand Royal Blue wanting to escape. Plagued by press and relentless fans, he had been driven to the edge of sanity. Had Richard opportunely died, giving Roy a way out? Perhaps it was Richard who had committed suicide and Roy had taken the chance to escape while he had it. Had Richard been murdered? If so, by whom? Murder was such a horrible, selfish mechanism. It didn't fit with the man Royal seemed to have been and I couldn't imagine *him* doing it. If a murder *had* been committed, I was determined to find out who and how. Even though the trail had long ago grown cold, the crime couldn't be allowed to go unpunished. If murder had indeed occurred, whoever had done it was cold-blooded and cruel and I aimed to find the killer.

I parked in the hotel lot and started back up to my room. Suddenly, I thought I heard footsteps behind me. I stopped in a pool of light and turned around to face a possible attacker. No one was behind me. Anyone could have been crossing the parking lot exactly as I was. I shook my head, feeling paranoid and foolish. But, it was the second time I had felt that same unease.

The minute I opened the door to my room, I knew someone had been there. Nothing had been visibly disturbed, but I felt a subtle disorder. The books on the nightstand were no longer in exactly the same places. The notepad I had left on the table was still there, but it had been moved. On it, I had jotted phone numbers and ideas regarding the case. The end of the bedspread was slightly disarrayed as though someone had lifted it and looked under the mattress. I went to the *lanai* and found the door unlocked. Someone *had* been there. I looked around. How had they gotten into my room? Surely not from the *lanai*. I was five floors up. And what had they been looking for? The business card with Willis' prints? It was already in the mail.

I was just about to take the direct approach and give Willis a call when I realized I *still* didn't have his phone number. He had said he would call me. I hadn't even turned away from the phone when it rang. It was Willis.

"This afternoon you asked me if I was psychic," I said. "I think *you* are. I was just about to leave and come see you."

"Wonderful!" he said, sounding genuinely happy. "Are you going to?"

"Not now," I said. "But I do need your phone number so I don't have to come up there every time I want to ask you a question." I knew I sounded grumpy, but I didn't care.

He told me his number then asked, "Is something wrong?"

"Willis, a little while ago, while I was out for dinner, someone came into my room. Do you have any idea who that might have been?"

He was silent.

"Do you think I did it?" he asked finally. His voice was deadly calm.

"No, I'm not saying you did it. But I do think your bodyguard/henchman guy might have had a hand in it. He's the one who threatened me with a machete."

"Harry didn't threaten you, Chey. He wasn't even close. I don't see how it could have been Harry. He was running an errand for me today."

"Do you know where he is right this minute?"

"Of course. He's right here. It couldn't have been him." He turned away and spoke in rapid pidgin to someone in the room. I heard Harry's sullen, stupid voice answer but the words were unintelligible, though I thought I heard the word 'bitch'. I could have been wrong. Willis' muffled voice raised in anger and then he was back on the line. "No, Chey. He hasn't been near Kona all day. Are you sure you're all right? Do you want me to come down there?"

"No," I said, convinced that he knew who had been in my room. Willis possibly had more than one thug hanging around his place. "It could have been anyone. I'll report it to the hotel."

"Chey, listen. The reason I called you was that I meant it about dinner tomorrow night. I'm eager to see you again." I had to bite back a bitter retort about his unique way of showing affection. But then, I wasn't sure that my intruder had been Willis or someone working under his orders. I thought suddenly of Jon-Paul.

"I'd like that," I said, and surprised myself by meaning it. I did want to see him again.

We made plans to meet in front of my hotel the following evening. I told him I would select the restaurant.

While I was getting ready for bed, I inspected myself in the bathroom mirror. Was this tired old body good enough to entice a sexually dysfunctional man into functioning? Assuming that was physically possible, of course. I was disturbed by the cold calculation with which I was approaching my "date" with Willis. I had always liked sex but I didn't make love without concern and I had certainly never deliberately, coolly gone to bed with a man for the sake of finding out who he was.

I tried calling Aïda and got no answer. Then I made another, local call. At last, I switched off the light and went to sleep.

TWENTY-THREE

Friday and Saturday, January 13 January 14, 1984

In the morning, I headed out of the Kona Surf and walked down Alii Drive letting the morning sun warm my muscles. A few cars went by, but the early traffic was sparse.

I didn't recognize the shrubs growing along the roadside, but huge orange butterflies did and bumbled crazily around them. The air was filled with the heavy smell of hot leaves and steaming earth. In moments my shorts and T-shirt were soaked, though I was only walking. I passed a man jogging in the opposite direction. His streaming face was fire red and his eyes were glazed. I hoped he didn't suffer a heart attack before he made it back to his hotel.

I passed the bank on the way back to the hotel room, its thermometer said the temperature was already in the low eighties at a little past seven o'clock. The day would be a scorcher, but I had things to do.

Back at my room, everything looked normal and undisturbed. I tried to convince myself that housekeeping had been responsible for the subtle changes I had noticed the evening before. Usually, though, housekeeping tends to make the place neater, not messier. And, unfortunately, King's warnings about a possible contract on my life did not reassure me.

I showered, shampooed, then settled on the *lanai* to dry my hair. While I combed and spread it out to the sun, I paged through my notes. A great listlessness moved over me while I read. No matter what the outcome of this case, someone would lose and I had the uncomfortable feeling that one of the losers would be me.

At noon, I gathered my notes and stowed them into my brief case. I wasn't going to leave them lying around the room for Willis' henchman or anyone else to find and help himself.

I pulled my hair into a ponytail then pinned it up off of my shoulders. I climbed into a swimsuit and moved out to the pool. The sun was hot but the breeze was cooling. I slipped off my cover up and spread on lotion.

I've never been much of a swimsuit person. I'd had the same one for twelve years until a girlfriend pointed out that no one who was really cool would wear one with underwires anymore. When I went shopping for another, I was amazed at what designers had been calling swimsuits.

A young woman on the other side of the pool wore one of those new suits that are nothing but a series of straps and a swatch of cloth the size of a large Band Aid. The rise of her hips hid the string that went around her waist and the entire back of the suit was hidden in the cleft of her behind. I had seen her before she had untied the string that held the top together and reclined face down on the lounge chair, and knew she *was* wearing a suit, but from the angle I was viewing her, it looked for all the world like she wasn't wearing a stitch.

I had carried the lyric sheets Easy had copied for me out to the pool. As I went over them, I became mesmerized by the poetry of Royal Blue's words. On the flight to the islands, I had begun, I thought, to detect a pattern and as I continued to read and think, I felt that there were definite messages in the words, as though he had buried a code deep inside his work. I wished that I could hear the melodies as well and read the words simultaneously. I felt the music itself lent depth and power to the secrets hidden within the lyrics.

Unlike the seemingly naked woman on the other side of the pool, I stayed out of the direct sun. The umbrella over my lounge chair filtered through enough of it for me to feel it, however, and I was sure that my skin was probably absorbing more than it should.

I must have dozed. The day had fuzzed out and been replaced by dreams of home and Easy. I awoke in time to turn, baste and finish up reading my Sue Grafton novel.

The afternoon had not been completely unproductive. And it had been wonderful. When I awoke for the second time I was drugged with sleep and sun. I ran an important errand in town and arrived back at my room in time for another shower. Then, dry and powered, I slipped on a *pareau*.

Islanders had known about the *pareau* for centuries but I had only recently discovered it. It was a large colorful piece of contoured fabric with two tails. You wrapped it around your body and tied it at the breast, back of the neck, waist or wherever the heck you wanted and you ended up with a cool, comfortable and incredibly sexy garment. I didn't know how I had survived without a *pareau* for thirty-eight years. But then, I had never been in the islands before. I had the slightly uneasy feeling that when I returned to Seattle, I wouldn't be seeing too many opportunities to wear either of the two I had bought.

I inspected myself in the bathroom mirror. The sun had given my skin a healthy glow which I realized would probably turn into sunburn at some point. For now, though, it looked great. It had done a passable job of disguising the bruise too, although I thought that it was finally beginning to fade. The little star shaped scar stood out in delicate contrast to my skin. Altogether, the *pareau*, along with the strappy sandals with the flirty heels I had found in the same shop, made me look and feel terrific.

At six, I stepped down to the lobby to wait for Willis. I relaxed on the sofa facing the front entrance and enjoyed the view. Pale skinned couples arrived with luggage and darker couples left. At intervals the breeze rushed through the lobby bringing a taste of flowers and of far off rain.

It was several minutes before I realized that I, myself, was being enjoyed. I looked up to see one gorgeous hunk of man watching me from the desk. He had a deep tan and blond hair. I could have had a son his age if I had started early. Nevertheless, I gave him a big wink just as Willis' car pulled up.

"Where to?" Willis asked, giving me an approving look as he opened the door for me.

"I took the liberty of making a reservation at the King Kamehameha," I told him.

He steered his dangerous little car onto Alii Drive.

"Have you ever been to the King Kam?" he asked, barely watching the road. I felt warm under his gaze and it wasn't from the sunshine.

"Once," I said. I didn't mention that my one visit to the hotel was the foray I had made to it that very afternoon. I smiled at him and leaned back to close my eyes. God, I could *so* get used to riding off to expensive dinners in shining red sports cars.

"I like the King Kam," Willis was saying. "It's one of the older hotels down here. Doesn't look very imposing from the outside but the food is excellent and so is the service."

"So I understand." I smiled at him. He continued to appraise me and I knew I looked good. "And does it have a view? It seems that everywhere I go, the view is touted as being the most magnificent in the world."

"And it probably is, too," he said, laughing. "I know this view isn't bad either."

"Watch your driving," I told him, but let my gaze linger on his for another moment.

We were ushered into a softly lit dining room to the music of clinking glasses and gentle laughter. We slipped into the *banquette* side by side. Willis touched my back and I felt the heat of his hand sear my bare skin. That evening, all I felt from him was a kind of contentment as though he was happily in the moment. In a way, I was a little disappointed. I don't know what I had been expecting. A big neon sign flashing on and off in his mind that said, "I am Royal Blue?"

We sipped our first glasses of wine. The soft beginning notes of "Can't Help Falling in Love" drifted from the shining grand piano.

After we had ordered, I cleared my throat. "Willis, there are a couple of questions I'd like to ask you."

He held up his hand then let it drop to mine. "Not tonight. Let's not talk about anything but us and where we are tonight."

"But, I—" I started to say, but he pressed a finger gently against my lips.

I laughed. "It *is* beautiful here," I said.

"Beautiful," Willis murmured. His lips were almost next to my ear.

The waiter was discreet and took his time serving and clearing away dishes. When we had finished, I knew I had eaten something wonderful and delicious but for the life of me, I couldn't remember what.

When the first few notes of "Unchained Melody" began, Willis stood. He held out his hand to me and said, "Let's dance. I love this song."

I slipped into his arms and we were soon lost in the lovely, lonely harmonies. When it ended, we didn't start back to our table, rather we stood on the dance floor so near I could feel his heat. Then "And I Love You So" began and I once again stepped into his arms. A little later, during "Hawaiian Sunset", his lips brushed my hair and he murmured into my ear.

When we at last sat down again, as "Are You Lonesome Tonight?" started, we touched the rims of our final glasses of wine and I looked up into Willis' face.

"Willis," I said. My voice seemed to have become

as thick as honey. My skin tingled. I watched him carefully from behind lowered lashes. "Let's go. I... There's a room waiting for us."

His mouth moved and for a moment I thought he was going to protest that he hadn't yet had enough wine and music and dancing. I slipped my hand on top of his and he nodded.

Silently we allowed the elevator to sweep us to the sixth floor. I unlocked the door to our room with the key I had picked up earlier in the day. I left the light off, moved to the window and stood with the starlight bathing my face. He was suddenly behind me, pressing himself very near.

"See? A view!" His voice was warm and soft. I turned toward him and moved into his arms. In a moment, I loosened my hair and sent it cascading down onto my shoulders.

He ran his hand down my back. I felt his body teeter midway between a chill and a meltdown. I slid my hand up to his chest and began to unbutton his shirt.

He stopped me. "Wait," he said.

"No," I whispered.

"I told you before that I'm unable..." he said. His voice had roughened. The mood shifted and almost faltered.

"There are lots of ways to make love," I told him. I had my lips pressed to his chest, but he understood me perfectly.

"You intrigue me, Cheyenne Bruce," he said.

"That's what I was hoping you would say."

He had been right. He'd had an injury that had devastated him. He had told me before that he had gotten it as a child, but I had thought perhaps he must have meant a young man, past puberty because I couldn't see how he could have achieved his normal masculine features with such an injury. Somewhere, a part of me was standing back and clinically watching the whole operation. I had come here as a detective, to do detecting and that's what I was doing. I was also enjoying the hell out of him.

He was skilled. More skilled than any man I've run into in a long time. Maybe all my life. I was aroused almost to the point of pain and then satisfied into a stupor. I was able, after a fashion, to reciprocate. It was different from any experience I have ever had.

* * *

T he morning had barely begun when I awoke. The stars were still hanging in the sky and soft trade winds were blowing past the open drapes. I could hear the surf pound outside. I sat on the bed half hoping I wouldn't wake him.

"Chey?" His voice sounded worried.

"I'm here," I said, sliding back under the sheet. "I was just looking outside."

"You've renewed me," he said, stretching. "I've not felt like this in years."

"What happened to you, Willis?" I had to know. He had said it had happened in childhood, but I could hardly believe it. If he *was* Royal Blue, obviously, he was not Aïda's father. The possibility remained that Renata had conceived with some other man. Also, Willis Henshaw could be Richard.

"I was bitten by a dog," he said. He didn't wince as he spoke but I did.

"Oh, God!" I remembered the dogs I had seen in Royal's home movie. I didn't see how this man would have been able to tolerate having not one but two of them. He *had* to be afraid of dogs.

"I was only a baby, Chey," he said, slipping his arm around me as if I were the one in need of comfort.

"You don't remember?"

"No, and very few people have ever known about it. My parents, of course. I was excused from showers all through my high school years. My folks cooked up a vague story about a back injury that kept me from most sports. I was a gym helper. You know, the guy who passed out the towels and took care of the equipment. I got my phys ed credits that way. I managed to slide through without anyone becoming overly curious. I don't know how," he said, laughing at some memory. "I wouldn't have been able to hide it from the army, probably, but I had asthma as a young man and was passed over for the draft.

"You...you never married?"

"Can you think of any woman who would want to marry this?" He waved his hand at himself. "I did learn a few basic skills, though."

That was true. He had.

"But you were so reluctant yesterday," I said.

"Some women aren't as sensitive as you are."

I felt a stab of guilt. *Sensitive? Me? I had been doing a job.* "Do you get negative reactions from most women? What do you tell them?"

"I explain to the few who get close enough that little Barney is missing and then they don't want anything further to do with me. One or two have been curious. Like you were." He pulled back and looked at me. "You laugh," he said.

"Little Barney?"

"Just because I don't have one doesn't mean I have to miss out on naming him. All men name their penises. Didn't you know that?"

"Yes, as a matter of fact, I did," I said, still laughing "I have suspected they did, at least. I've always wondered if anyone has ever tried to get a grant to study the subject." Suddenly, I was ashamed of myself. Willis had been right, I had been curious, but for vastly different reasons than he thought. "I don't think I was so much curious as challenged," I said.

He laughed. "I like you," he said. "You're honest." He let out a long sigh and slowly tumbled my loose hair onto his chest and shoulder, then played with the ends of it. "Did you know there are over 800 names for the male genitalia?"

I had to laugh. "I do now," I said. "And how, pray tell, did you come by that information?"

"When you lack a part of the body, you are a little more curious about it than other people." He was quiet for a moment. "And, how did I do?" He asked, finally.

I glanced at him quickly and saw that he was grinning. "You did splendidly." I searched his face. "It isn't possible for you to father a child." It both was and wasn't a question.

He shook his head against the pillow. "Nope. The doctors have a lot of long names of things that are severed and scarred and God only knows what. What it amounts to is that I can't have any kind of respectable erection, can't ejaculate and so, can't father children. One of my testicles was basically undamaged, so I get enough of whatever hormone I'm supposed to get in order to be male, but the main equipment is mostly gone. Why? Were you worried?"

"No. I was just thinking. What about

reconstruction, Willis? Isn't it possible with all the medical advancements...?"

He shrugged. "It's never been done. None of the doctors have ever offered anything like that. Besides, I've learned to live with it," he said. "Or, maybe I should say, 'live without it.'"

I thought I felt his muscles stiffen beneath my hands, so I let the subject go.

"I want to see you again," he said. His voice had a slight anxious edge. "When are you leaving? I have to be in Hilo all day today. In fact..." He leaned over to the night stand and glanced at his watch. "I have to leave soon. May I call you when I get back? Tonight?"

"Of course," I said.

We slowly dressed and he drove me back to the Surf in the early Hawaiian dawn. We kissed at the door with promises to see each other again before I left.

At first, I laid down on my bed, but I was too full of Willis and the previous night to sleep. I dressed again and slipped out into the fresh morning to walk in the garden.

No one was about except an aged gardener cutting palm fronds with a lethal looking machete. He grinned at me and continued to hack at the tough fibers.

I headed toward the lava cliff. There were no

beaches on that section of coastline, only black rock the mountain had spewed forth eons ago and from time to time ever since. There, at the water's edge the lava has been cooled into swirls and waves, what the Hawaiians call *pahoehoe*. I stood at the edge and watched the waves crash against the cliff. Suddenly, the ocean loomed, the land seemed to disappear and the sky skirled around me. Dizzy, I took a step back. I could still hear the *chump*, *chump* the gardener made chopping the dead fronds.

I continued my walk along the path. Brilliant green lawn and black rock offered startling contrast with the blues of the ocean and sky. The colors of the flowers lent pleasant punctuation points of reds, golds, purples and blues.

I thought about the lyric sheets again. Woven among the thousands of words that Royal Blue had written were many references to death, destruction and revenge. Of course, any songwriter can and did write about such topics for various reasons, but there seemed to be an inordinate number in Royal Blue's later songs. When I had listened to some of his music recently, there had been one song that my mind returned to again and again. I made a mental note to call Easy and get him to play it for me over the phone. It was Saturday, and unless he was out on an emergency call, he likely would be home and awake in an hour or two.

I walked until I came to the edge of the golf course and at the beach, a sign warned me of extremely hazardous conditions. I turned and walked back to the hotel. A snail with a spiral shell made its slow way through the garden. In an expanse of black rock, a brilliantly pink bougainvillea grew all by itself. Red birds landed, cocked their beautiful heads at me and at the snail and flew off again in flashes of scarlet. Because of a recent rain, a prickly pear cactus was about to burst into salmon pink bloom. It mingled with hibiscus and bird of paradise at the tennis court near the fresh water pool. I stood for a long moment, seeing nothing, then I turned back to the hotel.

Overhead I heard the fronds click against the sound of pounding waves. My walk had been meant to calm my swirling thoughts but it seemed to have stirred them up. Willis' face hung before me, as well as David's and Easy's.

❃ ❃ ❃

"Easy," I said, when he had sleepily answered his phone. "I'm sorry. I know I woke you, but I need you to do something for me."

"Anything," he said. One of the wonderful things about Easy is that I knew he meant exactly that. He would do anything I asked.

"Would you play a record for me?"

"What? Now? Over the phone?"

"Yes. I would like to hear 'Save the Darkness for the Night.' You have that, right?"

"Sure. What's up?" he asked. I could hear him rustling around. I wasn't sure how he was going to accomplish getting the phone close enough to his turntable without having to wake his neighbors with a blaring speaker.

"I've been going over these lyrics and I want to hear that particular song again."

After much delay, more rustling and some muttering on Easy's part, I heard the opening riffs of the song. It was one of those pieces with harsh keyboards, sharp edged guitar and pounding drums. Royal's voice was gravelly as he sang and I tried to keep track by following it with the lyric sheet.

"Like darkness invading the glory of light,

Dreaming your death disturbs my night.

The darkness invades the night.

It carries the guilt through my heart.

It bleeds and leads it into the night,

And shatters all of my peace".

After hearing the song twice, I thanked Easy and promised to explain when I got home. In a few minutes, we said goodbye. By then, I was convinced that "Save the Darkness for the Night" was a song about a man who was making plans to commit a murder. It was then that I made my decision.

TWENTY-FOUR

Saturday, January 14,1984

The day was going to be hot. There were no clouds in the sky except a fluff or two over the top of the mountain. I cranked up the air conditioner and settled back to enjoy the ride to Puako. I needed some time in Willis' house. Alone. Willis was in Hilo. All day, he had said. Of course, that didn't mean Harry wouldn't be there. He seemed to be everywhere, including my room. I had taken the precaution of calling ahead and had gotten no answer. That, of course, did not guarantee that Harry was not around. It meant only that he hadn't answered the phone. I was gambling, though, that Harry routinely tagged along with Willis pretty much everywhere he went.

It was muggy and silent in the little town when I arrived. I parked my car about a half mile down the road. I was sure that the village people would recognize me so I walked with confidence, hoping I looked like I belonged. If I could get my job done and get away, no one would know I'd been up to mischief. I had no plan to go to the police with any evidence of crime I might find. The police of Puako, if they existed at all, wouldn't be inclined to take the word of a hysterical mainlander over that of their beloved Willis Henshaw of the easy loans and the nightingale voice.

I knocked on the door, then pounded a little louder. Finally, satisfied that Harry was not in attendance, I tried the door.

It was way too easy to let myself in. The door was not even locked. I suspected it never was in this sleepy little town. Why should the residents lock their doors? They didn't expect nosy private detectives to come snooping around every day.

I didn't know what I expected to find. I never did.

It was dim and stuffy in the living room. Willis had bamboo blinds covering all of the windows. Or, what passed for windows, for there was no glass in them. I imagined he had storm windows stashed away for when the necessity arose. That day, the bamboo shades didn't move. There was no breeze.

I didn't necessarily like snooping around in other people's houses. Sometimes, though, it was the only way to find out what I needed to know. People were not always completely forthcoming with me, even my clients, so it was my job to learn what I could. I used to feel that I was committing an unforgivable sin by entering someone's home and looking through it. I suppose, technically, I was. But I was an investigator. I investigated. If that involved a bit of privacy invasion, so be it. I tried not to disturb anything and I wouldn't have dreamed of stealing anything. Except information.

The general feeling I got from Willis' house was the same as I had felt from the man himself. There was a deep sadness there, yet there was contentment as well. The sadness was enduring, as grief is and I could tell that it had come from long ago and it abided there. The contentment was newer, fresher in a way, as though it had only recently been discovered.

I stood in the middle of the room and scanned it. The house was small, there weren't many places to hide something as large as a stack of artworks or a million dollars. Not that I had expected the cash to be lying around, nor the paintings either.

Willis Henshaw was not a tidy man. Easy had told me that Royal Blue was famously neat and had a quick temper. Neither sounded like the man I had become familiar with at all.

I moved to the sideboard and opened one of the drawers. The top one held a tangle of tools, electrical cords and sandpaper. The second and third, similar items; drawer pulls, hinges and clamps of some sort. My heart wasn't into trying to sift through it enough for a search, so I saved it for later and moved into the stifling bedroom.

When Willis did go so far as to put his clothes away, it looked as though he jumbled them into the drawers straight from the dryer. He did have socks segregated from the underwear and aloha shirts separated from the running shorts, but everything else was piled in without regard for wrinkles. It only served to make my job easier. I didn't have to be careful that I was putting things out of order. There was no order.

I found nothing of interest in his bedroom beyond a rather sizeable stash of marijuana and a few odd pills that could have been aspirin and most likely were. His bed hadn't been made in what looked like weeks, if it ever was, and clothing lay in small piles here and there. I had to fight the urge to tidy up for him. A small jewel box on the dresser caught my eye, but I gave the bedside table a quick looking over first.

I found nothing but a prescription bottle of Meprobamate in the nightstand. What had I expected to find? Condoms?

I opened the jewel box and stirred my finger among the assortment of chains and old watches. Didn't the man get rid of anything?

I spotted a blue glitter among the other items. I pushed odds and ends aside and picked up a small ring with a sapphire heart. My own heart rose to my throat and fluttered there, my feelings spinning.

It was Royal's ring. His trademark. I shoved it into my pocket and made for the living room. So much for never taking anything. But, in my defense, I didn't mean to keep it.

The desk in the cluttered front room was locked but the two side drawers opened easily. In one, an address book shared space with a box of guitar picks, paper clips and an ancient stapler. The other held a bundle of papers bound with a rubber band. I spread them out and immediately spotted a birth certificate for Willis Raines Henshaw. It was certified by the State of Washington with a raised seal. I ran my finger over the rough raised lettering. So, it was not a copy. It was the real thing. Willis was who he said he was. If he wasn't Royal Blue, why then, did he have Royal's ring? I felt a disturbing wave of relief. And yet, as I looked at the paper, something wasn't right.

Suddenly I heard a heavy step on the porch and made a dive for the bedroom, the certificate still clutched in my hand. I heard the front door open. Frantically I spun on my heel looking for a hiding place. Under the bed? No. I pulled open the closet door and climbed in, stepping on a litter of shoes. I shut the door just as someone strode into the room. The closet door swung open a couple of inches and I peered out hoping whoever it was wouldn't look my way. I couldn't risk shutting the door and announcing that I was inside. Through the crack, I saw Harry, his eyes narrowed, standing in the middle of the bedroom. He must have spotted the open desk drawer. He went immediately to the jewel box and poked through it with his thick finger. His gaze swept the room and stopped at the closet door.

I moved to bury myself in among the clothes then realized there was very little of wearing apparel hanging there. My leg *thunked* against a piece of wood and I winced with the noise as much as the pain. I glanced down and saw the edge of a canvas stretched over a wooden frame. I heard Harry's thongs slap the floor as he stepped over piles of clothing and I bent to take a look at the canvas. It was a painting. And behind it another, and yet another. Though the closet was dark, the crack in the door afforded me light enough to see the paintings were all done by the same artist. Some were landscapes I didn't recognize. A few were scenes of Seattle and surrounding areas and there were some of Aïda—as a child as well as an adult. I'm the last person to be considered an art expert but I could recognize the style. The artist who had painted Aïda's portrait had painted all of them. Willis Henshaw had been lying to me about his paintings.

Just as I bent to reach for another, Harry's hand yanked the closet door open and grasped my arm. I pulled the painting along with me and we three tumbled to the floor, the painting landing on both of us.

"Goddamn!" he shouted. "What the hell are you doin' here again?" His huge face was suffused with fury. His hair, having come undone from his ponytail, crowded around his head like a black halo. He looked terrible and frightening. It was as if an angry Hawaiian god had suddenly come to life.

I pulled my arm away and scrambled to my feet heading for the door at a run. He was right behind me. His stride equaled two of mine and I never had a chance. He brought me down with a tackle that smashed my cheek into the floor. I felt my teeth crunch together and wondered if I had broken any of them.

He leapt upon me and grabbed my hair, jerking my head back.

"This time, I'm gonna take care 'a you," he said in a low growl. He dragged me toward the door and then thought better of whatever his plan had been, and dragged me back. My knees and elbows skinned along the floor while I scrambled to regain my footing. With a heavy shove he let go of my hair and pushed my face into the floor again. With thick fingers, he untied the string that held up his pants. For a horrified second, I thought he was planning to rape me, but he doubled the rope and tied my hands and feet together like a hog. As his fingers fumbled with the knots, I felt his malevolence as clearly as I could see the floorboards under my face. Momentarily I could see straight into the secrets he had hidden within himself. Then, nothing more than threat and hatred emanated from him in hot waves. The hard boards beneath me bruised my hipbones and immediately my back felt ready to break.

"Wills is going to have your balls for this," I said, through gritted teeth. "I'm supposed to meet him here."

He looked momentarily surprised and I felt a glimmer of hope. Then his eyes clouded over with pure malice and I knew I was finished. "The hell he is," he muttered. He watched me for a moment then went into the kitchen. I heard him pause briefly, but then he went out the back door. I heard his thongs slapping the stairs and I wriggled to see if there was any hope of loosening my bindings while he was busy outside. Pain shot through my back with even the tiniest shift in position. I learned my lesson after one half second and stayed still. There wouldn't have been time anyway, I realized, when I heard Harry in the kitchen again. He appeared in the doorway with a malevolent grin on his face and his machete in his hand.

TWENTY-FIVE

Saturday, January 14, 1984

Harry gazed down at me with such a pleased expression he almost looked like a kid at a birthday party.

"All *pau* for you, honey," he said. He deftly turned the huge blade and watched it, looking pleased as the light caught the shining surface.

"Harry, Willis is going to—" I started to say but he gave me a rather forceful nudge with his foot. It was a good thing he had been wearing rubber thongs or I would have been brain damaged.

"You shut up, *haole* woman," he snarled and pressed his finger against the machete blade until a line of blood appeared on his skin. He stuck the finger in his mouth and sucked at the blood. He laughed and I wondered why he didn't just get it over with. When I did nothing, he frowned and moved down to within an inch of my face.

"You scared, lady?" he asked, breathing his foul

breath onto me. I tried to turn my head but he grasped my hair and held my face toward him. "You scared?"

"Yes, I'm scared," I said. It seemed to be what he wanted to hear and, God knows, it was true enough. It did seem to satisfy him and I wondered if he would like it even better if I started to cry. I knew that in a few minutes, considering the pain in my back and shoulders, I may have no choice.

Imminent death is a great leveler. You can sit in your chair in the front of the television and say that you wouldn't beg or grovel in front of a bully who is intent on doing you grievous bodily injury, but there is no way of knowing how you would react. And the gut level instinctive reaction is to do any damned thing you can to make your assailant spare your life.

I was thinking of what I could offer him when he suddenly rose and stalked into the kitchen again. I breathed a sigh of relief that my end would not be coming immediately when I heard the refrigerator door open and shut. He returned carrying a beer.

What the hell? I thought and decided to try to reason with him, though I knew that reasoning was almost always hopeless when dealing with a homicidal maniac. And if the man sitting before me with a machete across his lap wasn't a maniac, I didn't know what one was. I was glad I had not brought my gun. He would have taken it from me and anything could have happened while he was playing with it.

"Harry, did you know that Willis has a lot of money?" He peered at me and said nothing. His small black eyes glared at me wetly. He took a giant slurp of beer then wiped the back of his hand across his mouth. "You know, I could help you get some of it."

He didn't say anything, just kept looking at me. I couldn't tell if he was considering asking me to help him or if he was considering chopping something important from my body. My arms and shoulders were aching but my legs and hands, by then, were numb.

"Look, Harry," I said. "Why don't you untie me and we can talk. I'm sure that I could arrange to get you some of that money. A lot of it."

"Couldn't do nothin', bitch. Shut up."

It occurred to me then that he was waiting. He'd been sitting on the sofa watching me for maybe fifteen or twenty minutes. Of course, in my state, it could have been only five or six. He had laid the machete in his lap as if to have it handy in case of sudden need. But beyond drinking the beer and looking at me he had done nothing. I wondered if he had called Willis and if he had been told to "watch" me, though I hadn't heard him talking on the phone. He could have, however, taken the phone receiver outside the kitchen door to do that.

We stared at one another for what seemed like

half the day. Periodically the pain in my shoulders and hips would bring me close to passing out. Thirst tortured me. One time I managed to turn myself onto my side, but Harry kicked and hauled me back into position, balancing on my aching hipbones. I felt like whimpering but knew it wouldn't help and would only make Harry happy.

"I know about your sister, Harry," I said, finally.

He stopped in the act of another kick.

"What do you know?"

I didn't know anything, really. When I had gotten that momentary glimpse into his secrets, I had seen a glimmer of a girl who bore a resemblance to Harry. I was only presuming that she was his sister. I knew that something had happened to her, an accident of some sort, and that she was no longer alive. Harry, for some reason, carried guilt for her death. Maybe he had been the cause of the accident. Or perhaps he merely believed he had.

"You don't know anything!" he shouted and I realized that I had made a serious mistake. Whatever it was that he had done, he was willing to protect the secret at all costs. If he had been waiting, he was now ready to kill me.

Just then, I heard footsteps on the porch and in another second Willis was in the room.

"For God's sake, Harry!" he shouted when he saw me. "What the hell did you tie her up like that for?" He grabbed Harry's machete and quickly cut the cord. I cried out involuntarily as my shoulders crunched back into their normal positions.

"Thank you," I said, immediately feeling foolish and irate at myself for having thanked him. It was his fault that I was tied up in the first place. Well, it was my fault, of course, for being there, but still...

"Now," Willis said. "What the hell is going on here?"

"First of all, Willis, I want that guy out of here," I said and was incensed to hear my voice shaking. "I'm not talking until he leaves." Tears were finally streaming down my face and I wondered if Harry was happy about that. They weren't tears of fear, though, as he would have preferred, but from pain at the blood rushing back into my abused limbs.

"Harry," Willis said. Harry got slowly to his feet and flashed me a shot of pure hatred from his eyes. He trudged to the front door and slammed it behind him. I didn't hear his thongs on the steps and I knew he was listening on the other side of the door. *What the hell*, I thought. *At least he's out of here and he doesn't have his machete with him.*

"Willis, you lied to me," I said. I spit the words at him, furious even though I had lied every bit as much as he had. Maybe more. After all, I had come after him.

He had the good grace to look momentarily ashamed, then he got an odd gleam in his eye and for the first time, I began to wonder if I should be afraid of him too.

"You were the one who came into my house uninvited," he said. He stopped and plucked his wrinkled and torn birth certificate from the floor where I had finally dropped it in my struggles with Harry. He smoothed it out and looked at it. "Are you satisfied now?"

"Forget it, Willis. I know who you are."

"Oh?" His black eyebrows lifted. "And who am I?"

"I know you aren't Willis Henshaw." I gestured at the birth certificate. "I didn't have much of a chance to look at it, but Harry saw to it that I had plenty of time to think about what was wrong with it. That state seal doesn't say 'State of Washington', does it? It says 'Slater & Washington.' I saw the embosser on Charles Harbor's desk. I know what you've done, Willis. Or should I call you Richard?"

"You can call me whatever you want." His voice was deadly calm but held a faint tinge of menace. "I don't think you will be telling anyone about what you've discovered, however." He smiled tiredly, then walked over to the painting that had fallen out of the closet. Harry had brought it into the living room and had propped it up where he could see it. It was another nude, viewed from the front. It wasn't Aïda, but it was a portrait of a beautiful woman and it was an exceptional painting. The skin looked almost as though it would feel smooth and warm. The velvet chair the woman was sitting on had texture and depth of color that I had seldom seen in a painting. Her gold hair gleamed and seemed to shift on the canvas.

He stood before it almost as if he were appraising it.

"It's lovely," I said, hoping it would prompt him to say something about it.

"Yes," he said as if he were thinking of something else.

"Why did you lie when you told me you had thrown the paintings away? If you had admitted that you had all of them, it wouldn't have told me a thing I didn't already know." He stayed silent. "Willis?" He still didn't respond. I grabbed his shoulder. I was surprised by the sudden surge of disappointment I felt from him. Disappointment and that ever-enduring sadness. It rocked me back on my heels. For a moment I wished that I had never met Aïda.

"Willis, don't you give a damn about your niece? She's grown into a lovely woman. She's beautiful. She's smart. The only thing that prevents her from being happy is that she is convinced that her father is alive. She thinks that you are her father."

He slowly turned to face me. From the pain etched into the lines around his eyes, I realized that I had touched some chord inside him and set it humming. I dug into my pocket and brought out the sapphire ring.

"You see, Willis? I know. I found the ring. It was Roy's, wasn't it? This ring was Royal Blue's trademark. As recognizable as Michael Jackson's glove."

He took the ring from my hand and held it in his palm, gazing at it as if he had never seen it before.

"What do you want from me? he asked. His voice was low and tired.

"All *I* want is for you to acknowledge to Aïda that you are Richard. You're the only family she has left. Go home to her. Or send for her and let her get to know you all over again. There's no reason not to. Unless..." A thrill of horror shook me. "Willis, did you kill Roy?" I asked him gently. "Is that what you've been hiding all these years?"

"You don't know what you're talking about," he said. "You have no idea what my family went through."

"Give yourself up," I said. "Let Royal rest in peace. Let Aïda have the closure she wants."

"I can't do that," he said. He sighed as if making a sudden decision, then grasped my arm and pulled me toward the door.

Just on the other side of it, Harry was standing with his ear to the wood. Willis hardly gave him a second look and steered me down the steps into the yard.

"What are you doing?" I asked and tried to pull

away from his grasp. From him I felt depthless desperation and despair. He seemed a different man entirely than the one I had taken to bed. If he had killed his own brother, he would be perfectly capable of killing me to keep his secret. But I had to try. I owed Aïda.

He steered me toward the street and his car that had been hastily parked there.

He pushed me into the passenger's side and hurried around to the driver's seat. His eyes shone with an unusual glow and I was growing more and more confused. Uncertainty and anxiety warred in me. My mind was whirling with the conflict between the two emotions. I briefly thought of leaping from the car, but I knew that he would have no trouble catching me. He could have, after all, enlisted Harry's help in subduing me. If I were to be harmed, I would prefer that Willis be the one to instigate it, so I stayed put. He started the car with a grind and sped down the narrow street.

"Where are we going?" I asked again. I thought my voice sounded remarkably calm. I didn't feel that way but I intended to go to my death, if that was what it must be, with dignity.

His jaw muscles worked but he said nothing. I put my hand on his arm. Immediately I felt a war within him as well. Heartbreak battled with longing. For a brief moment, my fear lessened a bit. "Willis, at least tell me the truth."

"I'm going to tell you everything," he said. "But not yet."

Out on the road, in moments, his speed had climbed to over 80. His words came back to me then. I wouldn't be telling anyone what I had discovered.

TWENTY-SIX

Hawaii is supposed to be sunshine, blue skies, palm trees, white sands, flowers and trade winds. We left the sunshine behind us and drove into a bank of clouds that turned the world into a steamy hell. Willis drove from Puako through Kona down Route 11, the Hawaii Belt Road.

"Where are we going?" I asked again. This time I heard the rough edge of fear in my voice and hated it.

He gripped the wheel with a fury and stared straight ahead at the road. I thought it was menace I saw glinting in his hard, cold eyes.

"I want to show you something." He turned and grinned at me and there was more threat in that smile than in a thousand frowns.

We sped through Captain Cook and the coffee mills, past thick glossily dark trees lining the sides of the road. The yards we passed were full to brimming with brilliant flowers. Bougainvillea bushes fell over fences and spilled their color onto the ground. Poinsettias and kukui trees stood silently while we raced our way toward what I was sure would be disaster.

"Are you going to tell me what's going on, Willis?" I asked, my own sudden sadness overcoming my anxiety. "I guess I should call you Richard."

"No!" he said. I snapped my head around to look at him. His voice had cracked on that short word. "Don't call me that. My name is Willis Henshaw. My name is Willis! Willis!" With each repetition of his name, he pounded the steering wheel and then he ground his teeth together and refused to say any more.

Each time we encountered another car on the road, Willis brazenly passed without regard to the yellow line or to the oncoming traffic. Twice, we narrowly missed hitting other cars and once, a pickup full of young men had to swerve off the road to avoid hitting us. Willis laughed as the sound of their horn echoed weirdly behind us. He pressed his foot to the pedal and shoved the little car forward into the clouds. I clutched the sides of the seat and prayed that when the final impact came, the seatbelt would save me.

At Hookena we sped past huge philodendrons and vines climbing over the road onto the telephone wire. Neat houses lined the highway. A school, quiet and dignified, stood oblivious to our passing. I was grateful that on Saturday no school had been in session. I silently pleaded with the residents to stay off the street for a little while, and then to please alert the police to the maniac driving the red Porsche.

At the edge of town was a graveyard where old monuments leaned or had fallen down. I could see the ocean from there. I wondered if the sight of it, plus the beautiful angel's trumpet trees would be among the last pictures in my mind when the end came.

Only for an instant did I think of trying to make a leap from the car, but the black lava rock on either side of us would have cut my flying body to shreds and it could be hours, maybe days before anyone spotted me. Well after Willis had had time to come back for me. The only thing I could do was try to reason with him.

"Willis," I said and put my hand on his arm again. I hoped that memory of the night we had spent together would somehow seep into his fury and soften him toward me. "I want to help you. I wouldn't do anything to hurt you."

"You had to come sneaking around, pushing your nose in where you have no business. If you had only left me alone."

I still felt that deep anguish coming from him. I didn't know if it was because of me, because of Aïda or if he already regretted whatever he had in mind to do.

"I *did* have business. I told you Aïda hired me to find her father. If you've killed him, then you have to pay for it. But why would you let Aïda pay too? If you have killed Roy—"

"Oh, I killed him all right," he said. He glanced at me, then shouted a mirthless laugh. "You look surprised. I thought you had it all figured out. Or didn't you think you'd get a confession out of me so soon? And so easily?"

"I thought I knew you, that's all," I said and turned away from his face. "I can hardly believe that you killed him. You seemed so gentle and so much like... like Aïda described her father to be. She told me he was a wonderful, kind and loving man and, frankly, that's what I thought of you until now. I thought I knew you."

"She said that?"

I glanced at him again. It seemed to me an odd thing for him to say. If he had killed Royal, why would he care what Aïda thought? "Yes," I said. "She loved her father very much."

"Why now?" he asked. "Why did she have to stir things up now?"

"She was only ten when her father died. She had to wait until her twenty-first birthday to inherit the first portion of his money. She couldn't afford to hire anyone until then. She didn't have any money of her own."

"Twenty-one," he said as if speaking to himself. "Of course, I know how old she is, but she's always been such a little girl to me."

I thought I saw a tear sparkle at the corner of his eye.

"Why you?" he asked then. "Why not some guy? Some struggling drunk private detective? Someone I could have kicked off my property and intimidated into leaving me alone? I thought all private detectives were alcoholic males until you came along."

"We're even, then. I thought all killers were cold blooded and evil. Willis, I know you are not that."

"You don't know anything about me." His knuckles were white where he clutched the wheel in a death grip.

"I know more about you than you think," I said, more to myself than to him.

We passed Manuka State Park and for a brief time, sunshine warmed the car, but in the distance, heavier clouds hung over the island. The lava that had flowed to the sea in ages gone by was sprinkled with a few brave trees. What dim music we had been hearing on the radio began to fade and soon there was nothing.

Willis still piloted the car like a rocket, passing

what cars we approached on the road and narrowly avoiding the ones coming toward us.

We neared the bottom of the island, where the South Point Road led to the southern-most point in the United States. It was a winding road, going downhill. Along the way, I saw nice homes and well-kept yards as we neared Na'akehu where it began to rain hard. The cane fields looked dismal as we sped beyond the town. I began to fear that the small car would spin off the wet highway and we would burst into a glory of flame that no one would see until way too late. Soon, I saw only farm houses and coconut palms waving in the hot, wet wind.

"You don't look much like Royal, yet you were identical twins." I peered at him. "You don't even have the same color eyes.

"Colored contacts," he said.

"And the spaces between your teeth?"

"We both had the spaces filled in with composite years ago."

"Composite? But how…"

"Simple. I had mine removed."

"Composite, contact lenses, hair dye, beard, suntan…" I stopped and shook my head. "Willis, would you at least tell me why you killed him?" I asked.

We were riding through pasture land now and rolling, choppy hills dotted with cows. Crickets flew across the road but in the rain they didn't sing. The car filled with the wet, pungent smell of a dead animal.

"He was evil," Willis said at last, when I had begun to doubt that he would answer me at all. "He was a terrible man who did unspeakable things. The world became a better place the minute he was gone from it."

"But surely the police would have…"

"The police!" He almost spit the words at the windshield. "What could they have done? They would have laughed. Besides, no one knew, no one could ever know what he did to my family! He deserved to die. That was the only way my family could be safe."

"Look out!" I screamed as he nearly sideswiped a gray Volkswagen coming the other way. "My God, Willis, slow down."

A sudden squall battered the car with heavy rain and, for a few minutes Willis lowered his speed to a saner level. Outside there was nothing but black rock and scrubby trees. The only thing to link us with civilization was a stretch of telephone wire on the side of the road and an occasional mile marker. Thankfully, the traffic coming the other way had lessened considerably.

"Willis, I find it hard to believe that Royal Blue was an evil man. I read Renata's diaries and, from what I read, Aïda's opinion of the man was right on the mark."

"You read Renata's diaries?" He looked at me and I saw his eyes were full of naked pain and longing.

"Yes. Aïda gave them to me so I could get to know her father. And, from what I read…"

"Okay!" he said sharply. "That's enough!"

His white knuckles still gripped the steering wheel in a death fury. "How did you know that I was Richard and not Roy?"

"You aren't Aïda's father. You must be Richard."

He nodded. "Yes, I am. But not like you think." For a moment he said nothing, but his mouth worked, his teeth gnashed and his jaw muscles bulged.

"Don't you understand?" He turned to me, his face suffused with pure hatred. For a panicked moment, I thought it was for me. "I killed Roy. I killed my brother." His eyes were filled with a terrible pain now. The fury was gone and in its place was enough guilt to last him the rest of his life and beyond.

The trees around us had become dry and sere as if the tops had been scorched by a great breath of wind from Hades. They were nothing but dead sticks poking out of the rock.

Willis, or rather Richard, stopped the car at the entrance to Volcano State Park and paid five dollars for us to get in. I was so shaken by what he had said and so startled that a man who had just confessed to murder was stopping to pay an entrance fee, that

I sat there next to him and said nothing. What, after all, could the young woman in the booth have done had I blurted that he was a killer? She probably would have laughed and waved us on through. Anyway, I wanted to hear the end of the story. I was more curious than I had ever been. Besides, I thought it possible his story might be the last thing I ever heard.

We drove onto the Crater Rim Road. Steam rose from the earth all around us. Here, there were few trees, few bushes, only the occasional clump of dry grass. The only tree that grew there was the Kiawe, and those were twisted into grotesque, tortured shapes. The earth smoked. There was no one else around. I was alone in hell with a madman.

"Richard...I'm sorry, I mean Willis, if you did kill Roy and if he did harm your family as you say, then you should face up to it. I'm sure if there are extenuating circumstances, if he harmed your family in some way..."

He laughed an ugly sound with absolutely no humor in it. "No," he said. "You don't understand and you never will."

"I will. Tell me what he did. I think I *could* understand."

"Do you understand how a man would feel if his brother raped his wife? Do you understand having to live with something like that?"

"Roy raped your wife? I...Aïda said you never

married. You said...I thought you said you had never married." Royal, a rapist? That went against everything I had ever heard about the man. I not only couldn't believe it, I was having trouble understanding it, as though he had said it in a foreign language and I had mis-translated.

"Oh, I was married all right." I saw the tight knots at the corners of his jaw. "Renata was my wife."

"But..."

"I am Richard." He looked my way for so long he nearly ran the car off the edge of the sharp cliff on my right. I gasped. "I am Richard. And, I'm Roy."

TWENTY-SEVEN

Saturday, January 14, 1984

He pulled the car over to an outcropping of rock next to the crater. He turned to look at me with fire and sickness burning in his eyes.

"Roy was the original Royal Blue," he said. His tight lips worked to form the words. It was as if each one caused him great pain as he shaped it and gave it voice. "He and I formed a band when we were only boys. We wrote our own songs and practiced. We were going to be 'The BlueStones.'" He turned to look at me, then stared across the bleak landscape. "The S in Stones was to be a capital letter. We thought it had a kind of sexual overtone, I guess." He laughed but it was a dead, dry sound. "We were twelve. He would sing sometimes and sometimes I would. We both played the guitar. We had cheap, crappy little guitars that our folks had given us for our birthday. He was good at it but he wasn't great." He looked at me again. "I *was* great."

I could think of nothing to say.

"We went along for years, playing and writing in the garage. When we were in our first year of college, there was a talent show and we did our act. We thought it would be a great joke. But Mickey Carrol was in the audience."

"He told me he had known you since you played with rubber bands and shoeboxes," I said.

"To him, we must have seemed like we were. We laughed and cut up all during our 'act', but I guess Mickey saw something and came to talk to us later. He wanted us to make a demo. A serious one without all the joking around. I didn't want to do it, but Roy did so I went along. He wasn't as shy as I was. His first record shot to the top of the charts.

"He got into drugs and booze almost immediately," he continued. "He quickly lost interest in performing. He liked the notoriety but the pressure was terrible for him and he couldn't take it. One night he was out cold when he was supposed to be on stage and Mickey talked me into putting on his makeup and doing the gig. I knew the program. I had listened and helped him rehearse enough. There was no problem. I convinced them all. That was in the very early days. We still had crowds and fans, but nothing like it was later on. He began to slip farther and farther away from us. He seldom sang and I took over for him again and again. We...He lost interest in it altogether and I became more and more popular. More and more Royal Blue. By the time I met Renata, I *was* Royal Blue."

"She didn't know that you were Richard and not Roy?"

"She never knew. I had essentially become Roy. I was using his name and he was using mine and, for all practical purposes, we had changed places." He stared out the window at a steaming vent. "We used to do that all the time as kids. Change places."

"And he raped her," I said quietly. "Why didn't you report it?"

"Renata begged me not to. And I was afraid that the truth about Roy and me would somehow come out. The truth about my injury, too. I didn't want the world knowing that, physically, I wasn't a man. I thought the truth would ruin our—my—career. As it was, he ruined my career anyway. Now, of course, I know it was selfish and childish of me." He stopped and buried his face in his hands. I could easily imagine that all around us were ghosts and demons, watching us from the fog. There were no birds, no butterflies, no wildlife at all. Only spirits.

"I didn't know what had happened until she told me she was pregnant. She had thought she could keep it from me. She didn't even tell me she was pregnant at first." He blindly watched the past, swallowed twice and continued. "Roy and I had been so close once. At least, I thought we were." He turned to face me. "I loved my brother." A ragged sob tore at his words. He sat for a moment with the past crowding him, pushing against him. "But he turned into a different person when he became Royal Blue. He thought he was entitled to anything. Even my wife. He raped her one night while I was in New York. She never said a word. Not one word! I thought...for a long time, I thought, God help me, that she secretly liked it."

I started to protest but he cut me off. "No. She... don't you see? She hadn't ever been with a man... really...not with a *whole* man. I thought she wanted to know what it was all about. She was a virgin, Cheyenne. I realize now, of course, that rape is a horrible, violent act, and it has little to do with sex. But, back then..." He breathed a deep sigh.

"If she hadn't gotten pregnant, I may never have known. I didn't blame her for any of it, Chey," he said turning his tortured eyes toward me again. "I loved her so much. It never changed anything about the way I felt about *her*. Still feel about her. And then, when she found out that she was pregnant, she had to tell me. When she did, we talked about...At first, we thought we couldn't keep the baby. Abortion wasn't legal then, but I knew a doctor... We were going to end it. Renata was going to go back to her music and try to forget. In the end, of course, neither one of us wanted to do it. Neither one of us *could* do it. My God, to think about aborting Aïda!"

"But Roy died when Aïda was ten. Why did you wait so long? Why, if you wanted to kill him, why not then? Was it because of your career? Why wait ten years to do it?"

"I didn't *want* to kill my brother! God, no! And it certainly wasn't because of my career. I would have chucked the whole thing and taken my family away. No, I was ready to give it up long before I did. I didn't *plan* to kill him all along. I watched him and kept my wife and daughter away from him as much as I could. But then, one day while I was gone, he...he attacked..." He took a long, shuddering breath. "He got to Aïda." He burst into terrible masculine tears and couldn't go on.

We sat in the car, silent except for Richard's sobs. All around us was desolation. In front of the car, at the crest of the hill, I could look down into the abyss of hell. We could have been the only survivors in the aftermath of some horrible catastrophe. The ground was hot and the rain was cool, so the fog crept over the landscape and turned the few, distorted trees into ghosts. I could almost feel Pele standing guard there. Her presence crackled through the air.

"I had to kill him then," he said. "I *had* to. She... Aïda was only eight." He looked at me with tortured eyes. "She was such a little thing. And so sweet. Oh, my God!"

"And she was his own daughter," I said slowly. "He had to have known that."

"She had fine, fine hair that looked like silk." He turned to me. "You know that shiny thread they use for embroidery? It looked like that." His smile was a horror mask. I thought of the little lock of baby hair Mickey kept hidden in his book-safe and nodded. "She was so tiny. Her little body... He beat her. She was unconscious for a day. He...we told her she had been in a car accident. She never remembered any of it, thank God."

"Yes," I said. "She told me she had been in a car accident. But, what did Richard—no, Roy—tell you had happened to her?"

"He said he had found her like that in the back yard. He said someone had come into the yard and hurt her, then had run off. The old 'bushy-haired stranger story.'" Tears streamed down his cheeks but he made no move to wipe them away. "That's what people always say when they make up a story to cover up their own actions. That it was a 'bushy haired stranger.' Of course, I knew it had been him. So did Renata. You could tell... Just by the look in his eyes, we could tell he had done it but we decided to stick to the car accident story. I think I had already started forming the first seeds of my plan in my mind."

"But, Willis, you still waited two years before doing it." I put my hand on his. I could feel his anguish burning its way into my mind.

"I had to plan. I told Roy that if he ever came near my family again, I would kill him. He knew I meant it. He didn't know that I had decided to see to it that he never hurt anyone else ever." He looked at me. "I had to make a plan."

"You got a new identity," I said."

"I went to Mickey and talked to him. After I had told him what happened, he helped me. He knew as well as I did what had to be done. I found out then that it wasn't the first time Roy had...hurt women. Some of them were just kids. After I got my new name, I started a sham company and paid myself so I would have some money to live on. I planned to go to either Hawaii or Australia and stay for a year, then have Renata and Aïda come to me. I kept up with my contracts for those two years. We never let Aïda out of our sight for a second." He stopped and ground his palms together.

"You built on Roy's addictions, too, didn't you? It's what I would have done."

He nodded. "I had to do drugs, or at least appear to, in front of people once in a while. The drinking part was easy. I let myself be seen chugging a bottle of vodka once." He shook his head. "It was just water. And I could water down my drinks or dump them out and replace them easily enough. But, yes, I had to make everyone believe that I was a roaring drunk with a hard drug addiction. And, meanwhile, that's exactly what Roy was."

"Aïda—," I began.

"She can never know about this," he said with an air of having come to an important decision. He reached to open his door, then came around and pulled me out with him. The air around us smelled like sulfur. He pulled me by my arm toward the edge of the crater.

"I never missed my career for a moment," he said.

His voice was conversational. I couldn't believe he was a man who may be intending to commit murder for a second time. Murder or, perhaps, murder and suicide.

"By that time," he went on. "I was so tired of the endless tours and the endless fans, I had to get out and the only way I could see was to fake my own death and change my identity. They would have never let me go." I didn't know if he was talking about the authorities or his fans. Either way, it hardly mattered.

I thought about the lyrics I had studied. It had all been there, spelled out for the world to see and to hear if it would. There had been rage and hate, yes, but torment and terrible pain as well.

"You put your intentions into your songs," I said, almost to myself.

He looked at me. "Did I?" He turned back to stare out over the abyss. "Maybe I did. God knows I was consumed with it."

"It *is* Royal's ashes buried in that grave in South Seattle," I said to convince myself. Odd. What the world believed, was true after all, though the truth they knew was far beyond what was actuality. "It's a shrine, you know. They bring flowers to him and fan club members come to weep on the grave every year on your birthday."

"He's welcome to it all," he said. He watched me as I stood next to him.

I was no longer frightened. From Willis I felt no violence at all. His anger seemed to have been spent. I knew that he would do me no harm. He was hurt, angry, and disappointed. He had killed, yes, but he was no killer.

"You can see why I said you'd never tell anyone what happened, can't you?"

Suddenly he dug into his pocket and extracted the sapphire heart ring. He studied it for a moment, then he pulled back his arm and threw the ring far out into the crater. I expected to see a tiny flash of fire when it landed, but there was no sign to mark its passing. The fog roiled around us silently and made our voices echo weirdly.

"Now, no one will ever know. There is no more proof."

"There's you," I said. "And there's me." I put my hand on his. His feelings of despair and hopelessness remained and I felt it emanating from him as easily as I could feel the heat-damp fog on my skin. I wished that I could take some of the hurt from him. It was so profound and heartbreaking I didn't see how he could endure. He let my hand remain. "And, Willis, there's Aïda. She's never going to let this go."

"Cheyenne, I think I know you well enough to know that you won't go back and hurt Aïda by telling her about this." He stared straight into my eyes and I wondered if that were true.

"What about the painting? What *should* I tell her?"

"I'll not sell any paintings. I never should have given that one away. I gave it to... to someone in payment for something he did for me. Tell her...Tell her it was copied from a photo."

"I tried that," I said. "She didn't buy it. After a moment, I asked, "Did you give it to Harry?"

He nodded. "I asked Harry to go to the mainland and find Aïda for me. I just wanted him to see her and tell me how she was. I paid for the trip and I let him choose a painting. I never dreamed he would choose that one and then sell it."

"Did he find her?" I tried to imagine what Aïda would say about being spied upon by Harry.

"No. He said he looked but couldn't find her."

I wondered if Harry had gone to the mainland at all. He had sold the painting just a few miles from home. I imagined him using the money Willis had given him for the trip and the sale of the painting to loll away the time in some posh hotel and then return to report that he had failed to find Aïda.

"Willis, something I can't seem to grasp is your

trust in Harry. I would think that you would surround yourself with people… well, not thugs like him."

"Harry saved my life once," he said, looking out over the caldera. "It was right after Renata died. I was so broken I didn't want to live." He glanced at me. "Harry wouldn't let me die."

I didn't think that Harry, on the best day of his life, would be enough to convince me to do anything, but I kept my thought to myself.

"Was it Harry who searched my room the other night?" I asked.

He turned to me with volumes of anxiety written on his face. "No, not Harry. It may have been Rainier Kaneko. Honestly, Chey, I never ordered anything like that. Harry could have been protecting me. He may have told Rainier to do it, although Rainier doesn't like Harry much. He isn't necessarily inclined to do what Harry wants." He shook his head doubtfully. "Was anything taken? I'll repay you for any damage. Any loss."

"No, nothing was taken. If it wasn't Harry… Would you find out from Harry if he asked Rainer to do it? If it was neither one of them, who was it?" *Could Jon-Paul have followed me to Hawaii? Or had he successfully accumulated the money to hire someone to kill me? Was that someone here on the island? Had they been looking for* me *that night?*

We continued to stand at the edge of the crater,

saying nothing. Finally, I asked, "Aïda paid me to find you. Shall I go back and tell her I didn't?"

He was silent for a moment. The air moved around us. The smell of sulfur was everywhere.

"I'm going to leave that up to you, Chey. I know that you won't hurt her, and I'm pretty sure you won't hurt me." He turned his back to me and looked out over the crater, his shoulders sagging from the weight of his terrible burden, though I thought that some of it, a little, may have lifted.

We stood in the mist silently for a long time. At last, he sighed and looked up. "Tell me about my daughter," he said. "What is she like now?"

"That painting you did looks just like her. She's a wonderful woman. Someone you can be proud of. She told me she plans to use her money to fund a foundation. She wants to bring music programs to underprivileged and ill children. She hasn't completed her plans yet, but to me it sounds like something you would approve of."

He nodded and swallowed hard. I thought he was, again, very close to tears. After a moment, he said, "I wrote a song about them – Aida and Renata – shortly after I left." He stared off at the mist shrouding the lower trees, probably not seeing them, but instead, seeing into the past. "It was the hardest thing I ever did, leaving them. But I did it *for* them. You understand, don't you?"

He turned a pathetic face to me and I felt a little of

his pain.

"Yes, I think I do," I said. I heard that my voice had gone husky.

"I wrote that song about them and no one has ever heard it." He mumbled a few bars of a hauntingly beautiful song of loss and grief, then his voice grew rough and he couldn't go on. I stretched out my arms and held him for a while.

"Willis," I said, thinking I might as well get used to calling him that since he wasn't Richard anymore. "Can you tell me how you did it?"

"Did it?"

"Yes. How you killed Roy."

"It wasn't hard. Not hard at all. It's amazing how easy it was, really. He had halfway killed himself already." He kept staring as though he found the desolate landscape fascinating, although there was nothing to see but the shifting mists and the ghosts that haunted his mind. "I made sure it all happened late at night, in my den. Renata and Aida were visiting Renata's mother that weekend. No one would see me coming or going. I played on the rumor that I'd been drinking and overdoing drugs." He laughed. It was a dry, sad sound. "I gave him some pills and a bottle of good Scotch. He was like a kid at a baseball card convention. I knew he would be. I knew he would want more and more and more. I gave him all he wanted. He thought I knew all the tricks, since I was the musician. I pretended to drink and take pills along with him. He got sleepy and sick and…I wrote a note…a suicide note and that was it."

He lowered his head into his hands. "He was my brother, Chey. I loved him once. But with the booze and drugs he became someone else altogether. He became an evil man. Can you understand how it was for us, knowing that he had…attacked our little girl?" He turned his tormented eyes to me. "I told you, it wasn't just Renata and Aïda. There were lots of other women he had hurt," he said. "I couldn't even count how many women. Young ones. He used to brag about it. I didn't believe him at the time, but later Mickey told me it was all true."

I shook my head and held onto him. I could feel the pain emanating from him. We both wept a little, I think. His tears were for the past, for mistakes and loss while mine were for empathy and helplessness in the face of his tortured heart.

"I could have stopped. I could have gotten him help, but I didn't, Cheyenne." He buried his face in my shoulder. "I didn't do anything. I just let him die."

"After he was dead, I put my identification on him, took his and left him in the den with the note," he said at last. "I walked out. I never went back. I didn't take anything with me, except the ring. If they missed it, they probably thought it was lost." He seemed to sink into thought for a moment. "I *did* have a couple of things with me; a tie clasp that Renata had given me before we were married, a gold chain she had given me for our first anniversary and a lock of Aida's hair from when she was a baby. I sent them all back to Mickey to hold for me. After Renata died, I couldn't bear to look at them." He sighed sharply.

"There were never any questions about his death though. Mickey arranged for a quicky autopsy from some doctor that he knew. I don't know about that. But there was never a question."

His wide shoulders sagged with the weight of many years of grief. He wore his loneliness like a heavy blanket. "I hope you will never in your life know how much I miss my family. When I heard that Renata had died, I almost died myself." He turned to me. "I wanted to. I thought about suicide but Harry wouldn't let me. And, I knew I couldn't kill again." His gaze bored into mine. "I killed Renata too, you know," he said softly.

"I know *that* isn't true," I said.

"Yes," he said. "Yes, it is. If I hadn't left, she never would have died. If I had told her of my plan, she would still be alive. But I didn't." His eyes began to tear again.

"What did you tell her?"

"Nothing! I didn't tell her anything. I didn't think she could play the part. It *had* to look authentic." He paused, then whispered "Oh, my God! If only I had told her. I think she died because I left. I know she did."

"She died from pneumonia," I said, watching him. I could tell he knew that and I watched him struggle with his feelings.

"You'll never know how much I miss her," he said softly after a while.

"I actually do know how much you miss your family, Willis. Like I said, I know more than you think."

He glanced at me with sad amusement. "I know, I know. You're psychic."

I nodded and he laughed tiredly, still thinking I was joking.

"You could have taken Renata and Aïda with you."

"I was going to send for them after the furor died down. But then Renata died and I found I couldn't go back. Aïda was being cared for and I knew I could never let her find out that her father was a murderer. Or worse, that I was not her father and that her father was a rapist and a child molester."

We turned and began the trek back to the car. He looked drained and white. I felt curiously weak too, as though I was recovering from a long, serious illness.

"Willis, why did we have to come all the way up here for you to tell me?" I asked him. "Wouldn't it have been easier telling me in your own living room?"

He smiled and shrugged. "Harry was there. You

saw him listening at the door. He has a tendency to do that. And I was angry." He flushed a little and looked sheepish. "I have an urge to drive when I'm angry. Drive fast. Bad habit, I know. I was furious at Harry for having treated you that way. I guess I was upset, too, that my whole life seemed to have fallen apart. Besides," he stopped and turned to me. "I had planned to bring you up here before you went home. Everyone should see Kilauea while they're on the island. I'm sorry if I frightened you. You don't deserve that."

"Well, I actually did deserve it. I *did* break into your house, after all," I said.

"My door wasn't locked, Chey. You didn't break in. Anyone is welcome in my home."

We were several yards from the car when I heard a scrabble of rock and glanced back to see a young man heading toward us. He waved and smiled and I gave him a tired smile in return. His dark hair was mussed and bruised looking circles ringed his eyes. It was a moment before he reached into his pocket and pulled out a gun which he pointed straight at us.

TWENTY-EIGHT

Saturday, January 14, 1984

"Don't go any farther, if you please," he said politely.

Willis stopped and turned to him. "What the hell?" he said. He sounded annoyed, as if he had had enough and wanted nothing more than to go home. "Who the hell are you?"

"It's Jon-Paul LaCross," I said. I would have known him even if I hadn't seen the star shaped ring glinting on the hand that held the gun. I had seen a picture of him in Mickey's condo.

"Mickey's nephew," Willis muttered as if he couldn't quite believe it.

"Very smart," Jon-Paul said. "Hello, Uncle Roy. I remember I used to call you that. It's been a long time. I'm not surprised you didn't recognize me. Now move over to the edge of the crater." He waved the gun. "I said move."

"Don't go, Willis," I said. "He can't shoot both of us." I stepped away from Willis and Jon-Paul tracked me with the gun. "Right now, you aren't in too much trouble, boy," I said slowly. "But if you shoot one of us, you will be."

"Oh, I don't intend to shoot just *one* of you," he said comfortably, almost as if he were enjoying himself. "Move over there next to him again. I intend to shoot both of you."

"You little son of a bitch," Willis said through clenched teeth.

I stayed where I was.

"What a thing to say to a guy who was like a son to you," Jon-Paul said.

"You were never a son to me."

"Sure I was. Don't you remember? You said you were going to leave me something in your will."

"I never said that," Willis said, his face a mask of rage.

Jon-Paul waved the gun as if to dismiss Willis' words "I was disappointed when you didn't. Doesn't matter though," he said congenially. "I know all about you and what you did."

"You don't know shit, you little twerp," Willis said, taking a step toward Jon-Paul. I put my hand out to stop him.

"Stay right there," Jon-Paul said. "Oh, but I do

know. I was there when you were talking to my Uncle Mickey, you know. I was hiding behind the couch. I heard every word. I'm sure you remember that day."

"You were a child. You don't know what you're talking about," Willis said. "What I *do* remember is you scheming to get money from your uncle Mickey. Even when you were a little kid."

"Oh, I'll get that soon enough. He's not going to last much longer."

"What are you talking about?" Willis turned and looked at me for an answer.

"He's dying," Jon Paul said, smiling pleasantly. "The old man is finally dying."

"Mickey?" Fresh pain welled in Willis' eyes.

I nodded and reached out again to touch him, but he was too far away. "He's very ill," I said quietly.

"Don't move!" Jon-Paul said. "Besides, I'm going to get yours too. At first, I thought you might give me a...let's call it a gift, if I didn't tell what I know. But I don't need to bother with that. I don't need to wait for the old man to kick off, either. I'm going to get your money soon enough."

"Mine?" Willis said. "You're not going to get jack shit from me, you little bastard."

"He's...He *was* engaged to Aïda," I said.

"Forget it, Jon-Paul," I said to him. "She knows all

about you. She won't marry you now even if I don't go home and tell her everything."

"Engaged? The hell you are!" Willis lunged forward and the sound of the shot echoed across the caldera. Willis crumpled at Jon-Paul's feet. I started toward him but Jon-Paul turned the gun toward me.

"I mean business," he said. His jaunty air was gone. His eyes were full of ice. "Move over toward the edge of that crater."

"You're a fool. Even if you have to push me over the edge, you're aren't going to get away with this."

"Oh, I think I will. The heat will destroy your body." He nodded at Willis' still form. "His too. No one will think to come looking for you here. You will have simply disappeared. I can push his fancy car into the pit, too. There won't be any trace of it." He nudged Willis with his foot. "Or either of you."

I wasn't so sure of that, but I stayed silent.

Around us the mists shifted and settled eerily.

"Move," he said.

I took a step, not nearer to the edge but closer to Jon-Paul. I wasn't going to make it easy for him.

"To the edge," he said. He strode over to me and gave me a push that sent me stumbling back. I made a grab for his arm but he yanked it away and swept his gun hand across my face, I nearly fell down. I could feel a warm line of blood drooling down my cheek.

He pushed the gun into my ribs.

"Turn around," he said through gritted teeth. "Now walk over to that edge. I don't have all day." I felt the barrel of the gun sharp against my bones. I took first one step and then another. The sulfur stung my eyes and the back of my throat. Near the edge I stopped and partially turned to him.

"It was you who searched my hotel room, wasn't it?" I asked him, thinking I could distract him. If I could engage him, I might be able to put him off guard.

"Oh, I'm disappointed," he said with a sneer in his voice. "I thought I was more covert than that. I didn't think you'd notice."

"What were you looking for, anyway?" I looked at him. I turned toward him a little more. If I could gradually turn to face him, I would have more of a fighting chance. He was an amateur. I knew I could get the gun away from him. "And how did you get in?"

"It doesn't really matter now, does it?" He reached out as if to give me the final push. I was ready for him.

"Freeze!" A voice broke the icy silence of those few seconds. I grabbed at Jon-Paul in the split second that he was distracted. As I grasped his arm the gun flew into the crater. He wheeled his arm and I almost followed the gun over the edge. Out of the corner of my eye, I saw Willis trying to struggle to his feet, an ugly blood stain had blossomed on his shoulder. The mist swirled in front of him and I could almost believe he wasn't real.

Jon-Paul turned around and we grappled. He tried to pull me to the edge. I twisted away and I made a grab for his arm. He swept it back and reached for the front of my shirt with the other. He wasn't a large man but he had strength and youth on his side and my recently abused joints and muscles made it hard to fight him. Nevertheless, I threw him to the ground. He was back on his feet in less than a second. He tried then to push me backward toward the pit. I twisted and grabbed the front of his jacket then hooked my leg behind his and threw him over my shoulder. His shout echoed all the way down the steep edge beyond the caldera's rim.

I fell to my knees and my head spun in horror and disbelief at what I had done. I crawled to the edge and looked over. The heated air coming from the crater was intense and terrible. Far below I saw the twisted body of Jon-Paul. Wisps of smoke were beginning to rise around him.

TWENTY-NINE

Saturday and Sunday, January 14 and 15, 1984

I heard Willis scrabbling weakly in the dirt as he sat down hard again on the ground. I rose shakily to my feet. I seemed to be moving in slow motion, but at last I reached him and helped him to rise. Together, half crouching, we stumbled to the car and I managed to get him into the passenger seat.

I stopped at the park gate just long enough to report Jon-Paul's death. The ranger looked at Willis in horror as I told her our names and said that we would be in Hilo at the hospital. Without taking her eyes from us, her hand reached into a box of tissues on the desk in front of her. From it, she handed me a huge wad of Kleenex. I pushed it onto Willis' wound, threw her a grateful thanks, then raced onto the highway.

The drive to Hilo was almost as harrowing as the drive to the volcano. I went just about as fast as Willis had on the way up. Thankfully, it wasn't nearly as far.

Willis came in and out of consciousness during the wild ride. At one point he muttered, "Don't tell the police," but I thought that ship had already sailed. Another time, he tried to holler "Freeze" again, though with a lot less force than the first time. In his lucid moments during that trip, I tried to give him the gist of what I was planning to tell the police so that he could be prepared as well. Willis' character and reputation was known not only in Puako but all up and down both coasts. The authorities would be ready to believe anything he said.

* * *

I told the police that Jon-Paul, angry over my part in his breakup with Aïda, had come after me and my friend with a gun, intent on killing me. Willis had tried to intervene and had been shot for his effort. The gunshot wound Willis had suffered supported my testimony. I had acquired a cut over my eyebrow from the blow Jon-Paul had dealt me in the ensuing fight. In the end, Jon-Paul had fallen over the rim of the volcano. There was nothing about that story that was not true. And it kept Willis' secret safe.

After he was admitted to the hospital and I had

dispensed with my testimony, the doctors told me that Willis' wound was serious but not critical.

I drove Willis' car back to his house and left it locked in his driveway and let myself into the house to pick up my briefcase. Harry was there and I informed him of Willis' condition with the briefest amount of information I could manage. He had questions but I avoided most of them. The man didn't like me any more than I liked him and we were both glad to make our exchange as brief as possible.

I gave my briefcase a quick look-through to make sure Harry hadn't helped himself to anything. I could tell that he had gone through it, but nothing seemed to be missing. The Guy Loring novel I had stashed into it was still there too. But then, I didn't see Harry as being much of a reader.

When I left, I took a few articles of clothing and toiletries with me that I thought Willis might need.

I stayed with Willis all night, sleeping an uneasy sleep on a lumpy cot the nurses had kindly brought in for me. Way too early in the morning, still the middle of the night, really, I was sitting in his bedside chair nearing the final chapters of *Still Life: Earth*.

"Do you often have crazy people chase you and try to kill you?" I heard a weak voice ask.

"More often than you would think and certainly more than I like," I said.

Willis looked a million times better than he had the night before, but he was pale and looked strangely vulnerable in the striped hospital gown. The bullet had been removed surgically and the doctors had informed me that it had not created any lasting damage.

"I see now where you got the scar." He raised a finger to my cheek and let it linger there. "I noticed it the other night," he said. "But I thought you were one of those chicks who would like a beauty mark but settled for a star shaped scar instead. I never connected it to Mickey's ring."

"Beauty marks are a little unimaginative. Scars are more my thing." I put my hand up and captured his. "I got this in San Francisco. Yes, it was a gift from Jon-Paul. At first, he just warned me off the case. Then, when I wouldn't give up, he tried to hire someone to kill me. I guess he didn't want to do it himself because he was really a cowardly little shit. But he couldn't find the money, so he was forced to try it himself. When I found you, he thought he had to get rid of us both. Almost did too."

"I'm harder to get rid of than that," he said. He shook his head and smiled tiredly.

He fell back asleep with the smile lingering on his lips and my gaze lingering on him. I liked not only his looks but the man inside. I wished that there was some way we could have continued our friendship but I couldn't see one. Before I went back to my book, I realized that I had thought about calling it a relationship before the word friendship had come to mind.

The dreadful nausea of realization continued to wash over me each time my mind returned to the depth of what I had done. It was as if it would not allow me a moment of peace at all. It was there always, in my head, waiting for me to relax so it could blindside me again. I had killed a man. I had killed a man. I had killed a man. It rang like a dissonant bell.

I pushed the thought away and opened my book, determined to enjoy the last of what had been a thoroughly absorbing novel.

Just as I finished the book with a satisfied sigh, I spotted the author photo on the back flap of the dust jacket and it stopped me cold. I actually felt my heart lurch. It was the eyes that I noticed first. At least the eye. He had a black patch over one of them. I looked at the cheekbones, the line of his chin, the lips. *He could be*, I thought. *But I don't see...* I stared for several long minutes.

Dazed, I stood, gave Willis a gentle kiss on the forehead and left.

❋ ❋ ❋

T he Hawaiian morning was just beginning to break. The sun was rising as I drove the lonely stretch of highway north then south. Along the way to Kailua-Kona I had plenty of time to think. I was torn. So torn I thought I must be bleeding inside. My mind kept changing itself. At one moment, I was convinced and at the next, I was chiding myself for being so idiotically stupid.

The book I had just finished seemed then to be as full of hidden messages as Royal Blue's music. Maybe, over the past few days I had trained myself to look for such things, but some of the pieces had begun to make sense. There was the undeniable undercurrent of regret, of recrimination and of loss. Deep and terrible loss. These things had been right there, in that book, seemingly for me to find.

I prayed that the bookshop would be open on that Sunday morning. It wasn't, but there was a woman doing some paperwork at the counter. She looked up, frowned and shook her head. I repeated my knocking until she reluctantly let me in. She was not the same person who had sold me the Guy Loring book, but I didn't care. I asked, begged, argued, lied, then bribed her for the information and, though I'm not sure which of my machinations had actually worked, she finally gave me what I had come for.

Without stopping to question the sanity of what I was doing, I climbed back into the car and turned north to the town of Hawi, at the very northern tip of the island of Hawaii. It was a small, quiet town that very likely hosted few tourists. But I wasn't there as a tourist.

According to the bookstore clerk, Guy Loring was something of a loner. He rarely did signings, never gave talks and wanted nothing more than to live quietly, away from the scrutiny of his fans. That was fine with me. I had no plans to disturb him.

I found the house, a small shabby box flanked by enormous poinsettias and fenced with broken, dirty white pickets. The yard was overgrown. It had that benevolently neglected look of many Hawaiian homes. Attached to the house was a large garage. A sun-bleached wood ramp connected the front door with the yard. For a few moments I thought I might march up to the door and knock but I kept thinking, too, that it wasn't too late for me to turn and run.

The picture of Guy Loring looked nothing like David. But there was something about the gaze of that one eye that drew me in and threatened to drown me. I had to know.

I sat in my car watching, alternately running the air conditioner and turning it off. I watched for an hour, two. At last, a car pulled into the driveway and a young woman got out. She walked to the door and went in without a knock. My heart sank. I didn't know what I had expected. A girlfriend? A wife? A maid?

I sat on. I studied the house and I studied the picture on the dust jacket, placing my hand over different parts of the face, mentally comparing. The chin was obscured by a beard but the nose was the same. The hair was long. The lips were David's. The cheekbones were too, until they weren't and then were again.

My rational mind, which seemed to have been absent that day, would have told me to simply go to the door, talk to the man for a moment and then leave. It probably wasn't David. It probably was. It could be. It couldn't.

I had been sitting in my car for more than three hours before the door opened again and they both came out onto the porch and headed down the ramp. The man was in a motorized wheel chair. He was missing an eye, an arm and a leg from his left side. My hand flew to my mouth and a tiny sob escaped. I didn't have to be physically close to him. A familiar feeling filled me and I was convinced that I had at last found David. Until, again, I wasn't.

THIRTY

Sunday and Monday, January 15 and 16, 1984

I pulled into the parking lot of the Kona Surf, then rode the elevator to my room. I slept the rest of the day away, awoke long enough to call the hospital to check on Willis. Harry, apparently, had come to take over command of the hospital. At least the floor where Willis was. I was allowed to speak to him for a few minutes and he assured me that he was getting along well.

"I'm going home tomorrow," he said. He still sounded too frail to be let loose, but what did I know?

"Send Harry home and I'll pick you up," I told him. In the end, we decided to do just that. I would spend my last day in the Islands with him and without Harry. But first, I had something to do.

The rest of that night was one of those white nights where you're awake but think you're asleep, and sleeping, but having dreams that convince you

you're awake. My dreams were nightmares of death. The terrible truth rang through my sleeping mind. I had killed. I would awaken and realize that this awful bell would never stop ringing in my head. I tossed, sat up, got up, returned to bed and tossed some more. At one point I knew that I had been sleeping because I woke up crying. At another, I felt that I hadn't slept at all.

* * *

Hawi struck me just as it had the first time, though it was too early for the air to ring with the sounds of children's voices and the barking of much-loved pets. The little yard was just as dry and neglected as it had been, yet I could see the appeal of living there. It looked like a home.

I parked just around the corner where I had a view of the house. At 8:00 o'clock, I watched the young woman arrive. I had come to realize that she didn't live there. I saw her leave again an hour later and even later return with groceries.

By then, I was convinced that Guy Loring was David. I could feel a David-nearness around the house. There was a soft warmth connected with it somehow. That little house wasn't the home of a stranger, but someone I knew and loved well. Again, I thought about going to the door. But, beyond that, I couldn't think. What would he do? What would he say? What would *I* say?

I was a cauldron of feelings. Hurt mixed with hope and blended with a heavy dollop of self-pity. There was a dash of anger stirred into that stew of confusion. I had fully intended to go to the door, tell the man that I knew he was David and see what happened, but I seemed to be glued to the car seat. I reached over to flip on the AC again and realized that the moisture on my face wasn't perspiration. I dashed it away, furious at myself as much as with him.

I stayed put for a while longer, watching and tormenting myself with doubt.

At last, I started the car.

Just before I drove slowly back to pick Willis up at the hospital, I whispered, "Goodbye, David."

THIRTY-ONE

Monday, January 16, 1984

"You might think about staying," Willis said later that evening. We were sitting on his porch and he was testing out his guitar strumming arm. "I mean...you know...staying."

I watched him for a moment and considered his words. "I don't think you mean that, Willis," I said finally. "I think you're feeling weak and vulnerable from your injury."

He shook his head. "I realize we don't know each other all that well, Chey, but I like you." He put down the guitar and turned to look at me. "More than you know."

I said nothing. I felt like I had had this conversation before.

"I know it would be a big change for you. I like having you around."

"It would be a *huge* change for me. My whole life is in Seattle."

"Don't be afraid to exercise your right to change," he said.

"What about my right not to change?" I felt my walls starting to go up and tried to fight down the flight response.

"That's an option, of course." He picked up the guitar again and strummed a chord then his eyes narrowed in a wince. Just a little one, but I saw it.

"Maybe you should put that aside for now," I said, but he ignored me and tried another chord.

"Does that mean you're turning me down?" He said it lightly but I felt, rather than heard, the pain under his voice. "I had no right to ask you in the first place, but, what do I have to lose after all?"

"I have to go home tomorrow," I said.

He looked up from his fingers in surprise. "I thought you planned to stay until Wednesday."

"I have to go. I've finished my job."

"You probably won't forgive me for saying this, but I think you're running away." His voice was gentle as only Willis Henshaw's voice can be, but the words stung nevertheless.

"Maybe," I said.

"I understand." His face didn't change.

"No, you don't. I didn't decide not to stay because

of your... injury. I didn't want to say "disability" but he knew what I meant. "That isn't important. Not to me, anyway. But I don't live here. This isn't my home."

"It could be." He strummed again. No wince this time. "It became mine."

"And, having left the mainland," I said. "Have you been happy?"

He gave a half smile, but otherwise said nothing.

"You left your family and your friends," I reminded him.

"Yes," he said. "There's that." He looked across the yard for a moment. "I miss Mickey. I wish I didn't know that he is dying."

"I talked to him a few days ago. He has kept your secret all these years."

"He helped me with becoming Willis."

"How did you do that? Your birth certificate looks authentic except for the seal."

He stopped strumming for a moment. "It wasn't so hard," he said. "I bought a pad of certificates at a supply house and wrote up the one I wanted. I used old man Harbor's book embosser on it when he was out of the room. I had the certificate and the name for two years before Royal died."

"What about a driver's license?" I asked.

"When I got here, I said I had lost mine. I had to

take the driver's test over, but that wasn't a problem. I had a birth certificate to prove I was Willis."

I looked at him carefully. "You did a very good job with disguising your appearance."

"I had been wearing those blue contact lens for a long time. They were Mickey's idea. Something about the Royal Blue mystique. I simply stopped wearing them. Roy and I had brown eyes. I had the composite removed from my teeth. The hair was easy. Both of us had been bleaching our hair for years." He laughed softly. "The beachboy look. I just let mine grow out.

"But you were always known for being extremely fastidious. And I don't understand about the dogs."

"Dogs? What dogs?"

"You owned dogs. I saw the movie of you and your family."

"Oh, and you wondered why I'm not afraid of them? Simple. I was too young to remember the dog that injured me. I was only three. It could have been a horse or a cow or a sparrow for all I remembered. But fastidious? I was never a clean freak." He laughed again. "My God, you've seen my house." He tilted his head back toward the front of the house. "That was the fabrication of a magazine reporter. We had money. It's easy being clean and tidy when you have a maid."

"It was you who went to Australia, then?"

He nodded. "I didn't become Willis Henshaw until I landed in Hawaii. Until then I was Richard Bluestone. Except for it being the hardest thing I ever did in my life, it was surprisingly simple."

For a moment, neither of us spoke.

"I'm homesick," I said finally.

He nodded. "I can understand, Cheyenne." He turned to look at me. "I truly can."

He picked a little melody out on the strings of his guitar.

"So, your case is solved," he said at last with a deep sigh.

I shook my head. "No, it isn't. It isn't solved."

"Do you know what you're going to tell Aïda?" He laid the guitar across his lap and looked at me.

"I…No."

"What about the truth? The man, Willis Henshaw, turns out to be just some guy. Not Royal Blue, after all. Just a poor sap who's had his world turned upside down by a sexy *haole* detective."

"But, *is* that the truth? You aren't biologically her father but blood doesn't always make us family. According to her, you were the best father in the world. So, are you her father, or aren't you?" I stopped and looked out over the yard. A red bird landed on the grass and flew away again. "The answer to that is both yes and no. You are the man she knew and loved as a father. The truth is, obviously, not always black or white. I've known that a long time."

"Truth is truth," he said. "I don't think there is a black or white about it."

"I have found that there are different sides to truth. What we believe becomes our truth, but sometimes that same truth is different for someone else."

He said nothing but continued testing his arm and strumming quiet chords.

"I have to go home now and decide if I should lie to a nice young woman so she won't be devastated by the truth. Either that, or go ahead and tell her the truth and mess up her life even more than it would be if she believed you were dead. And, in fact, mess up more than one life."

"It would mess up mine," he agreed, "but I don't see how she would be *more* devastated to know that I was alive."

"She would be crushed to know that you had willingly stayed away for all of these years, knowing that she is somewhere in the world thinking about you and missing you." I looked at him. "And loving you. Believe me. I know what I'm talking about."

"You could say, 'He's not your father.'" He picked up the guitar again and played with the strings. "That would be the truth."

"Yes, it would. But would that be fair?"

He leaned the guitar against the house and took my hand in both of his. I felt his dismay that I was leaving and it almost broke me to realize that *I* was causing pain for someone too.

"Unfortunately, nothing much in this life is fair," he said. "I'm sorry you have to be the one to decide."

He looked at me carefully now that he had set aside the guitar. "Are you...Is there...Are you all right?"

"Aside from the fact that I have killed someone, you mean?" I had meant it to sound lighthearted but there was no way to make light of that subject.

"That is something you will have to deal with," he said.

I nodded. "I don't know if I can, though."

"It's something you live with. It doesn't get better or easier or okay. It's simply something you have to live with."

We sat for a while. Willis picked up his guitar again and strummed. Each time it seemed easier for him. I was glad he had no residual effects from the bullet.

"Willis," I said after a few minutes. "Have you thought about the irony of you giving your painting to Harry and him selling it to Aloyse Kaneko who, in turn sold it to a woman who lives in San Francisco? And further, your daughter being the one person in the world to buy it?"

He nodded. "I thought of that. I almost came unglued when you told me that Aïda had bought that painting."

"Really? I didn't see any reaction from you at all," I said, surprised.

"Over the years, I've gotten very good at hiding my feelings, I suppose. Very accomplished at hiding," he said and played a discordant note, winced and replayed it. "It's funny how life works, isn't it? There are so many intersections in life. You never know who you're going to meet."

That I knew to be the truth.

"You know," I said, finally voicing something that I had been turning and turning in my mind. "You didn't actually, technically kill Roy."

"In the same sense that you did not 'actually, technically' kill Jon-Paul."

"I don't think it's the same thing at all. Dead is dead. I caused his death."

"And I caused Roy's. And Renata's." His voice was so gentle I felt like weeping.

"Willis, you said it doesn't get any easier. Are you sure?"

He thought for a moment, then shook his head. "It doesn't," he said with regret. "It's always there."

I nodded again and swallowed. He gave my hand a

squeeze.

We went into the house then, and thought of other things to talk about for the rest of the night.

THIRTY-TWO

Tuesday, January 17, 1984

Because of the time difference, the flight back to Seattle stretched out into an interminable day of travel. I didn't want to read. I didn't want to sleep because I didn't want to dream. I didn't want to think and I didn't want to wonder what I was going to tell Aïda.

I felt distinctly rumpled when the plane finally landed. Even the on-board exercises had done nothing to unknot my back and ease my depression. Instead, the plastic cheeriness of the flight attendant deepened my desire to be off the plane and settled into my own bed.

All the way across the Pacific I had swung between hoping Aïda would be at the airport to pick me up and not Easy, and hoping Easy would meet me and not Aïda. It didn't matter. I wanted to see neither of them just yet.

Aïda was standing in the throng waiting for

disembarking passengers when I saw her. I felt a strong urge to go the other way before she saw me, but she turned and caught me before I could act on it.

"Mr. Radford asked me to pick you up," she said, looking in seeming distaste at the frazzled state of the late-night travelers. "He was called out on some crime, I think."

"I appreciate it, Aïda," I told her, thinking that I would have preferred a cab.

She rode the subway with me to the baggage claim where I picked up my bag, then we walked out into the cool Seattle night. She hunched her neck down into the fur-lined leather jacket she wore and I crossed my arms across my chest and shivered in the wet air. I still wore my warm weather clothes and had brought only a light jacket against the winter chill.

She seemed to be waiting for me to begin the conversation that reared up in front of us both. Maybe she was allowing me time to collect myself.

We silently took the elevator to the huge circular garage and walked to the car. I was too dispirited and broken to say anything at all. She seemed unwilling to hear the words that would open forever a chest of secrets that she may be reluctant to hear.

"Let's stop for some coffee," she said. Her brown eyes looked around nervously and I realized she was as jumpy as I was. We found a Denny's on Pacific

Highway South and settled into a corner away from the truck drivers and after-movie goers scattered among the rest of the tables.

When the waitress arrived, Aïda ordered coffee and I ordered nachos and tea. The airline food hadn't been fit for a food fight, let alone human consumption and I had eaten little. Besides, I was trying to delay the inevitable as long as possible.

"So," she said, after the waitress had brought us the nachos, tea and coffee which Aïda shared with a cigarette. I left my tea to cool and picked at the plate in front of me. "Are you going to tell me or do I have to wait for the final report or what?" she said, sounding as disgruntled as I felt.

"I met with Willis Henshaw," I told her. She nodded. Of course, I had told her that much on the phone. "Aïda, Willis Henshaw is not your uncle Richard and he is not your father."

Her whole body seemed to slump.

"I'm sorry. I know this is not what you had hoped for." I put my hand onto her arm.

"I had hoped...When Uncle Richard didn't come to my father's funeral, and then we didn't hear from him again after that, everyone assumed he was dead. I guess I always half hoped it was him buried in my father's grave."

"I'm sorry, Aïda," I said again. "I know you are disappointed."

She sighed and looked up at the ceiling. "I'm not so much disappointed." She looked at me. "I feel... abandoned."

I nodded. I knew that feeling myself. "I wish I could tell you that Willis Henshaw was Royal Blue, that he was your father. Your father is dead." It *was* true enough. "Do you have any people? Any family you can connect with?"

She shook her head. "I literally have no one left," she said.

My heart broke for her. It was such a waste, after all. The man she had loved most in the world was alive and well in Hawaii and she would never know. I wished once more that I had never become involved in the case. Had never made the trip to Hawaii and had never uncovered any secrets, neither Willis' nor my own. "Your mother had no relatives?"

"I think she had an aunt somewhere. Someone living in Iowa." She sounded dispirited and I didn't blame her. An unknown great aunt in Iowa seemed a far cry from family at that point.

She took a long sip of her coffee and put it down. After she had digested the fact that her father was dead and had drained off the rest of her coffee, she leaned on the table and clutched her elbows.

"You know, Chey," she said, peering straight into my face and beyond. "I was molested as a child."

I must have paled, because she put her hand onto

my arm and murmured something about it being all right. "I was eight or nine. I don't really remember too much about it. Actually, I didn't even know what was happening until I grew a little older and found out a few things. I've had years of therapy and my therapist helped me to get most of it out and deal with it." She shook her head and paused with a piece of tortilla loaded with guacamole at her mouth. "I don't really understand why I brought it up just now."

"Do you know who the man was?" I ventured, not sure where we were going with it.

We picked at the hot cheese, olives and chips. Just two chicks hanging out on a Tuesday night, talking about child molestation and death. She put another chip piled with sour cream into her mouth. I was surprised, for some reason, that Aïda liked nachos. I had her figured as more of a *paté de foie gras* girl.

She nodded. "It was my Uncle Richard who did it. Isn't that an awful thing to have to remember? I think I may have been afraid that it was Richard who was living in Hawaii." She wiped her mouth and signaled the waitress for a refill of coffee. "I didn't really know him well; my parents never seemed very close to him, and I rarely saw him at all, but he looked exactly like my father. I had no reason to be frightened of him. He came into our back yard where I was playing and got me to go around the side of the garage with him. He…well, attacked me right there in the yard." She shook her head again.

"Then I knew he wasn't my father. For one thing my father would never, ever hurt me. Uncle Richard hit me and told me that if I told anyone, he would hurt my parents. I think he hit me too hard. I was unconscious for a little while. My parents told me I had been in an accident. I think they were hoping that I was too young to remember."

"I'm sorry you remembered it at all, Aïda," I said. "Sexual abuse is a horrible thing."

"Well," she said, with a dry little laugh. "I think I've dealt with it as well as anyone can. Of course, my mother and father never knew that I remembered it at all. I'm glad they never found out." She gazed at the window that gave back nothing but her own reflection.

"I guess I told you about it because I'm glad it isn't Uncle Richard living in Hawaii. If it was, I'd feel that I had to drag all of it back up again and see to it that he was prosecuted. If Willis Henshaw can't be my father, then I'm grateful he isn't Richard. If Uncle Richard is alive somewhere in the world, Australia, or wherever, I'm sorry that he's still living and my father isn't and I hope he stays wherever he is."

We sat quietly for a while, letting the normal, comfortable sounds of the restaurant surround us. A busboy clinked glasses behind the counter and sometimes one of the cooks would shout a word or two to one of the waitresses. Somewhere a television droned the news, too low for us to hear, but loud enough to keep the place from sounding empty.

"Tell me about Willis Henshaw," Aïda said finally. "Was he my father's friend?"

"Yes. A friend. Maybe the best friend your father ever had. He has some of your dad's paintings. He's a good man, Aïda." I considered how much to tell her. "I got to know him well. We...talked quite a bit. He's a generous, kind man. His friends and neighbors like him and he's respected in his community."

She gave me an odd look. "You sound like you're talking about my father. To his fans he was loud and used drugs and partied, but at home, he wasn't that kind of a person at all. He was kind and generous too."

I nodded. "I'm sure he was."

We were silent for another moment, then I gathered my courage and began. "There's one other thing that happened in Hawaii," I said, unwilling to broach the subject but knowing I had to. "I know the Hawaiian authorities notified you about Jon-Paul."

She nodded.

"You may not know that he tried to kill us. He, Jon-Paul, that is, fell...he fell and he died. I'm so sorry."

"Mickey called me and told me." She gazed at me.

"But there's something you don't know, Aïda." I tried to appraise her. My heart was beginning to thud and my fingers suddenly started to tingle. "I am the one who caused Jon-Paul's death."

She still said nothing. Her eyes had gone round.

"We were standing on the edge of the volcano caldera. He had shot Willis and he was trying to push me in. We fought and he...Jon-Paul fell."

"I'm sorry," she said. "I...I didn't know that part." She put her hand on mine and I felt that she held no blame for me. But, then, I had enough blame for myself. "You shouldn't feel that it was your fault, though." She peered at me. "I think you do."

"I killed him, Aïda. That's a fact."

"It's also a fact that he would have killed you if you had not protected yourself."

I said nothing. I felt there was nothing more to say.

"I knew I was going to have to get away from Jon Paul," she said after a moment. "Even before you and I talked about that. He had something...a violence about him, that I was pretty sure wasn't going to go away. I was going to break up with him when you came back. I think..." she stopped and stared at the fork she was turning over and over. "He might not have easily let me go."

"Do you think he would have made trouble? Done you harm?"

"Possibly. He had given me signs of it before. He got furious when I wouldn't let him have the ten thousand dollars he wanted. I...I honestly thought he was going to hit me. He didn't, but...He was terribly jealous too. And, of course, knowing what I know now..." She looked at me. "I'm probably lucky." After a moment she added, "I feel bad for Mickey, though. We talked for quite a while about Jon-Paul. He was pretty broken up."

"I thought you didn't get along with Mickey," I said. "You accused him of embezzlement."

"Yes, I did. At first. It was Jon-Paul who suggested it in the first place. After I talked to Mickey, I realized I was wrong. I think I knew all along that Mickey wouldn't steal from my father, but I must have wanted to hang some of the blame for his death on someone. I'm ashamed."

"Don't be. You can only do what you think is right. It's the best anyone can do. Sometimes we're wrong. It's life." I wasn't sure I believed my own words right then. "Now, I'm going to have to get home." I pulled my jacket around my shoulders. She bundled into hers and we headed out the door.

When we pulled up in front of the dark, looming house in West Seattle, I was shaken with an idea that I wasn't at all sure was a good one. "Maybe you should write to Willis Henshaw," I told her. "Tell him you'd like to talk about your father. Maybe you could talk about your Uncle Richard too. He's an understanding man. I liked him very much."

Aïda looked at me with her eyes wide. "That's a good idea," she said. "I think I might do that."

"I will call you with his address," I said, thinking I would ask Willis if he would mind. I had a feeling he would welcome knowing Aïda again as long as he could feel that he was still Willis.

She turned to me. "Thank you, Chey," she said. "For everything."

"I only wish I could have given you the news you wanted, Aïda," I told her, meaning it.

We hugged and we both cried a little for her lost hopes.

I got out and waved at her as she pulled away. It was late and I knew there would be a call on my recorder. I didn't want to hear it just yet. My life was waiting for me and my soul would need to heal its bruises. I walked toward the cold, dark house alone.

I turned on the entry light, gathered the accumulated mail from the floor and tossed all but one piece of it onto the coffee table. The house seemed to be waiting, perhaps for me to warm it, light it and begin to live again. The cold went straight to my bones, but I didn't switch on the heat. Instead, I lit a fire and pulled a chair nearer to it.

For a while I watched the flames and thought of Willis, Aïda, David and Jon-Paul. As I stared at the fire, I turned the envelope that contained the card with Willis' fingerprints over and over in my hands. The events of the last few days returned in random scenes. I felt Willis' warm arms enfolding me as we danced to "Unchained Melody". I saw him again spread his arms to the wind at Kamehameha's birthplace. Once more, I felt that almost physical twist my heart made when I saw the devastation that had happened to the man I believed to be David. I saw Jon-Paul's crumpled body beginning to smoke on the hot floor of Kiluea's caldera. I felt Aida's disappointment when I told her that her father was dead.

I sat for a long time, thinking, wondering, remembering. At last, I stood, and threw the envelope into the flames.

Epilogue

Those who had loved Royal Blue had been loving a man who was much more than a singer, more than an artist. He was a loving, compassionate man who willingly sacrificed himself for those he loved. I wish I could have done more to ease his mind from the burden of guilt that he had carried for so long. Instead, I took up my own burden and have carried it for years.

I think about Aïda Blue often. We kept in touch after I had finished her case. I know that she eventually did call Willis Henshaw and that she met him when she travelled to Hawaii a couple of years later. As far as I know, Willis did not reveal his true identity to Aïda, although I couldn't see how she would fail to recognize his voice, his laugh and his love for her. I do know that when she returned, she seemed happier and more at peace. Perhaps he did share his secret with her, but if he did, I never knew.

I had called Willis to tell him that I had suggested to Aida that she write to him. He had seemed glad, even grateful, but I couldn't be sure. It had been an awkward conversation between two people who, though strongly drawn to one another, were separated by something much more vast than an ocean.

Through the years, I have often wondered why I didn't feel the presence of Royal Blue when I was near and touching Willis. Gradually, I came to believe that he had so changed his life, so altered his inner self that he had become, in actuality, Willis Henshaw and discarded Royal and Richard completely. I was unable to detect the truth because Willis had so hidden it from himself that it was no longer a part of him.

For the rest of the years of my life, I have lain awake nights with the enormity of what I had done in Hawaii. I had always maintained that my own body could be enough of a weapon to protect myself. It allowed me the luxury of refusing to use a gun. What irony, then, to realize that those same self-defensive moves were the very weapon which would cause me to do something that I never thought I would do. I had taken a life, and, in so doing, lost something within me. It is a fact that one never moves past. It is there in our waking moments and it flavors our dreams. It colors our joys and adds something to our sadness.

Most people who have not experienced bereavement, whether from the loss of a loved one, or a part of one's self, believe that grief shrinks with time. I don't believe that is the case. I think that the grief remains the same but that, as time passes, we build ourselves a larger container to hold it. It's hard enough to deal with death and harder yet when you are the one who has caused it, no matter who the victim is. We are all haunted in one way or another by our pasts. Willis was right, it gets no easier. It is always there.

As for David, that question was eventually answered but that is a story for another day.

Cheyenne Bruce

December 2019

ACKNOWLEDGEMENTS

A giant thank you to my daughter, Carrie, my friend, Barb and my husband, Guy for their editing skills.

Thank you to Gale Peck at Iceberg Strategic Creative for the paperback cover design.

I would also like to thank my readers. I hope you enjoyed The Cheyenne Bruce mysteries as much as I enjoyed writing them. Please visit my website for updates and emails at https:// MasterPiecesUnlimited.com

BOOKS BY THIS AUTHOR

Always A Bad Sign: From The Case Files And Personal Journals Of Cheyenne Bruce, Private Investigator, Book One

In retrospect, aside from the fact that it was the last day of Jacob Levin's life, there was probably nothing unusual about that Monday in November of 1983. Until, that is, Jacob's wife, former screen star, Magda St. Martin called me for help. I was a private investigator. I was also a psychic.

Five years before, I had searched for Magda's missing teenaged daughter. I never found her and the case had haunted me for years. Now, Magda had lost two husbands and a daughter under mysterious circumstances. She wanted me to protect her from whomever was stalking her family and to independently investigate the case.

From the beginning, I knew that Magda, her secretary, Laurel and her gardener, Rolf were lying to me. As I uncovered secret after secret, I felt farther and farther from the truth until the final macabre moments.

The Book Of Signs: A Case From The Journals Of Cheyenne Bruce, Private Investigator, Book Three

Before the Whalesong murders, I had thought the life of a writer in a secluded, serene writer's colony, would be close to heaven. And Whalesong seemed the perfect spot for that life. A lovely island in the Straits, comfortable cabins in the woods, nothing to do but spend the day working at a task that one loves.

Little did I know that behind the idyll of Whalesong, lurked something much more ominous than I had imagined. It was a case full of dangers, deceptions and threats that I didn't yet understand. I didn't know that in the woods of a dark island in the San Juans, I would meet a group of people who had secrets and desires that, when exposed, would have lasting tragic repercussions for all of us.

Sign Of The Raven: A Case From The Files Of Cheyenne Bruce, Private Investigator, Book Four

In that summer of 1984, we residents of the Pacific

Northwest were familiar with serial killers. In the 70s, Ted Bundy had terrorized Seattle by charming then killing young women. In the 80s, Gary Ridgway hid his victims along the banks of the Green River only to return to their remains again and again.

These men were able to fulfill their horrible goals in plain sight because they appeared to be average, normal people. They had families, girlfriends and jobs. They acted like us. They looked like us. There were just like us.

The press never did name the perpetrator, nor did the authorities ever recognize the fact that a third killer roamed the area. I knew though, that in the colorful world of the local art scene, someone was watching, planning and waiting for the moment to strike. I knew about the killer I came to call the Raven.